CU00721661

The Mystery of a Techie's Murder

Mayur Varma Mysteries, Volume 1

Vijay Kerji

Published by Vijay Kerji, 2020.

THE MYSTERY OF A TECHIE'S MURDER

First edition. March 31, 2020.

Copyright © 2020 Vijay Kerji.

ISBN: 978-1393459927

Written by Vijay Kerji.

Also by Vijay Kerji

Mayur Varma Mysteries
The Mystery of a Techie's Murder
The Secret of a Strangled Woman
Mystery At The Mansion

Standalone
Love is Blind
A Friend In Need
The Ticking Clock
Lover's Courage
I Still Love You
Rohita - A Love Story

Watch for more at https://vijaykumarkerji.wordpress.com/.

Table of Contents

Chapter 01 - The Crime Scene 1

Chapter 02 - The Clues 5

Chapter 03 - Julia's Statement 9

Chapter 04 - Mr. Shekar Bedi Bereaved 17

Chapter 05 - Rahul and Harsha Reacts 23

Chapter 06 - The Trio Discusses The Old Cases............29

Chapter 07 - Mayur Discusses The Case with Aisha........37

Chapter 08 - Dr. Sunil's Findings 43

Chapter 09 - Mayur Meets Priya's Father 47

Chapter 10 - Secret About Praful and Harsha 53

Chapter 11 - Mayur Interviews Krishna Raj................61

Chapter 12 - Evidence of Praful 71

Chapter 13 - Evidence of Hemanth 81

Chapter 14 - Meeting with Dr. Sunil 91

Chapter 15 - Hemanth's Alibi................................... 101

Chapter 16 - Plan to Visit Bangalore 111

Chapter 17 - Mayur in Bangalore 119

Chapter 18 - Mayur Interviews Sumitra and Poonam.... 127

Chapter 19 - Poonam's Revelations 139

Chapter 20 - Poonam Argues 147

Chapter 21 - Mrs. Sumitra Bedi Meets Her Mother and Rahul 153

Chapter 22 - Evidence of Mr. Bedi, Poonam and Chirag 159

Chapter 23 - Miss Bedi's Greed 173

Chapter 24 - Evidence of Nayan 177

Chapter 25 - Mayur is Attacked 187

Chapter 26 - Mayur Calls Rahul 193

Chapter 27 - Evidence of Rahul 197

Chapter 28 - Evidence of Harsha 203

Chapter 29 - Check The Alibis 209

Chapter 30 - Returen to Hyderabad.......................... 217

Chapter 31 - Mayur With his Family......................... 225

Chapter 32 - Mayur Discusses the Case.. 229
Chapter 33 - News About Parthiv 237
Chapter 34 - Parthiv Dies.. 241
Chapter 35 - The Murderer 245
Chapter 36 - The Confession Letter.. 249

This is Dedicated to My Parents, who supported me grow my writing career

Chapter 01 - The Crime Scene

20TH OCTOBER 9 AM - Hyderabad

Detective Mayur Varma entered the bedroom of the Majestic Apartments. He fiddled with his car keychain. Priya Bedi's body lay in a pool of blood on the floor.

Mayur turned to Inspector Prakash Malhotra, who brought him there for an inspection. "You said you were already here this morning at seven."

The inspector nodded.

The blackish-red blood soaked Priya's sliced neck and it covered the carpet.

"Did you find the weapon?"

"No, the weapon is missing. The perpetrator might've taken it with him."

Priya lay flat on her back with her fair, square face tilted towards right. The bed lamp lit the room and the window and the balcony doors remained bolted.

Prakash had told Mayur the security guard had registered the complaint at around 7:00 AM.

"Did you interview the security guard?" Mayur asked Prakash.

"Yes, and he is the one who ushered me here in the morning."

"Was Priya staying alone here when the murder took place?" The junior detective Aisha Mishra asked.

"Her colleague, Julia, shared the flat with her," Prakash said. "But Julia had gone to Mumbai to meet her parents for two days. She is now traveling back to Hyderabad." He paused and then said, "Priya was alone on the weekend."

"How long did they stay in the flat?" Mayur asked.

"They stayed together for four months."

In her pale pink night suit, Priya appeared to be in her early twenties. Her wide-opened eyes and her swollen face added to the gruesomeness of the scene.

"Do you suspect any motive behind the murder?"

"Robbery," Prakash said. "There are some valuables missing. Priya always wore a gold chain and diamond earrings, which are missing. The contents of the closet are strewn around that shows the perpetrator had searched for valuables."

Mayur considered. The murderers had struck when Priya was alone in the flat. Was it a coincidence that Priya's roommate, Julia, was away? Or did the perpetrators know that Priya would be alone?

The room had a single cot with the bedspread on the mattress messed up. A pillow lay on the floor, away from the victim.

"Did you find the victim's cell phone with her?" Aisha asked.

"No," said Prakash. "That's one of the reasons why the robbery is the motive."

The bruises on Priya's forearms caught Mayur's attention. "Priya had protested before she succumbed."

"I too think so. But we can reach our conclusions only after Dr. Sunil conducts an autopsy," Prakash said.

The apartment security guard entered, breathing faster. He bowed to Prakash and his colleagues.

Mayur turned to the guard. "Were you on duty last night when the murder took place?"

"No, sir. Hemant Rathod worked in the night until this morning at six o'clock. I worked from six in the morning until five o'clock, sir."

"Would you like to share any information about Priya?"

"Well," said the guard. "I'd seen Priya outside her flat with her roommate and her colleague, Julia. She maintained a low profile and never came out of her flat alone in the evenings. She had been quite cheerful and happy whenever I'd seen her."

Priya might not have had any enemies in her life, Mayur thought. And she came from an orthodox family background as she never went outside alone.

"Was she upset lately for any reason?" Aisha asked.

"No, Madam. I have seen her cheerful while she went to her office along with Julia."

Mayur walked back to the main hall of the flat along with Aisha. They sat on a plush leather sofa. The room was spacious enough and well-furnished. A flat-screen television stood near the wall, opposite the seats.

Mayur glanced outside the main entrance. The yellow tapes cordoned off the main door of the guesthouse and the surrounding area. The forensic lab technicians were busy analyzing the scene. They wore light green masks and gloves.

Mayur's glance shifted towards Aisha. Her pink sari with a purple blouse contrasted with the yellow light from the chandelier. Her not so round but oblong, fair face matched her petite figure.

"Did you perform some special pooja at home?"

Aisha widened her eyes. "Yes. Today was my aunt's marriage anniversary. But how do you know about it?"

He winked at her. "The sandalwood paste on your neck is still fresh."

She touched her neck. "Oh, that's correct."

Prakash arrived along with the security guard and they sat on chairs. "I spoke with my boss this morning and told him about the case." He looked at Mayur. "He wants us to close this case early as the victim worked for an IT giant. We will have pressure from the company if we delay finding the perpetrator."

Mayur straightened his back. "Let's hope we will achieve some breakthrough soon." He forced a smile.

A couple of forensic experts approached, holding magnifying glasses. They wore white and green uniforms. Mayur and his colleagues exchanged greetings with them. The technicians continued to look for any shreds of evidence using their tools.

"Did you guys find anything significant?" Prakash asked.

One of the technicians turned to Prakash. "We've collected four important clues, sir." He paused for a moment and said, "A Pizza Hut cap, a shirt button of the Pizza Hut uniform, a cigarette butt, and footprints."

"Well," said Prakash, "that's a start."

Chapter 02 - The Clues

20TH OCTOBER 10 AM

Mayur's chest tightened. Pizza Hut cap? He remained silent, contemplating. Did Priya order pizza the previous night?

"Did Priya eat pizza last night?" Aisha asked.

"We haven't found any pizza either here or in the refrigerator."

"What about the box? Did you check the wastebasket?" Prakash asked.

The forensic expert shook his head in denial. "No, we haven't found any box either."

"Can we know if she called the outlet using her phone?" Aisha asked.

"Her cell phone is missing," Prakash said. "We need to find out which service provider she was subscribed to and find out her call details."

Mayur nodded. "That should give us a lead to proceed in the case." He looked up at the security guard. "Do you know when her roommate is coming back from Mumbai?"

"Julia madam should be here soon, sir. She is traveling on the train."

"When did you talk to her?" Prakash asked.

"This morning at around eight o'clock, sir."

"What about the cigarette butt?" Mayur asked, looking at the technician. "Did you find it here in the bedroom?"

"No, not here," the expert said. "It was lying in the living room, beside the couch."

"I don't think the pizza delivery guy would've smoked here," Mayur said. He turned to the security guard. "Did any guest visit the flat to meet Priya last night?"

"I don't think so," the guard said. "I'll cross-check the visitor's register and confirm."

"Was there any pizza delivery boy here to deliver the pizza last night?"

The guard put his finger to his lips. "Yesterday was Sunday and many residents would've ordered pizza, sir."

"Do you log the details of delivery boys?" Mayur asked.

The security plastered a smile on his face. "No, sir. Not for the delivery boys. But we do register the details of visitors who come to meet the residents."

Mayur sighed. It was indeed a lapse from the security point of view. He paused for a moment and then turned to the technician. "Are you sure the button belongs to the Pizza Hut uniform?"

"We will get it confirmed very soon."

Mayur turned to Prakash. "We need to inquire with the nearby Pizza Hut whether Priya called them the previous night."

"Sure. I will," Prakash said, looking at Aisha who was jotting on her notepad.

Dr. Sunil Hegde entered. They all exchanged greetings.

"Sunil, when do you think the murder occurred?" Mayur asked.

"I guess somewhere between eight o'clock and ten o'clock last night." Dr. Sunil looked at Prakash. "The victim's wristwatch stopped at nine-thirty. I can exactly tell the time of death only after autopsy."

"We're interested to know what the victim ate last night," Aisha said

"Sure," Dr. Sunil said. "I'll make all the findings available to you by tonight or by tomorrow morning."

The security guard's phone rang. He took it out from his pants pocket and glanced at the screen. "It's Madam Julia," he whispered and put the phone on speaker mode. "Hello, Madam. Where are you?"

"I'm calling from Nampally Railway Station," Julia said. "Is there any urgent matter you want to tell me?"

The guard darted his gaze between Mayur and Prakash. "Yes, Madam. I suggest you come to the flat soon."

"I'm starting now," Julia said.

A forensic expert approached with tweezers and a magnifying glass.

"Did you find anything significant?" Prakash asked.

They all looked at the tweezers eagerly with their eyes wide.

Chapter 03 - Julia's Statement

20TH OCTOBER 11 AM

Mayur looked at the tweezers through a magnifying glass. He gestured his colleagues to come closer.

"Yes, sir," the technician said. "These are a few strands of hair found inside the Pizza Hut cap." He held the tweezers in front of them.

Mayur looked at it through the magnifying glass. "It's good that you checked the inside of the cap. All these clues should definitely help us in our investigation."

"That's good," said Aisha. She turned and looked up at the guard. "What time will Julia arrive?"

"She left the Nampally Station a few minutes ago," Mayur said. "That means she will be here probably in the next twenty minutes."

"I too think so, sir," the security guard added.

Mayur was eager to interview Julia. He hoped she might provide him with vital leads in his investigation. Priya's murder during Julia's absence intrigued him.

"Is there any reason why you didn't tell Julia about the murder over the phone?" asked Prakash, looking at the security guard.

"I wanted to, but Madam Julia would be shocked to hear the news, sir. I thought it would be better to tell her in your presence."

"That's a good decision," Aisha said. "I'll take care of her if she doesn't take it well after hearing the news."

9

"I know Julia madam is very gentle in nature," the guard said. "She will not be able to withstand the shock of her friend's death."

"What's your opinion about Priya?" Mayur asked. "Was she mentally stronger than Julia?"

"Um... I've seen them entering and leaving the apartment, sir. So, I won't be able to comment much about it."

"Then, how come you told us Julia is gentle in nature?"

"Well, I remember an incident in the building," the guard said. "One of our residents once had let his dogs loose. At that time, Julia and Priya descended from the lift and walked towards the parking lot. The dogs started barking at them, coming closer. I noticed Julia was more frightened than Priya as Julia ran towards the security tower. Priya successfully calmed the dogs with some tricks. Then, the dog owner approached and took control of the situation."

"This clearly shows we should be cautious while we reveal the news to her," Prakash said. "What if we wait near the apartment gate to receive her?"

"That makes sense," Aisha said.

Prakash instructed his subordinates not to disturb the victim's body until Julia arrived. He walked everyone to the lift and then to the parking lot.

One of the constables arranged for a few chairs to be brought, but Mayur preferred to relax in the police Jeep. He sat in the passenger seat while Aisha in the back. Prakash slid behind the wheel. The security guard returned to his tower.

The crowd of people had dispersed. A few remaining men walked out of the place after seeing Prakash. Some gossiped about while standing outside the main gate.

"What do you think of the clues collected so far?" Aisha asked.

Mayur looked over his shoulder towards her. "The missing weapon indicates the perpetrator is clever enough. He had planned the murder beforehand."

"But I strongly believe it's a case of robbery," Prakash said.

"But the Pizza Hut cap and the shirt button rule it out," Mayur said. "I wonder why the murderer wore the uniform. Was he trying to avoid the security guards and not make them suspicious?"

The guard approached. "Sir, Julia called and said she will be here in ten minutes."

"Did she say anything else?" Mayur asked.

"She is keen to know if anything is wrong."

"Did you tell her what happened?" Aisha asked.

"No, ma-am. I didn't."

"I hope you have a plan to reveal Julia the information," Mayur said. Aisha nodded.

"You bring her straight to us when she arrives," Prakash said.

The security guard nodded and walked back to his tower.

Mayur leaned forward soon after the security went. "I wonder why the murder took place when Julia was away."

"Do you think there is any connection between Julia's absence and Priya's murder?" Prakash asked.

"You know the forensic experts found a cigarette butt in the living room. Maybe someone close to Priya met her before murdering her. He might have spent some time with Priya. And perhaps the perpetrator knew Julia was not in the flat and planned the murder."

"I think the footprints found at the crime scene should be a vital clue for us," Prakash said. "We can learn who visited Priya on that fateful night."

Mayur's glance shifted towards the approaching security guard. A short lady in blue jeans and a pink T-shirt accompanied him. Her short hair tied into a ponytail suited her square face.

"I think Julia is here," Mayur said. He waited eagerly for her to approach him.

The security guard introduced her to Mayur and his colleagues.

Julia furrowed her brows. "What's going on here?" Her lips trembled.

Aisha stepped out of the vehicle and held Julia's hand. "You need to steel yourself, Julia. We've some bad news."

Julia's gaze darted between Mayur, Aisha, and Prakash. She fixed her gaze on the security guard. "I've been asking you what the matter is. Why are you not telling me?"

"Okay," Aisha said. "Please calm down. Your flatmate, Priya is..." Aisha stumbled for words.

"Yes, tell me what happened to Priya?" Julia asked, her eyes narrowed.

"She has been found murdered in her bedroom," Aisha said with her tone lowered.

"What?" Julia widened her eyes. "Priya has been murdered? I can't believe this." She breathed rapidly, and she swayed. She held Aisha's hand tight.

Aisha grabbed her arm and prevented her from falling down.

Julia touched her forehead with her right hand and with her eyes remained widened.

"Why don't you relax inside the Jeep?" Mayur said.

"That's a good idea. Let's go and sit there." Aisha walked Julia to the back of the police Jeep and helped her inside.

Mayur sat back in the passenger's seat while Prakash slid behind the wheel. They sat in silence for a few moments; Mayur waited for Julia to recover from the shock.

"Julia," said Mayur. "We need your cooperation to find the perpetrator."

"I don't believe my friend is dead. I would like to go to my flat and see for myself."

"Sure," said Prakash. "Why don't we all go back to the guest house? We can interview Julia after seeing the crime scene."

Mayur nodded and stepped down from the vehicle. Aisha helped Julia to get out of her seat and Prakash led everyone towards the lift. He instructed the constable to remove the yellow tape to enable them to enter.

Mayur glanced at Julia as they entered the living room. Her fair face grew stony and her red open lips trembled. She seemed eager to see Priya with her curiosity filled eyes widening.

Aisha clutched Julia's arm tight when they entered the bedroom. They all stood in front of the victim.

Julia gave a loud cry and she covered her face with her hands. "No, Priya. I can't believe this." She sobbed aloud.

Aisha rubbed her back. "I'm sorry for your loss."

They waited in silence for Julia to calm down.

"Let's go back downstairs and discuss the matter," Prakash instructed a constable to take the dead body for an autopsy and he led them back to his vehicle.

Mayur sat in the passenger's seat while Prakash slid behind the wheel. Aisha helped Julia to the rear seat.

"I'm ready to provide any information you want to catch the culprit," Julia said. "I want you to get to the bottom of this crime."

"Thanks for consenting to cooperate with us," Mayur said. He paused. "Why did you go to Bangalore this weekend?"

"It had been many days since I visited my parents," said Julia. "I wanted to meet them soon and preferred to go on the previous weekend."

"When did you last visit?" Mayur asked.

"Um... exactly a month ago."

"Are you married?" Mayur asked.

"No."

"Are you engaged?" asked Aisha while she scribbled on a notepad.

"Is that question relevant?" Julia asked.

"Julia," Prakash said. "You've already promised us you'll cooperate. Please answer to whatever questions Mr. Varma ask you."

"All right," said Julia, her tone resigned. "I'm not yet engaged. But my parents are trying to arrange my marriage with one of my distant relatives."

Mayur waited for Aisha to finish taking the notes. "How long have you known to Priya?"

"Since April this year; almost six months. Priya was already staying here when I joined the guest house. It didn't take much time for us to get adjusted to each other. Priya was quite accommodating and jelled well with me."

"Where do you work?"

"Mind Tree Solutions."

"And who is your manager?"

"Krishna Raj," said Julia. "He is a native of Hyderabad."

"Did Priya work in your group and report to Mr. Raj?" Prakash asked.

"Yes."

"Did you join Krishna's team from the beginning or after some time?"

"I joined just one week after the project started."

"So, Priya came to Hyderabad one week before you?" Mayur asked. Julia nodded.

"Did Priya share any personal information with you?"

"Well," said Julia. "Can you be specific about the type of information you are interested in?"

"Was Priya married?"

"No. But she was engaged."

"Where does her fiancé live?"

"Bangalore," said Julia. "He has a wholesale garments business."

"How long had Priya been engaged?" Mayur said.

"She was engaged prior to coming here."

"Do you know the exact period during which she was engaged?" Mayur asked.

"I think she was engaged for five months before she came here. So, it was about ten months altogether. And her marriage got postponed because she was transferred to Hyderabad."

"May I know the name of her fiancé?"

"Nayan Chabra."

"Did Nayan ever visit Hyderabad to meet Priya?"

"No."

"Not even once?" said Mayur, his voice astonished.

"No, he didn't visit here at all."

"Did you ever ask Priya why Nayan didn't take an interest in coming here?"

"Well, she used to tell me he was always busy with his business."

"How often did Priya go to Bangalore to meet her parents?"

"On average, once every month."

"Did you guys plan to go on the same weekends?"

"We did plan to do that on two occasions. Priya had to stay back this time because she needed to finish her assignment on the weekend."

"Do you think Priya had anyone who wanted to harm her?" Mayur asked.

"Um... I don't think so. She was quite friendly with everyone at the office."

"Are you sure?" Mayur asked.

"Yes, at least for the duration of our friendship."

"Did she complain to you about any of her loved ones, including her fiancé?"

"No," said Julia, staring down. "*But she spoke with someone over the phone for a long time. I found her arguing with the person with whom she spoke.*"

"Do you know who the other person was?"

"No."

"Did you ever ask Priya about the matter?"

"No. I neither asked her nor did she tell me with whom she spoke over the phone."

"Why didn't you ask her with whom she argued?"

"Because I didn't want to interfere in her personal matter."

Mayur sifted his gaze towards Prakash. "We need to get more details about Priya's phone calls and find out whom she spoke to and for how long."

Prakash nodded. "Yes, I will."

Chapter 04 - Mr. Shekar Bedi Bereaved

OCTOBER 20 - 12:30 PM

Mayur knew Julia needed to rest after traveling overnight. She had yet to recover from the shock of her friend's demise. Julia would need a place to stay as the police cordoned off her guest house.

He along with Aisha and Prakash drove Julia to another guesthouse. They all sat in the living room of the alternate guest house.

Julia looked into Mayur's eyes. "Do Priya's parents know about the incident? Has anyone from the police department contacted them?"

"I called their home this morning and spoke to their housemaid," Prakash said.

"Did you tell them everything?" Julia asked. "Where were her parents at that time?"

"They were out for a morning walk. I avoided revealing the matter to the housemaid. I asked the housemaid to tell them to call me back urgently and left it at that."

Julia said she would freshen up and join them. She walked towards one of the bathrooms.

She returned, wearing a white mixed pale blue T-shirt and blue jeans. Her fair face glistened in the daylight, which streamed through a window. Her black hair was pulled back into a ponytail. A light green scarf was wrapped around it.

"Julia," said Mayur. "You said Priya had a younger sister," said Mayur. "How many siblings did she have?"

Julia swallowed. "Priya had only one younger sister, Poonam."

"Is she going to school?" Aisha asked.

"She finished her engineering course a few months ago."

"Didn't she get a job yet? What's she doing these days?" Mayur asked.

"Priya told me she did get some job offers, but Poonam is waiting for the right opportunity. Also, Poonam wanted to get married before she took a job."

"You mean Poonam is also engaged?" Prakash asked.

"Yes, Poonam is engaged to a Mr. Chirag Bakshi and Priya got engaged to a Mr. Nayan Chabra on the same day. The engaged couples also wanted to get married on the same day. I really feel sorry for Priya and her loved ones for their loss."

Mayur too grew sympathetic towards the Bedi family. Priya was their elder daughter and fate shouldn't have disfavored her. No doubt it would affect Poonam's future. He needed to help Priya's parents.

"What does Priya's father do for a living?" Mayur asked.

"He owns a jewelry business. It's located on the Brigade road, one of the popular streets in Bangalore."

"That means Priya comes from an affluent family."

Julia nodded. "Priya was also her parents' favorite daughter. In fact, they suggested Priya not accept the new project assignment at Hyderabad. They insisted she gets married to her fiancé. But Priya was keen to work on this defense project, that involved cutting edge technology. She was eager to take on challenging projects and grow her career."

"Thank you, Miss Julia, for answering my questions," Mayur said. "Did anyone from Priya's family visit Hyderabad?"

"No, as Priya often went to Bangalore to meet her parents and her fiancé. She needed to finish her assignment before today. That's the reason she avoided going there the previous weekend."

"Did she ever tell you where in Bangalore her parents lived?"

"Yes, in Malleshwaram."

"Is her mother a housewife?"

Julia nodded.

"You have told us Priya often spoke to someone over the phone arguing."

"Yes, I did."

"What were they arguing about? Or it's just that she spoke to her fiancé for a long duration?"

Julia stole a sideways glance. She paused for a moment and considered. "Maybe, she spoke to her fiancé, but she often closed her bedroom door when I was seated in the living room."

"Perhaps, she didn't want to disturb you," Aisha added.

"But it is possible Priya tried to cover up something. Or she just wanted some privacy?" Mayur turned to Julia.

"As I have already told you," said Julia. "I didn't want to interfere in her personal matters."

"All right, Julia," said Mayur. "One last question. In your opinion, did Priya really love her fiancé, Mr. Nayan Chabra?"

"Yes. Otherwise, she wouldn't have gone to Bangalore that often, you know."

"It could be that she went to meet her parents," Prakash said. "You told us that her parents loved her very much and she longed to meet them."

"But I don't see any reasons why Priya hated Nayan."

"I asked this question because you said Priya often argued with someone over the phone and it could be Nayan."

"Maybe," said Julia.

Mayur remained silent, contemplating. He needed to interrogate Mr. Nayan Chabra to get any leads in his investigation. He should also need to question her parents and sibling to find out about her past life.

"Should we call Mr. Bedi once again to claim the body?" Prakash asked.

"Yes, we should," Mayur said.

Julia cleared her throat. "Will it be possible to take the body to Bangalore soon? I would also like to go there to attend the funeral."

"That's right," Aisha added. "Mayur, what if you also join Julia in Bangalore? We may likely to get some clues over there."

"Yes," Mayur said. "You're also accompanying me. And we shouldn't delay informing Priya's parents about her death."

Julia fished out her phone from the purse. She gave Priya's father's number to him. "His name is Mr. Shekar Bedi," she said while she put her phone back in her purse.

"Thank you." Mayur pressed on the green button and put the phone on speaker mode.

OCTOBER 20TH - 1:00 PM - Bangalore

Mr. Shekar Bedi was seated in the living room. He ran his eyes over Poonam, Mr. Chirag Bakshi, Mr. Nayan Chabra, and Mr. and Mrs. Chabra, who sat on the couches opposite him. His wife, Mrs. Sumitra Bedi, sat beside Nayan's mother.

The and housemaid had told Mr. Shekar Bedi he had a call from Hyderabad. He had ignored her words as he was preoccupied with meeting Mr. and Mrs. Chabra

Nayan's father placed the coffee cup on the table. "When do you think we can arrange weddings?" He looked at his son and then fixed his gaze back on Mr. Bedi. "It has been almost a year since the engagement. Isn't it time we got things moving?"

Mr. Bedi's heart sank. He hadn't thought Nayan's father would raise the matter as Priya was working at Hyderabad.

"I know," said Shekar, trying not to sound harsh. "I'm waiting for Priya to finish her work and return. We've waited all this time. It's a matter of a couple of more months before we arrange their weddings."

"Uncle is correct," said Mr. Chirag Bakshi. "I too need some time so that I'll be free after finishing the ongoing project at my office."

"Yes," Poonam said. "We all need to wait for Priya to return. I don't think she'll agree to the marriage before her assignment gets completed."

Mr. Chabra looked at his wife for a moment and then stared back at Mr. Bedi. He evidently realized everyone's intention and decided not to hurry the matter.

"I too agree that we need to wait until Priya returns," Mrs. Sumitra Bedi said. She looked at Nayan. "I hope Nayan doesn't have any problems waiting for a few more months."

"Yes, Aunty. I can wait until Priya returns."

Mr. Bedi's phone rang. An unknown number lit the screen. His heart raced as the caller might be from Hyderabad who spoke to his housemaid in the morning.

He swiped the green button and said, "Hello, Shekar Bedi here".

"Hello, Mr. Bedi, I'm Mayur Varma, a private detective from Hyderabad."

Private detective? Mr. Bedi hoped Priya was safe there. "Hi. My housemaid said you called this morning. I'm sorry for not returning your call. Is everything all right?"

"No, Mr. Bedi."

"What? Did anything happen..." Mr. Bedi stopped short of his words.

"You need to steel yourself," said Mayur. "We have bad news for you."

"Bad news?" Mr. Bedi coughed. "I hope my daughter, Priya, is alright."

"I'm sorry to say that Priya is no more. She was found murdered in her flat."

"What? Priya...." Mr. Bedi's vision blurred. "No, Mr. Varma, I can't believe it." Nausea coursed through his stomach. Everything around him twirled. He looked at his wife and gave her the phone.

Mrs. Bedi spoke over the phone and then she collapsed on the floor.

They both started crying.

Poonam approached them. "What's the matter, Mum?" Her eyes darted between the phone and her fiancé, Chirag Bakshi.

Everyone approached Poonam and her parents.

"What's the matter, Shekar?" Nayan's father, Mr. Chabra, said. "Who was on the line?"

Mr. Bedi composed himself. "Priya is ...." He hesitated.

"Yes, tell us what happened to Priya?" asked Mrs. Chabra.

"Priya was found dead in her flat." Mr. Bedi hid his face in his hands and continued sobbing.

Poonam hugged her parents. She wiped the tears flowing down her mother's cheeks and she embraced her mother.

After a few minutes, Mr. Bedi sat straight. He couldn't believe Priya had been murdered.

Nayan, his eyes wide, stood beside his father, staring through the window.

Chirag, stony-faced, continued to look at Poonam, who was rubbing her mother's back to calm her.

Chapter 05 - Rahul and Harsha Reacts

20TH OCTOBER 1:15 PM - Bangalore

Priya's maternal grandmother, Mrs. Usha Bhatt, glanced at the wall clock. She stopped knitting a sweater for her son, Rahul. It was already half-past two and Rahul hadn't come to have lunch. *Is he busy teaching his students?*

The living room where she sat was spacious - around 25 by 30 feet large. A TV sat opposite a set of a sofas placed in L shape. A coffee table was placed in front of them. A couple of modern art paintings adorned the wall.

The cold breeze entering through the balcony door made her sneeze. The chill sent a shiver down her spine. Usha worried about Rahul's refusal to get married to a suitable girl. She had been insisting he marry because he'd turned thirty last month. But Rahul dodged the matter, citing one reason or another.

The doorbell rang. *Is it Rahul?* Usha rose, placing the woolen ball and partially knitted sweater aside. She walked towards the door and opened it.

"Hi, Mum." Rahul's fair and oblong face lit with a light smile. He stood tall - about six feet - and his neatly cut thick mustache appeared prominent above his thick open lips. His black-well-cut hair, applied with a cream, shone in the fluorescent light.

"Why are you so late?" Usha stepped aside, making room for Rahul to enter.

"I had to extend the class because the students had several questions." He let out a huge breath. "And I'm sorry for not answering your call."

"It's okay," said Usha. "The food is still hot. Go and freshen yourself up. I'll put the dishes on the dining table."

Rahul removed his shoes and walked towards the bathroom.

Usha went to the kitchen and placed the containers, containing spicy capsicum curry, sweet payasam, chapattis, and vegetable Palau on the dining table. She sat at the table in the dining room, waiting for Rahul to arrive. She needed to convince him about getting married. It's time for him to settle down with a family. Usha wanted to see the grandchildren and look after them before she grew weak.

Rahul arrived, wiping his hands on a pink napkin. He dragged a chair out and sat down.

"You must be hungry," said Usha. She placed an empty plate in front of him and served him curry and a few pieces of chapattis.

"Thank you, Mum. Yes, I'm hungry." Rahul took a bite of chapatti.

Usha waited for him to take a few more bites.

"Mum," said Rahul, chewing his food. "You know what, the student intake has improved in the last two years. I'm glad that my education institution, Excel Training Center, is growing."

"You've worked hard in the last two years, beta. And now it's time to reap the benefits. I think your brand name has become well known by now."

Rahul nodded. "I agree with you."

Usha waited another few moments. She drew in a huge breath, trying to gather enough courage to talk about his marital matter.

"Rahul," she said. "Don't you think it's the right time for you to get married?"

"Mum, ple-"

"Well," she said, "how long do you expect me to serve you? I too need someone who can help me with the household chores, right? And don't you think you need a companion at your age?"

"Yes, Mum. I agree with you. But I told you already, I need some time to decide."

"You've been saying that for so long, beta. I don't think it's good for you to postpone the matter any longer."

Rahul remained silent, staring at the plate. He narrowed his eyes and knitted his brows.

Usha started to serve him some more pieces of chapattis.

"No, Mum," Rahul said, pushing the plate away as his mother tried to serve him more food. "I've had enough."

Guilt coursed through Usha's mind. She should've discussed the matter after he finished eating lunch. Rahul seemed melancholic. Was he stressed about something? Usha tried to guess what bothered him. Was it Priya? "Tell me, Rahul. Are you worried for some reason?"

He remained silent.

"You need to tell me about your problem so that I can help you."

Rahul's glance shifted towards the framed photograph of him alongside Priya. He looked at it for a while and then back at his mother.

"I can understand you, Rahul," Usha said, trying to sound gentler. "You need to move on, beta. Priya is engaged. Forget about her." She paused and cleared her throat. "I can get you a girl who is more beautiful and accommodating than Priya."

But to her astonishment, Rahul washed his hands in a bowl and rose. He walked towards the living room.

She took a glass of water and followed him. "I'm sorry if I hurt you." She gave the glass to him and sat beside him. "We need to think of your younger sister, you know. She will finish her degree next year and we should arrange for her marriage. It's good for us if we arranged your marriage before thinking about your sister's."

Usha's heart sank as Rahul remained silent. She heaved a sigh and looked outside the balcony towards the neem tree whose branches shook in the wind. "I know Uncle Shekar is responsible for your betrayal. Had your father been alive, you wouldn't have faced this kind of situation." She covered her face with her hands and broke into a sob.

Rahul put his hands on her shoulder. "It is okay, Mum. Let's forget the past."

Usha's telephone rang. She put Rahul's hands aside and took the phone from the table. Vasant, her distant relative, had called her. "Hello, Vasant," she said, wiping a teardrop from her cheek.

"Usha, it's Vasant. I have some bad news to tell."

"Bad news? What is it?"

"Your granddaughter, Priya, is -"

"Yes, tell me what happened to Priya?"

"She is no more."

"What?" She turned to Rahul, who looked at her with 'what's-the-matter' expression on his face. Usha composed herself and said, "What are you saying, Vasant? May I know the details?"

"Priya was murdered in her flat at Hyderabad. The police found her body this morning."

Usha's stomach curdled. Her vision blurred and she rested her face on Rahul's shoulder.

Rahul took the phone from her and spoke for a few minutes before ending the call.

Usha wiped the tears flowing down her cheeks using the loose end of her sari.

"Mum," said Rahul. "Please console yourself."

Usha tried to compose herself. She sat straight and cleared her throat. "Did Vasant tell you anything else?"

"Not much," said Usha. "I would like to know more. I can't believe the news, you know. I also want to go and meet Sumitra immediately."

"Why would they want to see us, Mum? Don't you think we should avoid seeing Priya's father?"

"Because Sumitra is my daughter and she's lost her daughter, my lovely Priya. Don't you think we need to show our unity at this hour?"

Rahul remained silent. Usha wondered why he was not showing any emotions at the loss. Why was his face so stony after hearing this bad news? "I would like to speak with either Sumitra or Poonam," she said. "Can you call one of them?"

"Mum," said Rahul. "There is no rush. I think it would take a day for Priya's body to arrive in Bangalore." He cleared his throat. "I suggest you stay calm and not worry about it."

Usha's nostrils flared. How could Rahul be so unfeeling? She needed to act without any delays. She took her phone from the table and called Poonam.

"Poonam, what am I hearing, dear?"

"Yes, grandma." Poonam cried. "Priya is no more"

"I'm very sorry for the loss, dear. Tell me what really happened?"

"I don't have any idea, grandma. We just received a call from the police that Priya was murdered at her flat." She continued to sob.

"Don't worry, dear." Usha looked at Rahul, who was staring at her. He seemed to be trying to understand the ongoing conversations. "Is anyone going to get Priya's body?"

Poonam paused and said, "Papa is leaving for Hyderabad soon. The funeral will be taking place likely by tomorrow noon."

Usha didn't want to distress Poonam any further. She said she would meet her soon and ended the call. "God shouldn't have been so harsh on Priya. Poor girl. She would've got married had she not gone to Hyderabad."

"We should blame her father for the loss, Mum," Rahul said. "He made a mistake by sending Priya to Hyderabad even though she was engaged."

"He committed another mistake by forcing Priya to get engaged to that fellow - what's his name? Nayan Chabra."

Rahul inhaled a heavy breath. Usha made him angry by bringing up the past incident. "Absolutely, Mum. He is paying the price for his mistake he has committed. I think he will be ashamed to face us after what happened to Priya."

Mrs. Usha placed her hand on Rahul's shoulder. "Let's not harbor any kind of animosity. It's time for us to show our support to them. We both are going to meet them this evening."

20TH OCTOBER 4 PM

Mr. Shekar Bedi, saddened by the death of his daughter, sat in the living room. He made a few calls to his relatives and discussed the funeral arrangements.

His cell phone rang. An unknown number lit the screen. Who might it be? He hastened to grab the phone and answered. "Bedi here."

"Hello, uncle," the voice said. "Did you recognize my voice?"

"What the hell?" said Mr. Bedi to himself. "No. Who is this?"

"It's Harsha, uncle. How are you?"

"What the hell do you want?"

"Didn't I tell you you're going to get Priya in trouble? You hurt me by refusing my proposal to marry Priya. Now, it's your turn, Mr. Bedi. I'm happy to see you losing your lovely daughter."

"How dare you," said Mr. Bedi, his face flushed with anger. "I know it's you who murdered my daughter. I'll call the police and tell them about you."

"I'm glad to see you angry, Mr. Bedi. Good Bye."

Mr. Shekar Bedi gently tossed the phone on the table and heaved a sigh. He was already saddened by the loss and Priya's ex, Harsha's words added insult to injury. *It's time for me to inform the police about Harsha.*

Chapter 06 - The Trio Discusses The Old Cases

20TH OCTOBER 1:30 PM - Hyderabad

"All right." Mayur rose. "We will leave now. Julia, I hope you're attending work tomorrow."

Julia nodded. "I'll call Krishna and tell him I can only work tomorrow because it's already late."

"We're interested in meeting Krishna," Mayur said.

"We can go to his office along with Julia," Aisha said.

Prakash said bye to Julia and led everyone towards his vehicle.

The sun shone intensely in the middle of the sky. A not so warm wind swept over the apartment. The breeze lessened the warmth of the afternoon sunlight. A flock of pigeons took flight above a building. A few workers planted rose bushes between the lanes and watered the lawn. They wore soiled uniforms. A couple of kids practiced riding a bicycle.

Mayur and Aisha sat in their usual seats. Prakash drove the vehicle out of the apartment parking lot. Mayur remained silent until Prakash headed down the main street.

"I'm glad to see Julia accommodated in a different guest house," Mayur said. "She would have had a problem staying here at Hyderabad alone in a lodge if the second guest house was not vacant," Mayur said.

"Yes," said Prakash. "She is really shocked to see her friend murdered and would've gone back to Mumbai if there was no place to stay."

"We need to tell her to be cautious and not to venture outside at night," Aisha said. "Who knows if the perpetrator will strike once again?"

"You're correct," Mayur said to Aisha. "She appeared quite fainthearted and she will take some time to come out of the shock. If you were not with us, we would've found it difficult to console her."

Aisha turned to Mayur. "What do you infer after questioning Julia?"

"Well, I wanted to ask a few more questions, but she needed to freshen up because she traveled overnight. Though she told us some important details, she seemed to be hiding something from us."

"What is it that she hid from us?" Prakash asked.

"She said Priya argued with someone over the phone, but she hadn't asked with whom Priya spoke. Julia had been very close to her and I still believe Priya would've shared the secret with her."

Prakash cleared his throat. "What if Julia is telling the truth? We don't have any evidence to say she is lying, right?"

"But once she grew angry over Aisha when she asked her a question. Julia seemed off-balance with herself. If she were telling the truth, she wouldn't have gotten angry, right?"

Prakash remained silent, seemingly convinced that Julia indeed hid some facts.

"You suspected some connection between Julia going to Mumbai and Priya's murder. Do you still believe Julia deliberately went to leave Priya alone in the flat?" Aisha asked.

"Julia said she went to see her parents a month ago. Her plan to visit Mumbai again may not be connected with the murder. But Julia said Priya needed to finish her assignment and she decided to stay.

This we need to check with her manager Krishna before we come to a conclusion."

"I agree with your theory," Aisha said.

"We need to get Priya's call details soon," Mayur said. "The information should help us in our investigation."

"Sure, I will," Prakash said, negotiating a hairpin bend. "But for me, Julia appeared quite cooperative. She answered us truthfully even though she was in shock. And I didn't notice her getting angry while she answered except once with Aisha."

"I feel you didn't get much chance to interview Priya's father over the phone," Aisha said to Mayur.

"As you've seen," Mayur said, "her parents were not in a mood to answer any of my queries. They were shocked. No doubt it's reasonable for them to grieve about their daughter's death. I didn't want to ask them any questions in their current situation. We are going to Bangalore to attend the funeral and to enquire about the details."

"I wonder why no one from Priya's family or her fiancé, Nayan visited her in Hyderabad," Aisha said.

"I too am surprised by that fact," Prakash said. "Her parents would've come here at least once to see her."

"I remember Julia saying Priya's fiancé is a businessman," Mayur said. "It's quite likely that Nayan had been busy and couldn't visit. Priya visited Bangalore frequently and her parents didn't feel like coming to Hyderabad. Also, Priya was getting transferred to Bangalore after six months."

"You may be correct," Prakash said. "We need to prepare the list of suspects and interview them before we come to a final conclusion."

"I agree," said Mayur. "I'm not the kind of a person who would rush to close the case without thorough investigation."

Aisha patted Mayur's back. "I know your style of working on cases; slow and steady before ending it successfully."

Mayur looked at Aisha over his shoulder. "Thank you for keeping faith in me."

Aisha smiled back.

"We'll go to my office. I would like you both to go through a file related to robberies that have occurred in the city in the past two years." Prakash steered his Jeep towards the right and entered the police station. He parked the vehicle in a vacant slot and stepped out of the vehicle.

Mayur walked alongside Prakash and Aisha into the main hall. The police constable bowed and greeted. Mayur smiled at him and walked into Prakash's office.

The room was spacious. A teakwood table sat in the middle, next to a wide window. A globe was placed on the table, along with a pen stand and a couple of paperweights. A few files were strewn on the other side of the table, beside a local newspaper.

The photographs of Mahatma Gandhi, Jawaharlal Nehru, and Dr. Ambedkar adorned the wall. The entire room was painted in dark blue.

"Please take your seats." Prakash gestured them to chairs in front of the table. He walked to a large, Godrej locker and retrieved a couple of files. He flipped through the pages and then returned to his seat.

"Let's go through these files." He placed the files on the table and sat on his chair.

Mayur glanced at the files which belonged to robbery cases. He took the top one and started going through the details. The robbery had taken place in the Banjara Hills police station limits a year ago.

The victim had been strangled with a nylon wire and the house was burgled. The wounded survived after battling for her life for two weeks. The police were successful in arresting a couple of suspects. The case was pending in the criminal court.

"What do you think about the case?" Prakash asked.

"Well," said Mayur. "I don't see much connection between this one and Priya's murder. The perpetrator wouldn't have killed her if his intention was to steal the valuables. I don't think Priya was the kind of woman who would protest about handing over her jewels to the thief."

"I agree with you that Priya was killed unlike these two cases. But the victims in the previous cases were lucky to survive. The intention of the perpetrator in both the previous cases was to kill the victim. When they became unconscious, the thief hastened to rob the valuables before he ran away."

Mayur remained silent, contemplating. The missing valuables in Priya's case strongly supported Prakash's arguments. But he still believed the case didn't belong to the one they were looking at. Perhaps, the perpetrators took away the valuables to misguide the investigators.

Mayur didn't like to argue with Prakash. Prakash would be convinced as they proceeded with the case and got a few leads. Maybe, he wanted to please his superiors by closing the case soon saying it was linked to one of the robbery cases.

Mayur needed to be cautious not to annoy Prakash by speaking his mind. He needed the cases from him to investigate so that he would stay busy in his profession. He had developed a good relationship with Prakash. He didn't want to sever his ties and get himself in trouble.

He took the second file from Aisha and flipped through its pages. The victim, Anand Sexena, was suffocated with a pillow and he became unconscious. The robber took all his valuables away. Middle-aged Mr. Sexena got better after being treated in the hospital. The police concluded this case was also related to the suspects, who had been arrested. The case was pending in the court.

"The robbers who have committed the crimes are in police custody," Mayur said. "How is it possible to relate them to Priya's murder?"

"Well," said Prakash. "It's not yet proved that these arrested suspects have committed the crime. The suspects have so far denied the allegations made by the police. It may be possible that some other person is involved in all these cases. Or they're part of a larger group headed by a major rowdy."

"I think so too," Aisha said. "Why aren't the police successful yet in arresting these men to make them speak the truth? I know you've tough methods to make them spit it out."

Prakash's face lit up with a grin. Perhaps, he was boosted by Aisha's words.

"I know, but in spite of all our efforts, they're remaining tight-lipped. It is likely that they are not involved in the case, but we're not sure about that either."

Prakash's phone rang. He took the phone from his shirt pocket and looked at the screen. "It's my boss," he whispered.

Mayur continued to stare at Prakash until the conversation ended.

"My boss wants me to meet him urgently." Prakash rose. "I'm sorry, I was unable to spend more time on this."

Mayur and Aisha bade farewell to Prakash and then they walked out.

Aisha sat in the front passenger's seat while Mayur slid behind the wheel.

"I don't understand why Prakash is so reluctant to agree with my opinions. I have confidence that Priya's murder is not connected with the previous two robbery cases. I know Prakash is in a hurry to close the case. He's being pressured from his boss." He started the engine and eased his car out of the parking lot.

"Well," Aisha said. "He is saying so because the perpetrator took away the valuables from Priya. Also, the murderer has searched Priya's bedroom for anything which is worthy to steal."

"So, you're supporting Prakash's theory, then." Mayur chuckled while he headed down the main street.

"I'm only sharing his thoughts once again with you."

"We've been working with Prakash for the past few years and solved several cases. Have you come across an incident where I made wrong decisions or guesses?"

Aisha remained silent. Perhaps, she agreed to what Mayur said about his profession; she no doubt had confidence in him.

He turned his car left and entered Kamat Restaurant. He found a vacant slot amidst a crowded parking lot.

"I think you're hungry," he said as he walked towards the entrance.

They waited for someone to usher them to an empty table. A waiter in a red and white uniform escorted them to a corner seat, beside a window. They made themselves comfortable on the chairs.

"I feel sorry for Prakash," Mayur said.

Aisha propped her elbows on the table and looked at Mayur with a 'why so?' expression.

"He works hard and has tremendous pressure from his bosses. He often shared his bitter experience with me. The red tape bureaucracy is preventing him from making the right decisions."

"And thank God he is consulting you to solve the cases and see them solved successfully," Aisha said.

"Yes, I appreciate him for his efforts to remain truthful. He is ensuring that proper justice is delivered to the victims."

"You made a good decision to resign from your post and start your own detective agency," Aisha said. "You can continue your passion for solving mysteries. You're not under pressure from anyone and you can excel in your profession."

"Yes, you're correct." Mayur smiled.

His phone rang. It was his mother. She was annoyed as she wanted him to come home soon to see his sister, Apsara before she went to bed.

Chapter 07 - Mayur Discusses The Case with Aisha

21ST OCTOBER 7 AM

Mayur took a hot bath, which relieved him from his body ache. He had been working on Priya's murder case for more than twelve hours a day. It had been midnight when he returned home last night. He had to read the previous case files that Prakash gave him.

He wiped his wet body with a Turkish towel, wrapped it around him, and then walked to his bedroom. Standing in front of the dresser mirror, he took another soft towel and wiped his wet hair. His shiny, black hair touched his forehead. His oblong and well-chiseled face appeared fair and shone in the fluorescent lights.

After combing his hair, he went to his closet. It had been boring for him to wear a formal dress. He picked out khaki corduroy pants and a checkered white shirt and donned them. He went back to the dresser, smoothed out his shirt then went to the living room. His mother, seated on a couch. was chanting a prayer, holding a prayer book.

Mayur sat beside her. "I'll have breakfast in the restaurant."

Mrs. Varma closed the book. "I've prepared a vegetable sandwich for you. Why don't you eat it?"

He didn't want to disappoint her. She had been suffering from depression after losing his father five years ago. Mayur never forgot his mother's loss and did his best to keep her comfortable.

"All right," said he. "I like the sandwiches you make." He rose and walked towards the dining hall. But he needed to finish eating as it was already late.

"Don't be late in the night," Mrs. Varma said. "Apsara was angry yesterday. You promised to help her with the assignments, but you came back after she'd gone to bed."

"I'm sorry, Mum," said Mayur, eating his breakfast. "Today, I'll return early, promise."

"Mayur," said his mother. "You have been caring for Apsara a lot especially since your father died. Though she missed her Dad, your utmost care has kept her comfortable; you have been a Godsend for her, you know."

"Thank you, Mum." He paused. "When will she be back from her college?" he asked.

"Her college is open only for a half-day today," said Mrs. Varma. "She should be back by noon."

"Tell her I'll be back by five."

Mayur cared about his younger sister. He took an interest in grooming her with her studies. He helped her with her pre-university admission in one of the top colleges in Hyderabad. He never wanted to compromise her schooling matter.

Apsara had supported Mayur when he dated Shilpa, a receptionist at Leela Palace, two years ago. Mayur's mother had opposed his affair. Mrs. Varma wanted him to get married to someone who belonged to their caste. Also, she disliked Shilpa's profession - a helpdesk employee. Mrs. Varma came from an orthodox family.

Mayur became heartbroken when Shilpa told him she was marrying her distant relative. He hadn't expected she would reject him. It took almost a year for him to recover from the shock. Mayur asked Shilpa the reason for her such a decision. She told him she was under pressure from her parents. Mayur expected Shilpa's parents might not consent to their union. They didn't show much interest in talking to him when he met them at her house.

Mayur's mother also expressed her dissatisfaction when he introduced her to Shilpa. Caught in a dilemma and feeling insecure, Shilpa chose to marry her relative. Mayur didn't dare to go against his mother.

Their break up was also one of the reasons why he resigned from the post as a superintendent of police. He went into depression and his productivity lessened after Shilpa got married. Mayur resigned, to avoid the pressure from superiors, and the red-tape bureaucracy. He founded his own brainchild - Dolphin Detective Agency. He started working as a private investigator and consultant.

He wiped his hands with a napkin and rose from his seat. "Thank you for the tasty sandwich, Mum. Bye."

She insisted he drink a glass of milk, but Mayur hastened to put his shoes on and left.

He walked towards his car and pressed the remote to unlock the doors. The cold morning breeze sent a shiver down his spine. He slid behind the wheel, started the engine, and headed down the main street.

Mayur had told Aisha to be at the office half an hour early. He was expecting a call from Prakash and he wanted her to take notes of their conversation. He was dependent on Aisha for jotting the details. Her notes always helped him with the investigation. It had been common practice for him to go through her notes before he retired for the day.

He was fortunate to have Aisha as his junior. She was like a Godsend for him. He still remembered the day when he interviewed her. He had advertised for a personal assistant cum investigator in the local daily news. Though Mayur had received good responses from aspiring candidates, Aisha's resume stood out. She had a degree in law and a diploma in criminal justice. She worked as a junior consultant in one of the detective agencies in Delhi prior to coming to Hyderabad. Mayur became attracted to her when he saw her for the first time in the interview hall. Aisha had worked on many cases and helped her superiors.

He had not expected their friendship would turn into an intimate relationship. In the last few years of working together, they had become close. She had joined him on trips whenever the cases needed them to travel to different places. Mayur often enjoyed her company whenever they stayed together outside of Hyderabad.

Aisha stayed with her widowed mother. She didn't have siblings. Her mother didn't put any restrictions on her to stay away whenever the job required.

Aisha had told to Mayur she'd had a boyfriend when she worked at Delhi. But she always changed the topic whenever Mayur asked about her past. Aisha was keen to develop a new relationship with Mayur.

He steered his car towards his left and eased it inside his office complex parking lot. He hoped Aisha was not waiting for him as he was a bit late.

He exchanged greetings with the receptionist and entered his glass-walled office. He sighed in relief as Aisha wasn't yet in. After dragging his chair out, Mayur sat at the teakwood table.

A smell of jasmine room freshener filled the surroundings and it soothed his mind. The office floor looked quite clean as the cleaning personnel had done their job well. Mayur lit a couple of incense sticks. He chanted a prayer, to the statue of Saraswati—the goddess of knowledge and learning. He sat back in his seat, contemplating Priya's murder case.

Mayur had been waiting for Prakash's call to hear about Priya's call details. Prakash had assured him that he would get back with the findings the previous night. But Mayur hadn't received any calls from him. Maybe Prakash hadn't heard anything from Priya's cell phone service provider.

Prakash's opinion that Priya's case involved theft puzzled Mayur. He ought to prove that the murder was well planned. Mayur wanted a few leads which would take him towards success. He needed to be patient. He wished to hear from Dr. Sunil Hegde to read the autopsy report soon.

The Pizza Hut delivery boy's shirt button and cap intrigued Mayur. But why would the delivery boy murder Priya? The security guard mentioned that Priya wore expensive jewels. Did the delivery boy intend to steal the valuables? Mayur shook his head to flush all the possibilities from his mind. He could ponder the matter further only after hearing the facts from Prakash and Dr. Sunil.

His glance shifted towards the office entrance. Aisha, in her pale pink, creeper patterned sari, entered, smiling. Her chubby cheeks, highlighted with rose blush, shone in the fluorescent light. A pair of earrings dangled as she approached Mayur.

"Good morning," he said, smiling.

Aisha pulled a chair out and sat opposite him. "A very good morning. Hope I'm not late."

"No," said Mayur. "You're in fact on time. I got here a while ago."

She drew in a heavy breath. "Did you hear anything from Prakash and Dr. Sunil?"

"No, not yet."

"I assumed you hadn't as otherwise, you would've been on cloud nine."

He nodded, smiling. "You're correct." He took his phone and placed it on the table. "Let's call Prakash and see if he has anything important to share with us." He swiped the screen and called Prakash. He put the phone on speaker mode and listened to its ring. When Prakash answered, they exchanged greetings. "Do you have any update for us about Priya's case?" Mayur asked, his voice raised. He waited for Prakash to respond.

"Well..." Prakash stumbled for words.

Mayur waited for him to compose himself.

"I enquired with all the Pizza Hut outlets in Hyderabad," Prakash said. "They hadn't received any order from Priya from the Majestic Apartments that evening."

"Not even from the Hi-Tech City Pizza Hut outlet?" Aisha asked.

"Yes."

"Then why were the cap and shirt button found at the crime scene?" said Mayur. "Prakash, are you sure the button and the cap belonged with the Pizza Hut uniform?"

"Yes. Our technicians have confirmed it."

"Was someone close to Priya disguised and enter the flat?" Mayur asked.

"Quite possible. As I told you, the case involves robbery. The missing valuables reveal to us that person wanted to rob Priya."

Was Prakash correct in saying so? But the perpetrator wouldn't have to slit her throat.

"If the intention of the perpetrator was to steal the valuables, why would he murder Priya so brutally?" Mayur asked.

"Maybe Priya was reluctant to hand over the jewels and she protested," said Prakash. "And in the heat of the moment, the robber had murdered her without any options left."

Mayur's phone beeped with an incoming call. It was Dr. Sunil Hegde.

"Prakash," said Mayur. "Dr. Sunil is calling. I'll get back to you after speaking to him." He switched the call Dr. Sunil's.

Chapter 08 - Dr. Sunil's Findings

21ST OCTOBER 9 AM

"Hello, Dr. Sunil," said Mayur.

"Good morning," said the doctor. "I have the autopsy report with me. When can we meet?"

"As soon as possible," replied Aisha.

"What if we meet at my lab?" Dr. Sunil said. "We'll discuss the matter in detail."

"Sure, doctor. We'll be there soon." Mayur ended the call. "Let's call Prakash. It's better if we take him along with us." He called Prakash and updated him about the matter. "Let's go now."

PRAKASH DROVE MAYUR and Aisha to Dr. Sunil's office in his Jeep. He parked the vehicle in the parking lot and entered the suite of offices.

They met a lady receptionist. She spoke over the intercom and then ushered them to Dr. Sunil's office.

"Welcome," the doctor said, smiling. He gestured them to take seats. He sat on one of the wooden chairs.

"All right." Dr. Sunil handed a file to Prakash. "This is the autopsy report. If you've any questions, please let me know."

Mayur cleared his throat. "As you already know, the forensic experts have found a button that belonged to a Pizza Hut uniform. So, we're curious to know if Priya ate pizza on that fateful night."

The doctor took the file from Prakash. He flipped through its pages and then looked up at Mayur. "No, she hadn't consumed pizza that night. She had consumed orange juice and ate biscuits."

Mayur sighed. He needed to concentrate on the other clues—a strand of hair found inside the cap and footprints.

"Did she protest before the killer axed her to death?" Aisha asked.

"No," said Dr. Sunil. "You see there are no bruises on any place of her body which tell us she didn't protest and fight with the perpetrator. She had trusted the perpetrator before he killed her. The perpetrator is a left-hander because the cut is quite deep on the right side of the neck."

"Do you have anything else to share with us?" Prakash asked.

"Well, one other important point is, the weapon used is not the one used in the kitchen. It is quite sharp and the skilled perpetrator handled it without problems. He had used the weapon before in cutting meat or something similar."

"And there was no weapon left at the crime scene," Mayur said. "That indicates the murder is well planned and it's not a case of ordinary burglary."

Prakash's face grew pale. Maybe he worried about the mystery and it would prevent him from closing the case early. But at least, Dr. Sunil's findings convinced him that the case was not as simple as he had thought.

Mayur's chest lightened. He always looked forward to solving complicated cases instead of handling simpler ones. He believed the complex cases would give him good experience. They would develop his 'little gray cells'. He was eager to face riskier challenges and solve complicated mysteries. He never bothered about the time it took to solve the cases to bring the real perpetrator to justice.

"Can we know the time of death, doctor?" Mayur asked.

"It must have occurred between eight o'clock and ten o'clock," said Dr. Sunil. "That's around dinner time."

No doubt the perpetrator had come to Priya's flat disguised as a pizza delivery boy, Mayur thought. He turned to Prakash. "We need to interview the security guard who worked on the night of 19th October."

Prakash nodded. "Sure."

"So, the perpetrator is a left-hander, murdered Priya at around dinner time. And the case is not a suicide," said Mayur, looking at Sunil.

"Yes, that's right." The doctor paused. "And the body is ready for the cremation."

"We should not delay handing over the body to Priya's parents," Prakash said.

"Mr. Bedi has yet to arrive at Hyderabad," Prakash said.

Aisha's phone rang. She looked at the screen. "It's Julia calling."

Chapter 09 - Mayur Meets Priya's Father

21ST OCTOBER 10:30 AM

Aisha, her pulse quickened, put the phone in speaker mode. "Hello, Julia," she said. "Are you all right?"

"Yes, I'm fine," said Julia. "Priya's Dad, Mr. Shekar Bedi is with me at the flat."

Mayur's heart lightened. It would be better if they took the body soon for cremation. He cleared his throat. "Julia, Mayur here. Can Mr. Bedi take the body to Bangalore today?"

"Yes, he doesn't want to delay," said Julia.

"All right," said Prakash. "Please wait, we will come to the flat soon."

"Sure," said Julia. "Mr. Bedi needs your help."

"We'll help him out," said Aisha. "No need to worry." She ended the call.

Mayur turned to Dr. Sunil. "We need to go now. I know your findings will help us in the investigation."

Dr. Sunil handed the file to Mayur. "I wish you all the best. You can call or meet me any time you want. I'm at your service."

"Thank you, doctor," Mayur said. "We'll get back to you if required." He bade Dr. Sunil farewell along with his colleagues and then walked out of his office towards the Jeep.

"Dr. Sunil had some interesting findings for us," Mayur said.

Prakash started the engine and eased the vehicle out of the parking lot. "The fact that the perpetrator is a left-hander intrigues me."

"Yes," said Mayur. "It'll help us in identifying the culprit after we prepare a list of suspects."

"But can we rely on what Dr. Sunil said?" Aisha asked.

"We should because Dr. Sunil has made the right judgments," Mayur said. "He has helped us in closing the cases without fail before."

"And what's the significance of the Pizza Hut cap found at the crime scene?" Aisha asked.

Prakash looked at Aisha over his shoulder before he fixed his gaze back on the road. "I was hopeful that Priya would've called the Pizza Hut and ordered the food."

"Don't worry," said Mayur. "I'm confident we will make progress in the case when we get the telephone call details about Priya."

"It will be available by the end of the day," Prakash said.

He steered his car towards the right and entered Minerva Apartments. He parked his Jeep in a visitor's parking lot and stepped out of the vehicle. They all marched toward Julia's guest house.

Mayur was eager to meet Mr. Shekar Bedi because he has strong evidence in this case. He would reveal some important information which Julia and Krishna might not know. Mr. Bedi had known Priya since she was born and knew her better than the other suspects in the case. Mayur would make use of this opportunity to find out more about the victim.

They arrived at the flat. Prakash rang the doorbell and waited for Julia to open the door.

The latch sounded. Mayur stared at the door, his pulse quickening.

Julia, in her white and purple nightdress, opened the door. She smiled and stepped back, making room for them to step in.

Mayur shifted his gaze to the living room sofa. A middle-aged man sat on the couch, his face pale. He rose to his feet when Prakash entered the room along with Mayur and Aisha.

Mr. Bedi had fair skin. His pale oval and long face and his red, small, deep-set eyes showed his grief. His flat cheeks were sullen, and his thick open lips were dry.

"Please meet Mr. Shekar Bedi," Julia said.

Mr. Bedi shook hands with Mayur and Aisha. He broke into tears while Prakash greeted him. His emotion breached its limit when seeing Prakash in a police uniform. Mr. Bedi continued to sob aloud.

"I never expected it would happen to my daughter." He touched Prakash's shoulder.

Mayur needed to console Mr. Bedi. "Steel yourself, Mr. Bedi."

Mr. Bedi turned to Mayur and wiped the tears flowing down his cheeks. "My daughter was well brought up, sir. I don't know who did it, and I want the police to find out who killed her."

"Don't worry," said Mayur, holding Mr. Bedi's shoulders. "We're looking for the perpetrator, and we need your cooperation."

He sat him on a couch and gestured for Aisha and others to take their seats.

"We assure you that we will get justice for Priya," Prakash said. "Mayur is right that you need to cooperate with us in the investigation."

Mr. Bedi nodded, staring at the floor.

"Is it okay if we ask you a few questions?" Mayur said. Though Mr. Bedi was grief-stricken, Mayur wanted to get some vital information from him. He signaled Aisha to take notes of their interrogation.

"Mr. Bedi," said Mayur. "As a father, would you like to share with us anything about your daughter?"

Mr. Bedi stared down, seemingly contemplating. "Priya was our lovely daughter. Being the eldest of two children, she was honest and innocent. She always concentrated on her studies and never quarreled with anyone - either at home or at school."

"Did she get along well with her mother?"

"Yes. She was the eldest daughter and Priya's mother took extra care of her because she was innocent and naive."

"Did she study at college in Bangalore?" Mayur said.

"Yes. She completed all her studies at Bangalore."

"What was her response when her employer asked her to work in Hyderabad?"

"That's the mistake she made, Mr. Varma." His eyes filled with tears.

Mayur waited for him to gain control over his emotions. When he remained silent, Mayur said, "Please answer me, Mr. Bedi. Was Priya happy to move to Hyderabad?"

"She was reluctant in the beginning" He wiped his tears. "But she was eager to work on cutting edge technologies. It was she who decided to move to Hyderabad. We never expected she would meet such ill fate, you know." He burst into a loud cry once again.

"All right," said Mayur when Mr. Bedi composed himself.

"We should arrange for Priya's body to send it to Bangalore as soon as possible," said Prakash, looking at Mayur.

Mayur too didn't want to continue asking more questions as Mr. Bedi was in shock. He looked at him and said, "One last question, Mr. Bedi. Do you think Priya had any enemies in her life and did she share any of her secrets with you?"

Mr. Bedi looked sideways. He paused, seemingly trying to recall.

Mayur waited for him to answer.

"I already told you she was very innocent and was a very social girl. She didn't have any enemies in her life. But..." He mumbled.

"Yes, tell me," Mayur said. "You don't need to fear. We're all here to help you."

"My younger daughter, Poonam, told me once that Priya loved someone else before she got engaged."

Mayur's heart raced. Priya had an affair before her engagement with Nayan. Her ex-lover should be a strong suspect and should be high on the radar.

"Priya's avuncular uncle, Rahul, was unhappy over Priya getting married to Nayan. He had known Priya since their childhood. and intended to marry her."

No doubt Rahul should be another prime suspect based in Bangalore. *It's imperative for me to visit Bangalore and question all the possible suspects.*

Prakash rose and continued to look at Mayur with an expression of 'it's-getting-late'.

Priya's loved ones and suspects would answer after a few days, once the funeral was over. He needed to wait.

"All right," said he. "Let's go."

Prakash led everyone out of the guesthouse. He helped Mr. Shekar Bedi to take Priya's body in an SUV to Bangalore.

Mr. Bedi told him the funeral would be on the next day evening.

Mayur told him he would travel to Bangalore and attend along with his colleagues and Julia.

Chapter 10 - Secret About Praful and Harsha

21ST OCTOBER 11:30 AM

A damp, cold winter breeze that swept down the parking lot sent a shiver down Mayur's spine. He walked towards the Jeep along with Prakash, Julia, and Aisha. Mayur contented for sending Mr. Bedi off along with Priya's body after consulting Dr. Sunil.

They all sat in the vehicle.

Prakash started the engine and pulled onto the main street.

"Mayur," Aisha said. "Yesterday...someone..."

Mayur looked over his shoulder towards her. He raised his eyebrows. "Yes, tell me what happened yesterday?"

"I received calls from an unknown number." Her lips trembled.

"What's so special about it?" asked Prakash.

"I thought someone tried to threaten me as we're working on Priya's murder case," said Aisha.

"First, I want you to be cautious. But the call may be a hoax. We need to ignore them unless the caller threatens you."

"What did the caller say?" Julia asked.

"They didn't say anything. It was a silent call."

"Don't worry," said Mayur. "They had called the wrong number and disconnected it."

"But I received the call twice, you know."

"Aisha," said Mayur, pressing her hand. "You worry a lot." He paused, drawing a heavy breath. "Next time, you try to make the caller speak up and then call me immediately."

"I'm feeling scared, Mayur." Aisha fiddled with her watch. "It is better if Prakash can help us in identifying who makes such calls to us."

"But," said Prakash, "it would be hard for me also to find the caller. You try to be courageous. These things are common in our profession."

Aisha smiled, which wavered. "What is our next plan?"

Mayur looked at Julia, who was looking at him with her eyes wide. "Julia, what if we go and meet your manager at your office? I have a few questions for him to ask."

"Sure," Julia said. "But Mayur..."

"Yes, tell me."

"I wanted to tell you about Priya's close friendship with one of our teammates."

Mayur's pulse quickened. "Priya was close to someone?"

"Yes."

"Who was it?"

"His name is Praful," said Julia. "He has been working in my team. In the past month, I'd seen Priya spending most of her time with him in the office cafeteria. They also went to the malls and watched movies on the weekends."

"Do you think they were intimate?" asked Prakash.

"Yes. I learned Praful got sacked from his previous employer on sexual harassment charges." Julia paused. "I told you this because the information might help you in your investigation."

"Yes, definitely," said Mayur. "Thanks for revealing it. We're going to your office to meet Krishna and Praful. Also, I assume the security guard to be one of the strong suspects based in Hyderabad."

"Do you think the guard did it?"

"I suspect so. We know from everyone that Priya wore expensive jewels. The guard on duty could've stolen the jewels and killed her when she refused to give her ornaments."

Aisha nodded. "I also think so."

"I suspect Priya's colleague Praful committed the crime," said Prakash.

"Well," said Aisha, "you believed the case belonged to a robbery a few days ago. And now you're saying Praful is a strong suspect."

Mayur chuckled. "You are hastening the investigation without having patience. I hope you will start believing in us when we find the real perpetrator."

Prakash parked his Jeep in his office parking lot. "I need to attend an urgent meeting with my boss. I insist you both go and meet Krishna and Praful."

Mayur narrowed his brows. "But can you-"

"The meeting is quite important," said Prakash. "Otherwise, I would've joined you all, you know."

"All right," said Mayur. He bade Prakash Goodbye and walked towards his car along with Aisha and Julia.

When he pressed the remote, his cell phone rang. He dug it out of his pants pocket and looked at the screen. It was Priya's father. *Why is he calling?* Mayur swiped the green button. "Hello, Mr. Bedi."

"Hi, Mr. Varma," said he. "Are you free now for some time?"

"Yes, Mr. Bedi. Is there anything important you'd like to talk about? I hope everything is all right with your journey."

"Yes," said Mr. Bedi. "Are you alone? I would like to talk about a private matter with you."

"Pray, please proceed," Mayur said.

"I would like to extend whatever support you want in bringing the perpetrator to justice." He paused and then said, "I have a couple of issues to reveal it to you."

"Mr. Bedi, before you talk about the reason for your call, I have a few questions to ask."

"Please go ahead."

"Can I know more about Priya?"

"Priya was my dearest daughter. She was sportive and witty. She always made wise decisions and had been career-oriented."

"Did she got along well with her friends and loved ones?"

"Yes, she indeed was friendly with everyone. You know already how close she had become with Julia within four months of their stay. She was well-mannered and cordial with everyone at home as well."

"Please tell me about her decision to move to Hyderabad."

"You know that's the biggest blunder she ever made in her life." Mr. Bedi sounded emotional. "We pleaded with her not to go there as her wedding was in two months. But she wanted to work on a challenging and cutting edge technology project. She didn't want to lose the opportunity to work on the new project."

"Did she have any pressure from her manager to go there?"

"Yes. but Priya told me her project in the Bangalore office was nearing completion. There were lesser projects to work on because of the slowdown in the American economy. Priya didn't want to remain idle after the completion of her ongoing project in Bangalore."

"Did she ever complain about her manager or her colleagues to you or to your wife?"

"No. She was content working with her colleagues."

Mayur noted down the points in his notepad. "Okay, Mr. Bedi," he said. "What do you think about who murdered Priya? Do you suspect anyone from your family or from outside?"

"I have been pondering this matter and that's the reason why I called you, Mr. Varma."

Mayur waited in silence to hear from Mr. Bedi.

"I told you this morning, Priya loved someone else before she got engaged to Nayan."

Mayur wondered how Mr. Bedi knew about Priya's affair with Harsha. "Did Priya talk to you about it?"

"No, it was not Priya."

"Who was it, then?" asked Mayur.

"Priya's boyfriend, Harsha. He met me once at my place of business and sought Priya's hand in marriage."

"What did you tell him?"

"I asked him about his parents and what he did for a living."

"What happened next?"

"After hearing from him, I found he was unfit for Priya. He had a lower social status, and he also belonged to a different caste. It was impossible for us to allow him to marry Priya."

"What did you tell him?"

"Well, I told him he is unfit for my daughter."

Mayur paused and then said, "What was his reaction?"

"He became angry and we had a little altercation. He swore vengeance before I told my guard to take him away. He might be the one who did it, Mr. Varma."

Mayur remained silent, contemplating. *Perhaps, Harsha insisted Priya break her engagement with Nayan and elope. She would've refused his advice and that has forced him to kill her.*

"Okay, Mr. Bedi. Did you speak about this with your daughter?"

"No."

"Why?"

"Because Priya was willing to get engaged to Nayan and was ready to marry him. I knew she wouldn't defame her parents' social status."

Priya knew Harsha belonged to a lower caste and her parents wouldn't allow her to marry him. Then why did she involve herself with Harsha? She would've told about her boyfriend at least to her mother.

"All right. I've some more questions for you."

"Please, go on," Mr. Bedi said.

"Is your property be equally divided among your daughters?"

"Yes. I don't have any male heir to inherit my assets. I have written a will saying Poonam and Priya will share my property."

"And who will get Priya's share now? Is it Poonam?" Mayur asked, his tone curious.

"You're correct. But why are you asking this?"

"Well, there is a clear reason that the inheritance might be a motive for Priya's murder."

"You mean Poonam..."

"Not Poonam," said Mayur. "I suspect your son-in-law, Chirag."

"No, I can't believe this," said Mr. Bedi.

"Why not?"

"Poonam and Chirag were quite cordial with Priya and Nayan. But, Chirag, No. I can't believe he did this."

"I repeat, why do you think so?" Mayur asked.

"Chirag comes from a rich and well-known family. Being the only son, he will inherit all the small scale industries that his father owns. I can't think he would-."

"I don't buy your theory that rich people are not greedy. I've come across a couple of cases in the past wherein murders have occurred among the riches."

"But that may not be true in my son-in-law's case."

Mayur heaved a sigh. "Are you trying to protect Chirag?"

"Why would I protect him?"

"Your family name will become defamed and it might affect your business."

Mr. Bedi remained silent. It was possible he became ashamed that his social status would come down if Chirag had killed Priya.

"Mr. Bedi," said Mayur. "I want you to be honest."

"How dare you accuse me of something so horrendous, Mr. Varma? If I weren't telling you the truth, I wouldn't have called you, you know." He paused. "You should visit Bangalore soon. And it's time for me to say goodbye."

"Bye," Mayur said.

It is possible that Mr. Bedi is telling the truth. I need to go to Bangalore soon and find out more details.

Mayur told Aisha and Julia it was Priya's father who called him and updated them about what Mr. Bedi told him.

Chapter 11 - Mayur Interviews Krishna Raj

21ST OCTOBER 12:00 NOON - Hyderabad

Mayur sat in the car, his mood upbeat. He was curious to meet Krishna and find out more about Priya and her close colleague Praful. Aisha sat in the passenger seat while Julia in the back. The smell of jasmine perfume lingered in the air.

The morning traffic was moderate. A few cars carrying officials, who wore ties, sped past green city buses. The youngsters on their motorbikes sneaked through the passages between the automobiles. Rickshaw drivers, pedaling with difficulty, carried the passengers and khaki boxes. A few young kids in red and yellow uniforms pedaled their bicycles to get to their schools.

Mayur drove towards the Majestic Apartment to talk to the security guard. The security personnel on duty, in his pale-blue uniform, told Mayur the name of the guard was Hemanth. He gave him his phone number. Mayur jotted the details in his phonebook and then drove the car back towards the main street.

Mayur passed a heavy vehicle, carrying sacks of rice and belching out fumes. "May I know when your project at Hyderabad started?" he asked Julia.

"May this year. I can't believe it's been five months. It has been a pleasure working on the project, but Priya's incident dampened the spirits."

"What is the project's duration?" Aisha asked, looking over her shoulders.

"One year project, but it will extend for a few more months," said Julia. "We are lagging the design phase and the customer wants some more features to put in place."

"What's team size?" asked Mayur.

"Five excluding Priya."

Mayur needed to know more about Krishna. He might give him some vital information related to the investigation. "What's your opinion about Krishna?"

"Um...Are you interested to know something specific?"

"Did he like Priya?"

"Yes. He liked Priya because she worked hard and she was willing to learn new technologies. Priya was fond of using the latest software tools and we all learned from her about how to use them."

"Did she get along with Krishna and everyone in the team well?" Mayur asked.

"Yes," said Julia. "She was quite friendly to everyone. It's a great loss for us, you know."

"So, was Priya the top performer in your team?" Mayur said.

"Yes. She assumed more responsibilities and worked as a group leader."

"Was she aiming for a promotion?" asked Mayur.

"Maybe but I admire her for the contribution she had made towards the project."

"All right," said Mayur. "What Priya's father told me—Priya was fond of working on new technologies—is true."

"Yes, it's quite true."

"If she finished the tasks on time, why did she stay at Hyderabad on the weekend she died?" asked Mayur. "Why didn't she go to her home town?"

Julia remained silent for a few moments. "She was working on a few more tasks and she wanted to finish them before Monday."

Mayur was now convinced that Priya did well at her work. Her workplace challenges never bothered her. "What's your opinion about Praful? Is he a productive worker?"

"Yes, but...I ...re-"

"Tell me. You don't need to hesitate."

"He is not a good worker. He spent most of the time in the smoke room or in the cafeteria. He angered Krishna many times by not finishing the job on time. I remember Krishna arranging a few one-on-ones to make Praful work hard. But he remained lazy and passed his time in the smoke room."

"When did he join the organization?"

"A week before I reported. I've been observing him since then and his attitude has been disgusting. I wanted to ask Krishna what's the point in retaining him on the team. But Krishna said, 'Let the year-end performance appraisal period approach. I rate Praful as unsuccessful and I will talk to the management with the proof in hand.' I stopped complaining about him to Krishna then on."

"Where did he work before?"

"I don't know."

"Did he get along with Krishna and the rest of his team members in spite of not meeting expectations?"

"He behaved well and often initiated conversations with the team members on his own. Krishna got peeved because Praful didn't put enough hard work. He agreed to Praful's request to join him in the cafeteria. Maybe Krishna was hopeful Praful would change."

"What's your opinion about his close friendship with Priya?" asked Mayur.

"Well...I... really..."

Why is Julia stumbling? Is she trying to hide something?

"You can tell us without hesitation," Aisha said. "Did Praful get closer to Priya a few weeks before she got killed?"

"Mayur," said Julia. "I don't know what was the intention behind their closeness. But I agree that Praful took Priya to the cafeteria quite often. And I'd seen them quite close with each other a month before Priya...."

"Were they just friends?" asked Mayur. "Or had they crossed the limit and were intimate?"

"Priya was engaged, right?" asked Julia. "It's absurd to think she indulged in anything inappropriate with Praful."

Is it correct to consider Praful as a possible suspect? "Julia," said Mayur. "Don't you think you need to help us solve the case and bring justice to Priya's soul?"

"I know," she said, her voice trembling. "I've been answering all your questions so far, right?"

"But you're hiding something which might help us in solving the case," said Mayur.

"Priya was spending her weekends with Praful," said Julia. "They went to movies and eat out at restaurants. They looked for some privacy as Priya never invited me to join them. I wondered why Priya was behaving so, but I remained silent. Maybe Praful hypnotized Priya. He has those skills to lure a woman to his side, you know."

Mayur's heart lightened. "Do you think Praful seduced Priya?"

"Yes," said Julia. "He was a womanizer."

Mayur drove to Julia's office, contented. No doubt Julia's evidence made Praful strong suspect. He would interview Krishna and Praful to find out their sides of the story.

"One last question," said Mayur.

"What is it?"

"Was Priya attracted to Praful? Or did she consider him a friend?"

"I'm not sure," said Julia. "But as I said, she got closer to him in the last one month. She flirted with Praful and they often went out."

Mayur stepped out of his car and joined Julia and Aisha. "Thanks for answering me with patience. You've been very helpful in our investigation."

Julia smiled.

The five-storied glass-framed office building reflected the morning sunlight. It had a heightened, wide, wooden framed entrance in the center. A few people entered and left through the foyer.

Mayur stepped into the lobby along with Julia and Aisha. The main hall was spacious with a front desk located on the left. Two plush black leather sofas sat opposite to the right. Large-sized crotons adorned the two corners, beside a wide entranced lift.

A lady receptionist sat behind the help desk. Her large, open lips, smeared with red lip gloss, appeared like cherries. Her medium complexioned face was overly applied with talcum powder. Her short black hair was tied into a bun which suited her wide forehead.

Julia spoke to her about Mayur's intention to meet Krishna. The receptionist told Mayur and Aisha to take seats in the lobby and then spoke over the intercom.

Mayur waited for Krishna to arrive while Julia continued chatting with the receptionist.

A tall man with a thick black mustache and not so fair complexion stepped out of the lift. He looked at Mayur for a while before shifting his gaze towards Julia. She approached him and they both walked towards Mayur.

"Mayur, meet my manager, Krishna."

Mayur and Aisha rose. They shook hands with Krishna.

Krishna wore a formal suit—a blue striped white shirt and navy blue pants. His oblong and neatly shaved face lit with a light smile. He appeared handsome with a gold chain around his neck. "Let's go to the conference room." He led them to a room located to the right of the help desk.

"Krishna," Julia said. "I'll go to my workstation. Please let me know if you need me."

Krishna nodded. "Sure."

Mayur and Aisha sat opposite him.

"I'm shocked by the incident," Krishna said. "The Almighty shouldn't have been so unkind to Priya. She was so innocent and was liked by everyone on my team."

Mayur remained silent for a couple of moments before Krishna settled down. "We're confident that we'll find the perpetrator if all of you answer my questions."

"We'll be happy to assist you."

"May I know your age?"

"Thirty-two," Krishna said.

"Are you a native of Hyderabad?"

"Yes. Born and brought up here."

"Where did you study?"

Krishna told him the name of the school and where he finished his engineering course.

Mayur made sure Aisha wrote down everything. "When did you start your current job?" he said, looking back at Krishna.

Krishna wrinkled his forehead, seemingly annoyed by what Mayur asked. When Mayur continued to look at him, he said, "six years ago. I had worked for two years in a small start-up company before getting my current job."

"Are you happy working here?"

"Yes, I am."

"How many projects have you handled so far?"

Krishna looked sideways, seemingly making a mental calculation. "Four projects. For the past two years, I've worked as a team leader. There are five people right now on my team."

Mayur heaved a heavy sigh. "Okay," he said. "Thanks for answering my question. Your personal details are valuable to us." He paused and then said, "May I ask you a few questions about Priya?"

"Go ahead, please."

"What was your perception of Priya?" He looked into Krishna's eyes.

Krishna dropped his gaze. He said, after a few moments, "Are you interested in any particular information?"

"Anything which would help us in the investigation."

"Well," said Krishna. "I already told you, everyone on my team liked her. She was a hard worker and never said no when I assigned her any more work. It's a great loss for me and my company, you know."

"We know from a reliable source that Priya grew closer to Praful in the last month," said Mayur. "Would you like to tell us more about the matter?"

Krishna's face grew pale and he stared down. Why he remained silent? Mayur couldn't wait any longer to hear from him.

"Yes, tell me, Mr. Krishna," said Mayur. "I would like to know more about Priya's closeness with Praful."

Krishna forced a smile. "I agree that Priya was spending more time with Praful in the last month. I had seen them together in the office cafeteria flirting. I had worried why Priya behaved so as her productivity was coming down because of that. I wanted to caution her about her attitude. But before I spoke to her, she became dear to the Almighty."

"But you said Priya worked hard and other team members liked her," said Aisha.

"Yes, that was one month before she died. Priya was with us for five months and in the last couple of weeks, she became closer to Praful. As I said, I wanted to warn them, but I thought they might become offended. I was waiting for the right opportunity to speak to them."

"You made a good decision," Aisha said. "We have considered Praful as one of our strong suspects."

A bead of sweat formed on Krishna's head. He seemed to have scared about telling Praful's involvement in the case.

"Don't worry," said Mayur, trying to make him feel comfortable. "We won't tell Praful that you told us about him."

"That would be great."

"We know that Praful got sacked by his previous employer because of sexual harassment."

"Yes, he was."

"Why did you hire him, then?"

"Well, I came to know about it only after Praful joined us. I was helpless, you know."

"Can you tell us about his work ethics? Did he work well and contributes to the project?"

"He is not that an efficient worker," said Krishna. "But I'm extracting the work by using repeated follow-ups."

"Did you ever think of cautioning Praful about his underperformance?"

"Yes, I did. But I liked to wait until this year-end performance appraisal."

"You said you wanted to caution Priya about her reduced work performance."

"Yes, I did hint to Priya that her productivity had decreased in the last month."

"What was her response?" Aisha asked.

"She apologized and told me she would improve."

Mayur remained silent for a few moments. "A couple of more questions about Priya. How often did Priya go to Bangalore?"

"She told me she went there for almost every fortnight."

"Julia told us she worked on that fateful weekend."

"Yes, I remember she went to the office on that Sunday."

"Did you assign her any more work to complete?" said Mayur. "Julia said Priya had planned to visit her parents on that weekend."

"There was an important assignment we needed to work on. We worked together until the evening and fixed the bug. But I had never expected Priya would face such a situation soon after she went to her apartment."

Mayur heaved a sigh of relief. He didn't have anything more to ask Krishna. "We'll meet again when we need more information about the investigation." He looked at Aisha and then back at Krishna. "Can you please send Praful to us?"

Krishna rose. "Sure. I will. It was good to meet you both." He shook hands and walked out of the meeting room, closing the door behind him.

They sat in silence for a moment until Aisha said, "Krishna seemed honest to me."

"I too think so, but we need to verify if Praful was intimate with Priya. We'll get a clear picture only when we interview Praful. We should check if any of the forensic evidence found at the crime scene proves he is guilty."

Chapter 12 - Evidence of Praful

21ST OCTOBER 1:00 PM

Mayur and Aisha sat in silence for a couple of minutes. There was a perfunctory knock and the door opened. A young man in his late twenties entered, looking at Aisha first and then at Mayur. His gaze fixed back on Aisha. His lips quivered into a grin. He sat opposite her on the couch.

His square and fair face glistened in the daylight. He stood tall, around 5' 9" as his head almost touched the door frame. His black, well-combed hair shone with hair oil applied to it. His dark, almond eyes locked onto Aisha's. He was clean-shaven.

Praful's intense gaze at her irritated Mayur. But he needed to remain calm. His angry response would offend Praful, making him not cooperate in the investigation.

Mayur stretched out his hand. "I'm Detective Mayur Varma." Praful shook his hand. "And this is my junior, Aisha Mishra."

Praful's face lit with a wide grin but didn't last long. "Hi, good to meet you," he said, looking at Aisha.

"Mr. Praful," said Mayur. "I hope you know why we're here." He tried to read Praful's face for any sign of guilt, fear, or embarrassment.

Praful held his shoulders tight and tried to gather the courage to speak with confidence. "Yes, Krishna did tell me."

"Are you comfortable answering a few of my questions?" Mayur asked.

Praful nodded, smiling.

"Your full name?"

"Praful Dinesh Chawla."

"Where did you work before?"

"I worked for a startup company called Logic InfoTech," said Praful.

"Why did you leave it?" Mayur asked.

"Well...I was..."

"You can answer me without hesitation and we will keep it confidential," Mayur said. "What's the reason?"

"I was looking for a promotion," said Praful. "And a pay hike."

Krishna had told Mayur about Praful's sexual harassment incident. What a lying scoundrel. Getting honest information won't be easy.

"Did you get the pay hike and the desired position by joining your current employer?"

"Yes, sort of."

"But I've learned that your last employer sacked you because of sexual harassment."

"Who... told...you..." A bead of sweat formed on Praful's forehead.

"I want you to tell the truth, Mr. Chawla," said Mayur. "It's important that you cooperate so that we can catch the murderer soon."

Praful's face grew ashen.

"Mr. Praful," said Aisha. "We'll protect you if you cooperate with us in the investigation."

Praful took out a handkerchief from his pants pocket and wiped his forehead; he swallowed. "I agree with you." He looked into Mayur's eyes. "Please don't disclose this to anyone. I'll cooperate with you in the investigation." He switched his gaze between Aisha and Mayur. "I didn't kill Priya. I swear in the name of God. I'm shocked, you know."

"All right," said Mayur. "We want you to be honest and save yourself from conviction by behaving so."

Praful nodded.

"What your father do for a living?"

"He works as a deputy manager in a cooperative bank."

"What about your mother?"

"She is a housewife." Praful leaned forward. "Are these questions relevant?"

"Yes," Aisha said. "Mayur wouldn't ask you anything which is not connected to the case."

"What's your opinion about Priya?" Mayur asked, after a moment of silence. Though he realized Praful was a good friend of Priya, he needed to find out more details about her.

"Oh, no," Praful said. "I miss her a lot, Mr. Varma. It's a great loss for all. She was quite friendly with everyone on the team and I respected her for her work ethics."

"How close were you both?"

Praful narrowed his brows. "Well, it was as good as my friendship with other members of the team."

"Was your friendship limited to the office cafeteria?"

Praful breathed fast. He nodded. "Yes."

"But we know you went to movies and malls with her."

Praful's face fell. "Well...I really..."

"Mr. Praful," said Aisha. "You please tell us the truth. Otherwise, we'll take you to the police station and punish you to reveal the facts." She paused and then said, "Now, tell us the facts without fabricating them."

"I agree that we visited malls and watched movies together," said Praful. "But if you think I'm the one who killed her, you're wrong. I swear..." Praful touched his Adam's apple. He then wiped the tears from his face using his handkerchief.

"Did Priya share any information about her family members?" Mayur asked.

"Um...she did tell me that she and Nayan got engaged. But..."

"What else did she share?" asked Mayur. "Was she happy about marrying Nayan?"

"Yes, but she told me it was her father who liked Nayan and insisted she marry him. I asked whether she loved anyone else, but she never revealed any of her personal matters. She came from an orthodox family and her parents forced her to accept the alliance with Nayan."

"Did she tell you how she felt about staying away from her parents?"

"Oh yeah," said Praful. "She had said, 'It has been choking for me to live with my father in Bangalore, obeying his orders. I'm happy to be away from him for at least one year.' I wondered whether she loved her fiancé."

"But she went to Bangalore often on the weekends, right?" Mayur asked.

"She loved her mother. Though she felt irritated having to agree with her parents' orders, she was dear to her mother. She had said, "if it were not for my mother's love and affection, I wouldn't have visited Bangalore. My mother knows I didn't like Nayan, but she too was helpless. She feared my father about the customs and rituals of society. She wondered what our relatives would say if I married someone against my parents' wishes.""

"Did she say anything about her avuncular uncle, Rahul?"

"Rahul...? Well... she did mention him."

"What did she say?"

"She had said, 'Though I liked my uncle since I was a child, I never had any interest in marrying him. But Rahul grew obsessed with marrying me. I realized his love towards me when he confronted my father after I got engaged with Nayan.' In fact, it seemed Rahul often had talked to her over the phone when she was in Hyderabad. She had said, 'Rahul had been insisting we elope and get married in a temple with our friends' support'. But Priya loved her mother. Though her father had been orthodox, Priya didn't want to hurt him and defame his status in society."

"Did she mention her ex-boyfriend, Harsha?" asked Aisha.

"No, she didn't," said Praful. "I wondered if she ever had a boyfriend in her life as she came from such a conservative family."

"You agreed that you spent weekends with Priya watching movies and eating out at a restaurant."

Praful nodded. "Yes, I agree."

"How close were you both?" Mayur asked. "Was your friendship limited to spending time together or were you bother intimate?"

"No, Mr. Varma," said Praful, his eyes wide. "We were just good friends and nothing beyond that. Priya was engaged and she never thought of indulging in anything immoral."

"What about you?" Mayur asked. "Were you attracted to her?"

"You're wrong about me, Mr. Varma," said Praful. "I considered Priya as a good friend. I tried to relieve her from homesickness when she stayed away from her loved ones."

"All right," said Mayur. "I would like to know where you were between eight and eleven o'clock on that eventful evening."

"Um..." Praful looked the window with his finger on his lips. "I was at home with my parents."

"Are you sure?" asked Aisha.

"Yes," Praful sounded confident while he lifted his chin.

"When did you last see Priya?" Mayur asked.

"On Friday."

"So, you didn't work on the weekend."

"Um...Yes... that's...correct," Praful said, his voice trembling.

Mayur sat in silence for a moment. He needed to check with Krishna to find out whether Praful had not worked on that weekend.

"Okay," said Mayur. "Why didn't you attend Priya's funeral?"

"I had urgent work to attend. But I'm still disappointed about not making the event."

"Who told you about Priya's death?"

"I heard it from my colleagues. I came to the office on Monday morning as usual and my colleagues were talking about it in groups. At first, I couldn't believe it, but when the news app started broadcasting the message, I realized Priya was no more."

"What's your opinion about Krishna?"

"Oh, I enjoy working with him." Praful smiled. "I'm lucky to be part of his team."

But Julia and Krishna had told that Praful was not that productive in the last month. Why did Praful make contradictory statements?

"One last question, Mr. Chawla."

"Yes, please ask."

"Are you married?"

"No."

"Do you have a girlfriend?"

Praful's' face lit with a light smile. He nodded.

"All right," said Mayur. "You may need to visit our forensic lab for a DNA test. We'll take you there in a couple of hours." He studied Praful's face for any signs of embarrassment. Although Praful's face was ashen, he gave his consent by nodding.

Mayur remembered Dr. Sunil saying the perpetrator was a left-hander. He needed to check Praful's orientation. "Can I have your telephone number, please?" He took the scribbling pad from Aisha and gave it to Praful.

Praful took his pen from his shirt pocket using his left hand, sending a cold shiver down Mayur's spine. Praful wrote on the pad using the left hand. It was imperative to conduct DNA tests as early as possible.

Mayur needed to check if Praful's shoe size matched with that of the one collected at the crime scene - a size nine print.

"And may I know the size of your shoes, Mr. Praful?"

"It's size eight."

"Are you sure?"

"Yes, I am."

Mayur told him to remove his shoe and checked the size. He made sure number eight was printed on it and then said to Praful, "you can go. Send Krishna in."

Krishna entered with his brows joined together. Mayur gestured for him to a seat.

"Did I disturb you, Mr. Krishna?" asked Mayur.

"It's okay," said he. "Are you done questioning Praful?"

"Yes, but I need to verify some of the things he said."

"Pray, please ask."

"He told me he hadn't worked with her on the evening Priya got murdered. Is that true?"

"No, it's not true," said Krishna. "He did attend work. In fact, Priya accompanied him in the evening when she left the office."

Mayur's chest constricted. He looked at Aisha. "Why did Praful lie to us, then?"

"He feared the conviction," Aisha added.

Mayur turned to Krishna. "He told me that his performance on the team has been satisfactory and he got along with you and other team members."

"Liar," Krishna said.

Mayur thanked him for the interview and bade him goodbye. He walked back to the parking lot and slid behind the wheel.

"What do you infer after meeting Praful and Krishna?" Aisha said as Mayur steered his car out of the parking lot.

"Krishna tried to help us," said Mayur. "He is very much affected by the loss. His suspicion about Praful's involvement is reasonable. We also found Praful lying to us which makes me put him on the top of the list. But Praful gave us some important details about Priya's parents and Rahul as told by her. It showed not all was well with Priya's life after she got engaged to Nayan." He paused. "We were unlucky that Praful's shoe size didn't match the one found at the crime scene. I'm betting on the DNA match."

"Prakash should arrange for DNA tests soon," said Aisha. "Are you updating him about the details?"

"Yes, we're going to his office now."

Mayur steered past a school bus that contained students in green checkered shirts. He honked at a truck, which was loaded with wood, to clear the way and turned towards right to enter Prakash's office.

He entered Prakash's room along with Aisha, smiling.

"Please, welcome." Prakash gestured for them to take seats opposite him.

Mayur and Aisha made themselves comfortable on wooden chairs.

"How did the interview go?" Prakash asked.

"It went well," said Mayur. "We've some positive news to share with you."

Prakash's face lit with a smile. "Tell me what?" He leaned forward.

"First, let me tell you about Priya's project manager, Krishna. He is quite cooperative and seemed confident. He seemed to have treated Priya and the rest of his team members well."

"Did he put any pressure on Priya and make her work overtime?" Prakash asked.

"No," Aisha added. "We heard from Julia and Krishna that Priya assumed more responsibilities on her own. Krishna had treated Priya well; there is no doubt about it."

"And what about his claim that Praful was a womanizer?" Prakash asked. "Did you find Praful suspicious about the case?"

"That's what I was talking to you about," said Mayur. "Praful lied to us saying he didn't work on that Sunday. But Krishna told us he did work and left the office along with Priya. Also, Praful didn't accept he was sacked because of the sexual harassment. But he later agreed when we insisted he tell the truth."

"No doubt he had a motive to kill Priya." Prakash straightened in his seat. "I had a doubt that Praful is a strong suspect after what Krishna told me about him."

"But he has an alibi saying he was at his home with his parents," Aisha said.

"Aisha," said Mayur. "We can't believe him. It may be another lie to misguide us."

"Yes," said Prakash. "We should verify the alibi and find out if he is behind the murder."

"We should also conduct the DNA test on him without delay," Mayur said. "I suspect that the tests will be a match for Praful."

"Sure, why not?" said Prakash. "I'll take him to our forensic lab this evening."

"That's a good decision," said Mayur. "I would like to go with you."

"Okay," said Prakash. "What other new information have you collected?"

Mayur told Prakash Praful was intimate with Priya and he ventured out to malls and movies with her.

"Is he a native of Hyderabad?" Prakash asked.

"Yes. Born and brought up here," said Aisha. "His father works in a cooperative bank as a deputy manager."

"So," said Prakash, "what's the next plan of action? We are almost done with the case if the DNA test is a match for Praful."

"But I've got a disappointing fact to share with you."

"What?" Prakash asked.

"Praful's shoe size is size eight," said Mayur. "The footprints size we found at the crime scene is a nine."

"You mean Praful didn't go to Priya's place on that evening?" asked Prakash.

"That's what it seems to show," said Mayur. "But we'll proceed with the DNA test and see the outcome."

Prakash nodded. "All right."

"We also need to interview another suspect based in Hyderabad before we go to Bangalore."

"Who is it?" Prakash knitted his brows.

"Hemanth," said Mayur. "The security guard who worked at the Majestic Apartments on that eventful evening."

"Haven't we met him yet?" Prakash asked.

"No. Hemanth works between eight o'clock onwards until six in the morning."

"When are you planning to interview him?"

"Now. We'll call and tell him to come here for the interview." Mayur took out his phone from his shirt pocket and showed Hemanth's number to Prakash.

Prakash glanced at it. "You want me to call him?"

"Yes." Mayur nodded.

Prakash took his phone from the table and tapped on its screen.

Chapter 13 - Evidence of Hemanth

21ST OCTOBER 2:00 PM

"Hello, Hemanth," Prakash said. "I'm Inspector Prakash." He waited for a few moments. "We would like to question you on Priya's murder case. Oh, yeah. That's correct. I'll send my constable to bring you here...That's perfect ...I'm looking forward to seeing you. Bye." Prakash tapped on the red button.

"Did Hemanth agree to meet us?" Aisha asked.

"Yes. I'll send my constable to him." Prakash rang the handbell.

A constable in a dark khaki uniform with a brown belt buckled around his waist and holding a cane entered. His enormous black mustache stood out on his papaya shaped, semi-dark face. His potbelly made him look more like a joker than police personnel.

Prakash told him to get Hemanth from his house. He gave him the necessary details - a phone number and the house address.

"We can wait here until Hemanth arrives," He said to Mayur. "It'll not take more than twenty minutes."

A sudden air gushed into the room through the windows. The main door with their drapes fluttering and rocking like swings in the garden. Prakash placed the paperweights on the sheets to prevent them from flying away. A sound of rain pattering on the rooftop echoed in the room followed by a rumble of thunder. The rain intensified within a few minutes, lashing the windows and the parking lot tin shed. An acrid smell of wet soil filled the room. It started out like a thunderstorm and converted into a steady downpour. The raindrops danced on the windowpanes.

Mayur exchanged small talk about the change in the weather with Prakash and Aisha. "Did we update you about the possible suspects' list which we have prepared?"

"No, not yet," said Prakash. "I can't wait to see it."

Mayur took out his phone and opened the word document. He glanced over the list of suspects and then gave the phone to Prakash. "Everyone listed there has a strong motive to kill Priya."

"Can I know more about Rahul?" Prakash asked.

"Rahul is Priya's uncle - her mother's brother," Aisha said.

"His motive?"

"He was betrayed like Harsha," said Mayur. "Rahul knew Priya since their childhood. Everyone in their family had decided about his marriage with her."

"Why didn't they marry, then?"

"Because of Priya's father," said Mayur. "He wasn't comfortable with Rahul's social status and his profession."

Prakash looked back at the phone screen. "What's Harsha's motive?

"He too got betrayed. He dated Priya before she got engaged to Nayan."

"No doubt these two have strong motives." Prakash continued to read the list and said, "What about Nayan?"

"Nayan had a girlfriend before he got engaged with Priya."

"What about Chirag and Poonam?" asked Prakash. "I see them on the list."

"As you already know, Priya's father had written a will saying his property should go to his daughters. After Priya's death, Poonam inherits all the family's assets."

Prakash gave the phone back to Mayur. "You need to go back to Bangalore without further delay."

"But we need to conduct the DNA tests on Praful and Hemanth with the clues we've found at the crime scene," Mayur said. "We may get some surprising results and there'd be no need to go to Bangalore if we found the DNA match with any one of them."

Prakash nodded. "Sure. I'll try to arrange for the DNA tests after we interrogate Hemanth and make the results available." He paused for a moment and then went on: "Mayur, I'm getting pressure from my boss to close the case early. It's better for us to hasten the inquest."

Mayur's chest constricted. Goosebumps erupted on his skin. "What are you saying, Prakash? Are you going to punish someone who is innocent?"

"Well," said Prakash, forcing a smile. "I didn't say that. We're investigating the case and finding the culprit. I only meant not getting lackadaisical in our approach."

"Have you seen me lackadaisical?" asked Mayur, his breath increasing.

Prakash smiled for the second time, trying to clear the air. "I'm sorry if I offended your feelings. You know how my boss is, and you're well aware of how the police department works. It's not new to you."

Mayur inhaled a deep breath. There's no reason to get angry with Prakash. He was used to his repeated advice to close the case. "I can understand your situation, Prakash," Mayur said. "But you know my method of investigation. We'll achieve success only when we investigate the case thoroughly. My aim is to find the culprit and not to close the case to please the higher authorities."

Aisha straightened in her seat. "Okay, okay." She smiled. "Let's not go deep into the matter. We know we'll solve the case with our own and unique approach. Let's abide by the rules which Mayur has laid out."

"Sure," Prakash said. "I apologize to you if my request has annoyed you."

Mayur sighed. "It's okay."

Approaching footsteps echoed in the hall. It was the constable, who had gone to get Hemant.

"Sir," the constable said. "Hemanth is here."

The constable got drenched in rain with his uniform wet and his hair messy. He breathed heavily with the raindrops trickling down his medium-sized chin.

Prakash rose. "Bring him to the interrogation room." He looked at Mayur and Aisha. "Let's go and interview Hemanth." He led them outside towards the interrogation room.

The room was around 25x25 feet large. A medium-sized table sat at the center and a few metallic chairs stood around it. The ambiance was dark and a white light bulb hung on the ceiling at the center of the table. The light bulb illuminated the table and the chairs around it. An acrid smell lingered in the air.

Mayur sat between Prakash and Aisha. The constable entered along with a man in his early thirties. The man's medium-dark face appeared frightening in the dim light. His well-cut medium-thick mustache was prominent in his oval face. His dark, curly hair was scary in the dark ambiance of the surroundings. He wore a checkered blue shirt that got tucked inside his navy blue pants.

Hemanth held a raincoat and he placed it beside a chair. He was not as drenched as the constable because of the cover, though a few raindrops rolled down his cheeks.

Prakash gestured for him to a seat in front of them.

Hemanth sat opposite Mayur, twisting his watch in his right hand. He continued rolling his shoulders as Mayur waited for him to settle down.

"Hello, Mr. Hemanth," Mayur said, focusing on his eyes. "I'm Mayur Varma, a private detective. Meet my junior, Aisha, and Inspector Prakash."

Hemanth smiled. "Oh, yeah. Hi," he said, his voice wavering.

Mayur wanted Hemanth to feel comfortable. "Are you still feeling uncomfortable?" asked Mayur. "Don't get agitated. We want you to answer a few questions about Priya's murder."

"Please proceed," Hemanth said. "And I'm not disturbed. I'm comfortable to face this interview."

Mayur suspected Hemanth tried to hide his agitated feelings because his lips trembled. "May I know your full name?"

"Hemanth Rathod." He stared at Mayur.

"And your qualifications?"

"I studied a pre-university course before joining 'Squad Help.'"

"How old are you?"

"Twenty-five," Hemanth said with a light smile. His eyes gleamed.

"Why did you drop your studies?" asked Mayur. "Was there any financial problem?"

"Yes," said Hemanth. "I was not able to pay the college fees and took this job."

"Where do you live in Hyderabad?"

Hemanth told him the place of his house.

"Are you staying alone there?"

"No. My parents are with me." He leaned back.

"It looks like you're unmarried."

He nodded.

"How long you have been working for your current employer?"

"Seven years," he said, fixing his stare on Mayur.

"When did you start working at Majestic Apartments?" Mayur asked, continuing to look into Hemanth's eyes.

"I've been working there for four years."

"Where did you work before that?"

Hemanth told Mayur about his previous place of work.

"Why did you move to the Majestic Apartments? Did you ask for a change of place?"

Hemant swallowed. He avoided direct eye contact. "Well," he said, "it was the manager's decision to shift me to a new place. And it's the second place in my tenure as a security guard."

"Okay," said Mayur. "What's your opinion about Priya? Have you ever seen or met her while performing your duties?"

Hemanth opened his mouth and then closed it, struggling to find the right words. "I've seen her only a couple of times. I can't comment more about her."

"What are your duty timings?"

"From eight o'clock at night to six o'clock in the morning." Hemanth's voice lacked enthusiasm.

"Had you ever met her after the eighth?"

"I told you already, Priya rarely came out of her flat at night."

"But you'd seen Priya a couple of times," Aisha said.

"Yes."

"Was she alone when you saw her?"

"Her flatmate accompanied her."

"What's your opinion about Priya, then?" Prakash asked.

Hemanth crossed his arms across his chest. "What do you mean, sir?"

Priya wore expensive jewelry and was a potential target for robbers. Mayur wanted to find out if Hemanth had a motive to steal her valuables.

"What did she look?" He raised voice to enable Hemanth to hear amidst the sound of pattering raindrops.

"Well," Hemanth pursed his lips. "You can look at her Facebook page to know her better, sir."

"But Mayur would like to hear that from you." Prakash grimaced.

Hemanth lowered his brows. "She was pretty."

"Did you notice anything else which caught your attention?" Mayur asked. He wanted to know if Hemanth would say anything about the expensive jewels which Priya wore.

Hemanth darted his gaze between the three interrogators. "Maybe she dressed well."

"Did you notice Priya wore expensive jewels?" Aisha asked. She seemed to understand what Mayur expected to hear from Hemanth.

Hemanth jerked back. "Oh, yeah," he said, his voice wavering. "I agree with you she did have some shiny ornaments on her neck and earlobes."

"All right," said Prakash. "Where were you on that eventful evening? Were you working?"

"No," said Hemanth, his voice hardened.

Surprised, Mayur looked at Prakash. Prakash also seemed to have bewildered. Was Hemanth telling the truth? "Where were you between seven and nine o'clock that evening, then?"

"I was in a meeting," Hemanth said, gripping his chair's armrest.

"You attended a meeting?" Mayur said. "With whom?"

"My manager at Squad Help had convened a meeting."

"About what?" asked Prakash.

"We discussed a range of topics from our salary to our growing client base."

"Who is your manager?" Mayur asked.

"Dhananjay Sharma."

"Are you sure you attended it?" asked Mayur. "We'll call Dhananjay and verify it."

Hemanth licked his lips. "You can. And you'll come to know that I was not at the apartment on that night."

There was no hint of suspicion in Hemanth's voice. *Is he telling the truth?* Mayur needed to check his alibi.

Prakash took Dhananjay's phone number and his address from Hemanth. "We'll call him very soon."

Mayur remained silent, contemplating the clues which the technicians had gathered. He needed to know the details of the security procedures in the apartment.

"What are the rules you'll follow when visitors arrive at the apartment?"

"We maintain a visitor's register," Hemanth said. "We will ask the guests to enter their details."

"What kind of details?"

"Their names and addresses, and whom they want to meet in the apartment." Hemanth bit his lip, seemingly waiting to end the interrogation.

"You know we've collected a Pizza Hut cap and a shirt button of a Pizza Hut uniform at the crime scene," Mayur said. "We suspect that the perpetrator forgot to collect it after murdering Priya."

Hemanth sighed, closing his eyes. "How is it relevant to me?"

"It's relevant," said Mayur, his tone raised. "Did you also register the delivery boys' details who deliver the food or any other stuff to the residents?"

Hemanth breathed noisily. "We do register, but sometimes we'll be lenient on them because they'll be in a hurry to deliver the items."

"Did someone else work in your place on that evening when you attended the meeting?" Mayur asked.

Hemanth looked expansive, seemingly trying to recall his memory. He said, "One of my junior colleagues was there on that evening."

"Can we talk to him?" Prakash asked.

"Why not?" Hemanth gave the telephone number of the junior guard, inhaling a deep breath. He seemed to have exhausted as the interview got extended beyond their schedule.

Mayur straightened. He took a pack of Marlboro cigarettes and offered one to Hemanth.

Hemanth smiled. He took the cigarette from his right hand.

Mayur offered one to Prakash and took one for himself. He took out the lighter from his pants pocket and lit the cigarettes. "Do you smoke regularly?"

Hemanth dragged a puff and inhaled the smoke. He remained calm, seemingly relaxed. "Yes, I smoke often."

Mayur let out some smoke and looked at Prakash and then at Hemanth. "Do you know our forensics team has collected a cigarette butt at the crime scene?"

Hemanth's face grew ashen. He looked at Mayur with his brows knitted, eyes wide.

"We're going to conduct a DNA test to find out if the DNA of the cigarette butt is a match for you," Prakash said. "Do you agree to give your DNA sample?"

"Okay," said Hemanth sounding compliant. "I will."

Mayur remembered Dr. Sunil saying the perpetrator was a left-hander. But Hemanth held the cigarette in his right hand. And he also needed to check Hemanth's shoe size. When Mayur asked, Hemant said he wore size nine shoes.

But I wouldn't conclude anything until the DNA test results announced.

"The rain has stopped. Let's go to the forensic lab now." Prakash rose. "We'll pickup Praful on the way." He called the constable and instructed him to escort Hemanth outside. He led everyone out of the interrogation room, towards the parking lot.

The heavy rain fell for a half an hour and changed into a light drizzle. Mayur looked forward to seeing the DNA tests before leaving for Bangalore.

Chapter 14 - Meeting with Dr. Sunil

21ST OCTOBER 2:30 PM

Mayur stood beside the Jeep along with Prakash, Hemanth, and a constable. He was eager to go to the forensic lab for DNA tests. Both Hemanth and Praful had volunteered to give their DNA samples. This made him feel contented.

Aisha approached Mayur. "I have an important function to attend. Is it okay if I go home?"

"Oh, it's all right." Mayur smiled. "I can manage with Prakash. By the way whose function is it?"

"One of my close friends is getting married."

"Oh, I see." Though Mayur also needed to go to his office to prepare the next plan of action, he was curious to meet Dr. Sunil.

Aisha bade everyone goodbye and walked out of the premises.

Mayur sat in the vehicle along with others.

Prakash started the engine and eased the Jeep out of the parking place.

A cuckoo sounded, perched on a branch of a neem tree. Out in the street, a motorcycle roared by. An ice-cream seller called out to grab the attention of a boisterous crowd of hot and sweaty children.

"We're going to Hi-Tech City first to get Praful," Mayur said. He called Praful and told him to join them at the forensics lab.

Prakash arrived at the Hi-Tech City software development center and parked his Jeep. He sent his constable to escort Praful from his office by giving him Praful's location.

Mayur stepped out of the vehicle, went towards the shade of a banyan tree, and lit a cigarette. Prakash joined him and he lit a Marlboro. They took a couple of drags in silence.

An ATM located beside the main gate reminded Mayur of a robbery case that had happened five years ago. He was working as a police officer and had accompanied two constables in a van. They carried fifty thousand rupees in cash to load an ATM in Secunderabad. The constables were inside the van and Mayur drove his Bullet motorcycle behind it.

Near an intersection, a couple of masked robbers attacked the van driver. They rendered him unconscious and opened the van doors. They shot the constables in their knees and took control of the vehicle. When Mayur took out his revolver, another masked robber hit Mayur's hand hard using a cane stick. The pistol slipped from Mayur's hand. But Mayur continued to chase the van for a couple of kilometers. He held the collar of the man behind the wheel through the window. The driver lost the control of the van and it rammed into a compound wall, injuring an elderly woman.

Mayur fought and knocked the robbers down. A crowd of people helped Mayur and his colleagues recover from the incident. He called the medical emergency team and moved the constables to a hospital. He underwent treatment for his minor injuries. He had to lie to his mother at home when she asked the reason for his bandaged forehand.

"Mayur," said Prakash, alerting him. "What are you thinking?"

"Oh...I...was..."

"Don't worry," said Prakash. "You won't need to investigate at Bangalore once the DNA test results arrive. I'm sure it's either Praful or Hemanth who did it."

"Oh," said Mayur. "Let's hope so."

Praful arrived along with the constable. He wore a white-blue checkered shirt and navy blue pants. His square and fair face, applied with a cream, glistened in the daylight. He went and sat in the rear seat of the Jeep.

Mayur and Prakash threw the butts on the pavement and pressed them under their shoes. They all sat back in their seats. Prakash drove the Jeep ahead.

Traffic was heavy. A couple of cows and buffaloes tread on the road, disrupting the traffic flow. A red city bus honked to clear the path ahead. A few motorbikes eased through the passage and moved along. Impatient Prakash honked the horn until the animals cleared out of the way.

He entered the parking lot of the Forensics Department and parked the Jeep.

"Dr. Sunil is available," Mayur said, looking at the doctor's car. "We can discuss the case with him while we wait for Praful and Hemanth to give their DNA samples."

"How long does it take for the results of the test to arrive?" Praful asked, his voice wavering.

"It takes twenty-four hours," said Mayur. "We'll know the results by tomorrow." He waited for Hemanth to add his comments, but his silence intrigued him. Why did Hemanth behave so erratically? At times, he spoke with confidence but appeared suspicious most of the time.

Prakash led everyone inside the main hall of the laboratory. The room was spacious with a reception desk positioned in the center, facing the main door. A medium-sized Ganesha idol sat at the back of the counter. A pale-brown sandalwood garland hung around its neck and was lit with a diya at its base. The hall was well lit with a set of LED bulbs embedded within the ceiling. Two leather couches sat on the right side of the help desk.

The receptionist wore a green polka-dotted silk sari. Her lips were smeared with red lipgloss. Prakash told her the purpose of their visit and the case they have been investigating. She smiled and spoke over the intercom. After exchanging a few words, she turned to Prakash.

"I'll take them inside to collect the samples." She looked at Mayur. "You remain seated." She escorted Hemanth and Praful towards a lift.

When they went out of earshot, Mayur said, "I would like to meet Dr. Sunil."

"Sure."

They walked towards a passage to the right side of the lift where the doctor's room was located.

The door was ajar. Mayur knocked before peeping inside. Dr. Sunil, in his white apron and a stethoscope, hung around his neck, was busy reading a pathology book.

Mayur entered. "Hello, Doctor."

Dr. Sunil looked at Mayur. "Oh, Mr. Varma. Welcome." He rose and smiled at Prakash who followed Mayur. He waved them to seats opposite his. "How is the case progressing?" He sat back.

Mayur straightened in his seat. "It's progressing well, Doctor. We have interviewed two important suspects and have brought them here for DNA tests."

"That's interesting," said Dr. Sunil. "Do you think one of them committed the crime?"

"Well," Prakash said. "They do have the motive to kill Priya. One of them is a security guard of the apartment and works at night."

"And what's his motive?" asked Dr. Sunil.

"Maybe he got attracted to Priya's jewels. We found him suspicious when we asked a few questions relevant to the victim's ornaments."

Dr. Sunil sighed. "With the moral values declining every day, no doubt he might have tried to rob Priya and killed her." He shifted his gaze towards Mayur. "What about the other suspect? Is he motivated for the same reason?"

"No," said Mayur. "Praful was Priya's colleague. He seemed to have developed a close relationship with Priya in the last month. Maybe they had skirmishes over their relationship and he ended up killing her."

"But I heard from Julia that Priya was already engaged, right?" Sunil asked.

"Somehow, Priya got attracted to him. Her project manager told us that Praful is a womanizer. He had been sacked from his previous employer because of sexual harassment charges."

"Very interesting findings," said Dr. Sunil, his eyes widened.

They sat in silence for a few minutes. Mayur remembered Dr. Sunil saying the perpetrator might be a left-hander. He had checked both Praful and Hemanth about their orientation. He had found only Praful was a left-hander.

"Doctor," Mayur said. "You mentioned in your autopsy report that the perpetrator is a left-hander."

"Yes, I suspect it because the cut is deep on the right side of the victim's neck."

"And Praful is a left-hander."

Prakash looked at Mayur with his eyes widened.

"Are you sure about it?" asked the doctor.

"Yes, I've got it verified."

"But you can't arrest him based on that information alone, right?" Dr. Sunil asked.

Prakash shook his head. "We need to wait until tomorrow for the DNA test results to arrive."

An approaching footstep echoed from outside. Hemanth and Praful arrived, accompanied by the constable.

"Did you give the samples?" asked Prakash.

The constable nodded. "Yes, sir. The results will be available in twenty-four hours."

22ND OCTOBER 9:00 AM

Mayur glanced at the wall clock in his office while he flipped through the pages of Aisha's notepad. She should be here anytime so that he could go to Prakash's office with her. Mayur wanted to be with Prakash and discuss his next plan of action once the results of the DNA tests arrived.

Aisha had noted that Hemanth's had attended a meeting at his manager's house. Mayur needed to verify this alibi with the help of Prakash.

But what if the manager lied and tried to shield Hemanth? Should Mayur interview the remaining security guards and check Hemanth was also there?

His gaze shifted towards the entrance. Aisha, in her blue mixed purple silk sari, entered, smiling. Her well-cut hair was entwined into a medium-sized braid and a jasmine string dangled in it. The smell of the flowers filled the room.

Mayur smiled back. "You look so beautiful."

Aisha sat opposite him. "Thank you." Her face blushed.

"You've done an exceptional job of taking the interview notes," said Mayur. "I admire your diligence and concentration."

Aisha leaned forward in her chair. "It's my job and I understand that I need to work efficiently."

"I was going through your notes about Hemanth's alibi," Mayur said. "We need to visit Hemanth's manager and check if Hemanth attended the meeting on that evening."

Aisha widened her eyes. "What if his manager, Dhananjay, tries to shield Hemanth to save his company name?"

"I was thinking about that."

"Do you have an alternate plan to verify his alibi?"

"We need to meet a couple of other security guards who attended the meeting along with Hemanth."

Aisha nodded. "That makes sense." Her eyes glinted. "We can check with the junior guard who worked in place of Hemanth at the Majestic Apartments."

Mayur's phone rang. Prakash's image lit the screen. He took the device from the table and said, "Hello, Prakash." He paused, looking at Aisha. "Do you have any good news for us?"

"Well," said Prakash. "I called the forensic lab. They said the results will be available by noon. We need to wait for a couple more hours."

Mayur sighed.

"Are you coming to my office?" Prakash asked.

"Yes, I am," Mayur said. "I leave here in the next fifteen minutes."

"Is Aisha joining you?"

"Yes, she will."

Mayur ended the call and turned to Aisha. "We're going to Prakash's place. We will discuss the next plan of action there."

"What's your opinion about Hemanth?" Aisha asked. "Do you think-"

"His behavior was confusing. At times, he seemed nervous, and sometimes, he seemed cooperative and confident. His shoe size is nine, conforming to the one found at the crime scene."

"Do you think he stole the valuables and murdered her to avoid getting caught?"

"He had seen Priya a couple of times when he worked the night shift. No doubt he got attracted to Priya's jewels." Mayur paused contemplating the type of ornaments Priya wore and their total worth. "So far, we haven't made any inquiries about the type of jewels Priya wore. Have you come across anyone talking about their total worth?"

Aisha straightened. "We should've asked Julia about it." She paused for a moment. "What if we call her now?"

"Let's wait until the results got declared. If we find Hemanth's DNA a match with the cigarette butt, we'll call her."

Aisha nodded.

"Let's go now." Mayur rose. "It's better for us to be with Prakash."

Mayur walked towards his car. He slid behind the wheel while Aisha sat in the passenger seat.

Out in the street, a motorcycle roared by and a heavy truck rumbled by.

Mayur parked his car at the police station and stepped out. He walked towards the main entrance along with Aisha. The constable in the main hall stood up and saluted. Mayur returned the greeting by slightly bowing his head. He walked towards Prakash's office.

In his tight-fitting Khaki uniform, Prakash looked handsome. His semi-dark face was lightly rubbed with the face powder. His large, deep-set eyes glinted as he looked at Mayur and Aisha.

They exchanged morning greetings.

Mayur dragged over the wooden chair and sat opposite Prakash. Aisha also pulled out a chair and sat beside him.

"Did you call the forensic technicians?" Mayur asked, his voice curious.

"No, but I'm sure they'll get back to us soon."

"OK," Mayur said. "I hope something positive will come out very soon."

"Let's hope so," Prakash said.

"By the way," said Mayur. "How much Priya's jewels were worth."

Prakash rubbed his chin. "Do you think it's important information?"

"Yes," said Mayur. "The perpetrator would be highly motivated if the jewels were valuable."

Prakash's face lit with a light smile. "That's a good thought. I admire you," said he, "should we ask Priya's parents and find out?"

"We should," said Aisha. "We can also speak to Julia about it."

"We'll do it after we get the DNA test results," Mayur said.

"I have told my travel agent to book tickets for you and Aisha," said Prakash.

"Oh, did you?" asked Mayur.

"Yes," Prakash said. "You need to attend Priya's funeral this evening. Also, I don't want you to waste time here if the DNA tests fail. Sometimes, you may not get the air tickets because it's a holiday season."

Mayur remained silent, controlling his urge to argue.

Prakash's phone rang. He took it from the table and said, "It's from the forensic lab."

Chapter 15 - Hemanth's Alibi

22ND OCTOBER 10:00 AM

Mayur liked listening to the conversation between Prakash and the forensic technician. He whispered to him to keep the phone on speaker mode.

He tapped on the screen. "Hello, Inspector Prakash speaking."

"Hello, sir," said the technician. "I would like to share the DNA test results with you."

"Please tell me."

"We tested Praful's DNA sample for a match with two important clues - a cigarette butt and a strand of hair."

"What's the outcome?" Prakash sounded impatient. "Is it positive?"

"No," said the technician. "The test is not a match with Praful."

Mayur's chest constricted. He had believed Praful wanted a sexual favor from Priya and had killed her when she resisted.

"What about Hemanth?" Mayur raised his voice. "Is his DNA a match with any of the clues?"

"Yes," said the technician. "The DNA of the cigarette butt is a match with Hemanth."

Mayur's heart lightened.

"Interesting," said Prakash. "I knew the bugger did it as he was lying when we interrogated him." He thanked the technician and ended the call. "Mayur, I don't want to delay arresting Hemanth and filing a charge sheet against him. We can close the case with this outcome."

Mayur remembered Hemanth's alibi. Hemanth had claimed that he had attended a meeting with his manager, Dhananjay, at the time of the murder. "Hemanth told us he wasn't at the apartment when the murder took place."

"Mayur, I told you he is a liar," Prakash said. "I don't believe him anymore. Let's close the case by arresting Hemanth."

"But you know that's not the way I work," said Mayur. "We must verify his alibi before coming to a final conclusion."

"How can you trust a liar, Mayur? I don't-"

"We have to prove that he lied to us," said Mayur. "I'm not trying to shield Hemanth, but we need to make sure he murdered Priya. What if he attended the meeting and was away from the Majestic Apartments?"

"But, Mayur you-"

"I know you're eager to arrest him," said Mayur. "You can do it after we verify his alibi. What if Hemanth has a cast-iron alibi?"

Prakash lowered his gaze. He seemed to have convinced about what Mayur had said. "Okay. But have you observed something while we interviewed him?"

Mayur had noticed Hemanth's erratic attitude while he answered his questions. But he wanted to find out if Prakash wanted to talk about the same matter. "What?"

"He often lacked confidence when he replied to our questions. He seemed afraid of telling the truth." Prakash widened his eyes. "Didn't he act like a chameleon?"

Aisha straightened in her seat. "I agree, Prakash, but there is no harm in meeting Dhananjay and to verifying Hemanth's alibi. We are one step away from success, right?"

Mayur nodded. "Yes."

"All right," said Prakash. "I'm sure Hemanth's alibi will be proven false and he is the one who killed Priya."

"Before we meet Dhananjay," said Aisha, "we should call Julia to find out how much Priya's jewels are worth. I'm sure they were highly valued as otherwise, the murderer wouldn't have stolen them."

Prakash's eyes glinted. "Yes, we should."

Mayur took his phone before Prakash reached out for his. "Let me call Julia." He tapped on Julia's name, put the phone on speaker mode, and placed his phone back on the table.

"Hello, Mr. Varma," Julia answered.

"Hi, Julia."

"How is the case progressing?" she asked.

"We've achieved a breakthrough," Mayur said.

"Oh, congratulations," Julia said. "I'm glad you've made progress."

"Thank you," Mayur said. "We wanted some vital information from you. Do you have some time to speak with us?"

Julia paused and said, "Go ahead. I am happy to answer you."

"You told us that Priya possessed expensive jewels," said Mayur.

"That's correct," Julia said. "She was fond of ornaments, being a daughter of a wealthy jewelry merchant."

"Can you tell me the total cost of the jewels?" Prakash said.

"Well," said Julia. "I remember we had a discussion about it. Priya told me her diamond necklace cost around six lakhs rupees."

"Six lakhs?" Aisha exclaimed. "No doubt the killer had great motivation." She paused and said, "What about the remaining jewels?"

"Priya wore ear and nose rings. I'm not sure about their cost, but they too were made up of expensive diamonds."

"Did she have any valuables in her closet?" Prakash asked.

"Yes, as she wore different jewels every week."

Prakash turned to Mayur. "No doubt it's Hemanth who committed the murder. He had observed Priya before he struck. Maybe he teamed up with the other security guards who worked during the daytime."

Mayur gestured for Prakash to remain calm by raising his hand. "Julia, do you know the worth of jewels in total?"

"Um... no. I didn't think it was important for me to ask for those details. I discussed the necklace with her because it was intricately carved."

"All right," said Mayur. "Would you like to share anything else with us?"

"I remember Priya telling me her mother often suggested she not wear the jewels when she went out alone. Priya asked me to join her whenever she wanted to go out."

"Okay. Thanks for sharing this useful information," Mayur said.

"I suggest you also contact Priya's parents," Julia said. "I'm sure they will be able to tell you more about the matter."

"Yes," said Prakash. "We will do that."

Mayur ended the call. He looked at Prakash, whose face was lit with a smile. He seemed to have contented to know the facts. "No doubt the perpetrator got motivated to rob Priya as the necklace alone was worth up to six lakh rupees."

Prakash nodded. "What if we talk to Priya's parents and find out more details about it?"

"I'll do it now." Mayur took his cell phone and tapped on the screen. He once again placed the phone in speaker mode.

"Hello, Shekar Bedi here," Mr. Bedi answered.

"Hello, Mr. Bedi," said Mayur. "I'm Mayur Varma here. I hope you reached Bangalore."

Mr. Bedi coughed and paused for a moment. "Hi. Yes, I arrived here well." He paused and said, "How is the investigation progressing? I hope you've achieved some success."

"Yes, Mr. Bedi" Mayur said. "We've crossed a major milestone."

"Congratulations," said Mr. Bedi. "I know you'll succeed in your investigation and bring justice to the departed soul."

"Thanks for keeping faith in us," Prakash said.

"I and Aisha are traveling today to attend the funeral," said Mayur. "I hope all the arrangements are made." He paused. "Mr. Bedi, we wanted to find out some vital information from you."

"Please ask."

"Was Priya fond of wearing diamond jewels?"

"Oh, yes," said Mr. Bedi. "She loved to wear expensive diamonds. I remember her spending hours together in my jewelry shop. She combed through every ornament. She was passionate about wearing jewels and often changed them once in a month. She used to rush to my showroom when new stock arrived."

"But didn't you warn her of possible theft?" Aisha asked.

"I did, but she had said she would be careful. She used to keep her necklace at home when she went out late in the evening as we warned her not to wear them after dusk."

"Do you know the worth of the jewels she carried to Hyderabad?" Aisha asked.

"Um... I'm not sure about it." He paused and said, "Why don't you speak with her mother?"

"Is she around?" Aisha asked.

"Yes, she is. Please wait for a moment."

There were a rustling sound and background conversation. Mrs. Bedi said, "Hello, Mr. Varma."

Mayur greeted her and they exchanged small talk. He told her the breakthrough they'd achieved in their investigation. "Mrs. Bedi," he said. "We would like to know the details of the jewels Priya carried with her when she came to Hyderabad."

Mrs. Bedi paused for a moment. "I told her not to carry the diamond necklace, but she didn't listen. I did expect she would get herself in trouble." She broke down.

"It's all right," Mayur said. "Please try to calm yourself."

"You know, Mr. Mayur," said Mrs. Bedi. "I want you to arrest that rascal who killed my daughter. Priya's soul will rest in peace only when you arrest the culprit."

"Don't worry," said Prakash. "We're working towards it and it's only a matter of time before we achieve the success."

Mayur repeated his question about the cost of Priya's jewels.

"Her necklace was worth around six lakhs rupees," Mrs. Bedi said. "She also took with her a few gold ornaments which were worth around four lakhs rupees."

Prakash looked at Mayur with his eyes widened. "Ten lakh rupees. No doubt the perpetrator had a greater motive to rob Priya."

"Okay," said Mayur. "Mrs. Bedi, did Priya share anything suspicious about her safety?"

"Um...no," she said. "She always told me she got out of her apartment with her colleague Julia and she was safe. I had told her not to wear the necklace at night. But I don't know whether she cared for my suggestions or not."

"All right," said Mayur. "Thanks for cooperating with us, Mrs. Bedi. We'll get back to you when needed."

"You're most welcome."

"So, the details confirm that Hemant had a motive to rob Priya," Prakash said. "We shouldn't make any delays in arresting him."

"But we'll do it only after verifying his alibi."

Prakash rose to his feet. "Because you insist, we'll meet Hemanth's manager, Dhananjay. But I know it's going to be a waste of time."

"Let's go." Mayur rose. "We'll know only when we meet him." He walked out of the office towards the police Jeep along with others.

They all sat in their usual seats.

The sun shone in the middle of the sky and the winter cool breeze diminished the intensity of the sunrays. A couple of crows hopped on the ground below a Peepal tree. The pale green leaves wavered in rhythm with the gentle wind. A few bikers went past a green city bus, which was crowded with passengers. A few passengers hung on the steel bar on the footboard of the vehicle.

Prakash passed a heavy vehicle and then said, "What if Dhananjay lies to us to protect Hemanth?"

"We do have a solution for it," said Aisha. "Hemanth had told a junior guard who had worked in his place on that eventful night. We can question him if we suspect Dhananjay."

"That's a good plan," said Mayur. "We'll also ask Dhananjay for the list of security guards who attended the staff meeting."

Prakash eased his car into Dhananjay's office parking lot. They stepped out of the vehicle and marched towards the entrance. Prakash spoke to the help desk employee and told him of his intention to meet Dhananjay. The receptionist, clad in a dark blue business suit, spoke on the intercom. A red lipgloss smeared her lips and talcum powder covered her face. She hung the receiver back and said, "Please follow me." She led them towards Dhananjay's office, which was located on the right side of the lobby.

The office was spacious. A large mahogany table sat next to the wall, opposite the main entrance. The room was lit with fluorescent bulbs. The intricate woodworks decorated walls and ceilings.

A man wearing a sky blue shirt with a security guard emblem printed above the pocket sat at the table. His fair and square face was applied with facial cream. His thick, black hair glistened with hair oil.

The lady introduced the person as Dhananjay and left.

Dhananjay waved for Mayur and his colleagues to take seats opposite him. His eyes were wide open and his face was ashen. He seemed surprised that the police were visiting his office.

Mayur sat beside Aisha and Prakash. They shook hands with Dhananjay and exchanged greetings.

"Mr. Dhananjay," said Mayur. "Have you heard of the murder of a software engineer, Priya Bedi, at one of the apartments where your guards work?"

Dhananjay bit his lips. "Murder at the apartment? May I know the name of it?"

"It is Majestic Apartments," Aisha said.

"Um...oh, yes... I have heard about a woman in her company guest house had been murdered. Can I know more about it? I've been busy with other works so I didn't inquire much about the incident, you know."

"A software engineer got murdered in her flat," said Mayur. "And your security staff was on duty at that time."

"Yes, yes. What was the date and time of the murder? I forgot what my employee who worked there told me about it."

"It had occurred on the nineteenth of this month, somewhere between seven and ten," Prakash said.

Mayur waited for Dhananjay to mention about the meeting he had convened at that time of the day. But he remained silent. Mayur said: "We know that one of your personnel, Hemanth Rathod, was supposed to work there."

Dhananjay gasped. "But I remember our staff attended an official meeting on 19th evening. And Hemanth was part of the meeting."

"Are you sure he attended, Mr. Dhananjay?" Prakash asked, leaning forward.

"Yes, I'm sure he attended it."

Prakash looked at Mayur, his face fallen.

Mayur turned his gaze back to Dhananjay. "Can we get the list of other staff members who attended the meeting?"

"Sure. I'll ask my secretary to make the list available to you."

Aisha straightened in her seat. "Hemanth told us a junior guard was working there when he attended the meeting. Can we know his details?"

Dhananjay looked in her eyes. "Okay. I'll tell my secretary to provide you whatever details you want." He rang the handbell. A lady in her mid-thirties approached. Dhananjay instructed her to furnish whatever details Mayur wanted.

They exchanged a few more words until his secretary gave Prakash a set of papers. Mayur thanked Dhananjay and they bade him goodbye.

"So, the junior guard who worked in place of Hemanth on that eventful night was Chetan." Prakash flipped through the pages.

They walked towards their vehicle and sat in their usual seats.

Mayur took his phone from his shirt pocket. "Can you give me the junior guard's phone number? I would like to ask him a few questions."

Prakash read Chetan's phone number.

Mayur called him.

"Hello, Chetan here."

"Mr. Chetan. I'm Detective Mayur. This is about Priya's murder case at the Majestic Apartments."

"Oh, Detective...Mayur..." Chetan sounded shaky.

"Do you know about the incident?"

"Yes. I know about it."

"The murder happened on the 19th of this month between 7 pm and 10 pm. May I know where you were at that time?"

"Well," Chetan said. "I remember I got deputed to work there between 7 pm and 10 pm."

"Who sent you there?"

"My boss, Dhananjay."

"Did you notice anything suspicious when you manned the apartment?"

"Um...nothing, sir," said Chetan. "Nothing unusual happened."

"Did any visitor or any delivery boy come between those hours?"

"I remember a few visitors entering the apartment."

"Did they register their details in the logbook?"

"Yes, they did," said Chetan. "You can get more details by going through the register."

"Okay," said Mayur. "What about the delivery boys? Did anyone deliver food like pizza to the residents?"

"I did notice a few delivery boys entering the gate."

"Did you tell them to write their names in the register book?" asked Mayur.

"Unfortunately no, sir."

"Why?" Mayur asked.

"It's usual for us to let the boys in without registering their details."

"One last question, Mr. Chetan," said Mayur. "Did Hemanth come back and continue his duty after he finished attending the meeting?"

"Yes, sir. I left at ten o'clock soon after Hemanth returned."

"That's all we need, Chetan. Thank you for cooperating with us." Mayur ended the call. He turned to Prakash, who was listening to the conversation all ears.

"Do you remember what Hemanth had told us?"

"Yeah, he said he returned to the apartment only at seven in the morning the next day," Prakash said.

"Why did he lie to us?" Aisha asked.

"Maybe he feared of conviction."

Chapter 16 - Plan to Visit Bangalore

22ND OCTOBER 10:30 AM

Mayur's stomach growled. A Kamat Hotel signboard caught his attention.

"Would you like to eat something?" he asked Aisha.

"Yes," Aisha said. "What about you, Prakash?"

"Yes, I'm also feeling hungry," Prakash said. He steered the Jeep into the parking lot of the hotel. "Let's discuss the details over snacks and coffee." He turned the ignition off and stepped out.

Mayur led them inside the restaurant. The smell of hot South Indian masala food permeated the air. The hotel had a lobby next to the main door and a staircase which led to the A/C section. Beside the counter, a non A/C section sat. The waiters, holding large aluminum plates, were busy serving food to the patrons. The section was full of customers and the loud chitchat filled the surroundings.

They went upstairs, took the seats, and ordered the food.

Mayur propped up his elbows on the table and clasped his hands. "So, we're traveling to Bangalore and attending the funeral this evening."

Prakash sipped water. "Yes, the flight tickets are ready."

Mayur leaned forward. "It has been two days since we're working on this case. We waited to see if either Praful or Hemanth had committed the crime. Now, we don't have any strong evidence to prove they're guilty. Hemanth has a cast-iron alibi that he attended the meeting. Why should we waste our time at Hyderabad?"

"Shouldn't we further investigate Hemanth's involvement in the crime and prove him guilty?" Prakash asked. "We have two strong evidence against him, the cigarette butt and the footprint size, which are a match for him."

"The cigarette butt was there to misguide us. We should rely on Dr. Sunil's findings that the perpetrator is a left-hander. Hemanth is a right-hander and we verified it during the interview."

"What do you think of the footprint?" Aisha asked.

"Well, it may be a coincidence that Hemanth wore size nine shoes." Prakash remained silent, staring down.

The waiter arrived, holding a large platter containing three crispy, brown masala dosas. The smell of hot food wafted in the air. He placed the plates on the table and left.

Prakash cut a piece of dosa and took a bite. He chewed the food. "What if we don't succeed even after interrogating the remaining suspects?"

"Prakash," said Aisha as she chewed the food. "We should believe in us. You need to look back at our past records. Didn't we solve many cases which you've brought to us?"

Prakash took another bite of dosa in silence.

"Aisha is correct," said Mayur. "We should believe in ourselves. Otherwise, we won't achieve success."

"But you know one thing, Hemanth lied to us," said Prakash. "He told us he never returned to the apartment after he attended the meeting. But the junior guard, Chetan, said Hemanth did return."

"Okay," said Mayur. "Let's not go so deep into the matter. You know Dhananjay's secretary gave us a list of security guards who attended the meeting. If you doubt Hemanth or Dhananjay is lying, we can interview other guards from the list and verify the fact."

Prakash remained silent. He seemed to have given up his hopes on Hemanth's involvement after what Mayur told him.

"Still, I still don't want to remove Hemanth from the suspect's list," said Mayur. "If we get any more strong evidence against him, we'll take further action."

Prakash ate his last bite of dosa. "All right. Let's not delay your visit to Bangalore." He placed the fork and spoon on the plate. "I'll inform my constable to arrange the flight tickets for you. So, when do you plan to leave?" He looked at Aisha. "This afternoon?"

"Yes, by all means," said Mayur. "What do you say, Aisha?"

Aisha finished chewing her food. "I'm okay with it."

"Let's hope you can make some progress," said Prakash.

The waiter cleared the table. Mayur ordered three cups of coffee.

"It's time for us to find out the cell-site data of each of the suspects living here and in Bangalore," said Mayur.

Prakash agreed to research on the cell site data on each of the suspects.

"The Bangalore visit is an opportunity for us to go deeper into the case and find the real culprit."

"Do you think the suspects based at Bangalore have a motive stronger than Praful or Hemanth?" Prakash asked Mayur.

The waiter arrived and placed the steaming coffee cups on the table. The aroma of the strong beverage permeated the air.

Mayur took a cup and sipped the coffee. "The inheritance was their motive if they did it. The other factors could be betrayal and jealousy." He looked at Aisha and then shifted his gaze back to Prakash. "We'll get to know the details only after a thorough investigation. I hope something positive will emerge out of our visit in the next couple of days."

They finished their coffee. Prakash paid the bill and they walked towards his vehicle. He eased his Jeep out of the slot and joined the main street.

"Your flight departure is at twelve o'clock." Prakash steered his vehicle towards the right.

Mayur looked over his shoulder towards Aisha. "I'm okay with it. What about you, Aisha? Will you be comfortable traveling?"

Aisha waited for a few moments and then said, "I'm also okay with it."

Prakash nosed his Jeep inside the police station and parked in its usual slot.

"We'll call you after reaching Bangalore," Mayur said as he stepped out of the vehicle.

"Sure," said Prakash. "I'll send my constable to hand over the flight tickets to you soon." He smiled at Aisha. "I wish you the best."

"Thank you," said Mayur. "And don't worry. I'm sure we'll be successful in our efforts and close the case in the next two to three days."

They bade Prakash goodbye and walked towards Mayur's car. He opened the front passenger's door for Aisha before he slid behind the wheel. She sat, heaving a sigh. "What if we go to my home and meet my mother?"

Mayur eased his car out of the parking lot. *Does Aisha want me to talk about our marriage?* "Should I meet?"

"Yes," said Aisha. "She might not agree to send me to Bangalore as we have decided so soon." She turned to Mayur. "I want you to convince her so that we can go together."

Mayur often avoided meeting Aisha's mother as she spoke about their marriage. She knew Aisha was dating him and she was apprehensive about Mayur not marrying Aisha. Mayur needed to somehow convince Aisha and avoid going to her home.

"Your mother knows your job requires you to leave the station. She will not prevent you from performing your duties."

"I know," said Aisha. "But she feels happy to see you before we go to Bangalore."

Mayur remained silent. He needed Aisha to go with him as she would play an important role in the investigation. He didn't want to disappoint her and go alone to Bangalore.

"All right," he said, steering his vehicle to the left. "I hope your mother doesn't bring up our marriage matter as she has on previous occasions."

"Well," Aisha said, her voice raised. "I'll try to dissuade her if she brings up the matter."

Mayur nodded. He wanted to assure her that he was also eager to make a decision and would decide in a couple of years. But he was apprehensive about his career. He needed to grow his brainchild, 'Dolphin Detective Agency', and solve many more cases.

He hoped Aisha would wait until they achieved their goal and she would support him as his junior. He considered himself lucky to have her with him. Mayur parked his vehicle outside Aisha's house.

She rang the doorbell and waited for her mother to open the door.

Aisha's mother, in her pale blue embroidered sari, opened the door, smiling. "Welcome." She stepped back, making room for them to enter.

"What a surprise, Mayur," Aisha's mother said, as she sat on the couch. She gestured for him to take a seat.

Mayur sat on a smaller couch. "Aisha might have already mentioned to you that we are going to Bangalore today."

"So," said Aisha's mother. "At what time are you leaving?"

"Mum," said Aisha. "We're planning to travel at twelve o'clock."

Her mother shrugged. "Aisha, is it necessary for you to go?"

Aisha licked her lips. "Yes, Mum. We need to investigate an important case. Mayur needs my help."

"Well-"

"Aunty," said Mayur. "I need Aisha to go with me and we should be back in two days." He needed to make Aisha's mother become aware that Aisha's trip outside of Hyderabad was part of her job. He cleared his throat. "Aunty, you need not worry and put restrictions on Aisha to go outside Hyderabad. You know well that traveling is part of her job and she can't avoid it."

"I'm not preventing her from doing her job," said Aisha's mother. "But she should've told me well before time so that I would've arranged for someone to stay with me."

"You let Aisha perform her job, Aunty. I know she enjoys doing her detective work and let her come with me to Bangalore. I promise you that she will be safe and I'll be with her all the time."

"Aisha," said her mother. "Did you tell Mayur about the hoax call you received soon after you started working on this case?"

"Yes, Mum," said Aisha. "But I don-"

"I don't understand why you chose this profession," her mother said. "It makes your life risky and you receive all these threatening calls from the murderers. Who knows the person who called you is serious about his threat?"

"You don't worry, Aunty. We have police protection and we work for one of my ex-colleagues, Prakash Malhotra. You need to trust my words that we're safe."

Aisha's mother sighed. "I know you'll not listen to my words. I only pray to God that you will return safe." He paused, looking at Aisha. "You can go, but return as soon as possible."

"Thank you, Aunty."

Mayur bade Aisha and her mother goodbye. He told her he would meet her at the airport.

22ND OCTOBER 11:00 AM

He arrived at his house and his sister, Apsara, approached him, smiling. "How are you, brother?"

Her round and fair face glistened in the evening sunlight. She locked her small, black eyes onto Mayur's. Her black curls touched her not so wide forehead.

Mayur smiled back. "I'm doing well. How about you?"

"I'm all right." She took his leather office bag. "Thank god you arrived early today." She walked alongside Mayur towards the porch. "I missed you."

"I know it has been several days since we spent time together." He stepped into his home, sat on a chair near a closet, and removed his shoes.

Apsara placed the bag on the table and flopped on the couch.

Mayur rose and collapsed beside her.

His mother arrived. "It's good that you came home early." She sat on a chair.

"Is there a reason you came home so soon?" asked Apsara.

Mayur looked at his mother before fixing his gaze back on Apsara. "I'm going to Bangalore now."

Mrs. Varma leaned forward. "But you said you may not need to visit?"

"Yes, Mum," said Mayur. "What I expected turned out to be untrue. We're going to interview the suspects living in Bangalore."

"When will you be back?" asked Apsara.

"I'll return in two-three days."

He exchanged a few more words before he left for his room.

His father's large size photograph, fixed on the wall, caught his attention. His father had been a brave police officer. Mayur remembered an incident of his visit to a shopping complex along with his father. He needed to buy material on his birthday and his father took him to a nearby market. While they were walking on the street, a couple of women walked, holding shopping bags. One of them wore expensive gold necklaces. Mayur stood along with others for the crowd to disperse. A young man put his hand inside a woman's chest and pulled the chain. The women started shouting. Mayur's father told Mayur to stay there and ran after the thief. After chasing him long, he caught him and recovered the ornament.

Mayur's eyes moistened. It was a great loss for him and his family members losing his father. *My father's soul would rest in peace if I continue to work as a private investigator.*

Chapter 17 - Mayur in Bangalore

22ND OCTOBER 11:30 AM

Mayur placed his medium-sized luggage in the living room and sat beside his mother on the couch. "I'll leave from here in the next ten to fifteen minutes." He turned to his sister, Apsara. "Do you want me to bring you anything from Bangalore?"

Apsara licked her lips. "First, tell me do you need that luggage if you're planning to go for only two days?"

Mayur sighed. "I don't—"

"Yes, Mayur," said his mother. "Are you visiting for more than two days?"

"No, Mum," said Mayur. "My plan is to return in a couple of days."

"Why are you carrying that much of luggage, then?" she asked.

"Mum," said Mayur. "In case I need to extend my time, I'll need more clothes, right?"

"It's all right," said his mother. "We asked you to return soon because we'll feel secure in your presence."

"Don't worry. I'll come back soon."

"The marriage broker called me this morning," said his mother.

Mayur wanted to avoid talking about his marital status. "Mum," he said, "I need to leave now to go to the airport. Please allow me to leave."

"But Mayur, you need to answer me. When are going to get married? Apsara can't until yours gets completed. Don't you care about your sister's well being?"

Mayur's heart sank. He should answer his mother because he didn't want to disappoint Apsara.

"Yes, Mum, I agree," said he, "but I would like to see Apsara get married before I do. I don't need to settle down before she does. I'll be happier if you speak to your marriage broker to find a suitable groom for Apsara."

Apsara blushed. "I would like to study for a master's degree next."

Mayur rose and walked towards the door. "It's getting late for me. Please let me go." His pulse quickened, he stormed out of the hall.

He walked towards the main street, hired a taxi, and got in. A Hindi song of Kishore Kumar soothed his mind; a smell of jasmine air purifier filled his nostrils.

The sky was bright and the Sun shone in the middle. A few pigeons took flight above a dilapidated building. The driver steered the car onto the highway which was full of vehicles. The bright sunlight lit the asphalt road, which shone like a dark carpet.

At the airport, he paid the meter charges and then waited for Aisha to arrive. A few SUVs qued up near the curb and the people stepped down with their cabin luggage. The travelers and their loved ones were clad in new suits and attractive silk saris. The kids ran and chased one another beside the street, creating a commotion.

Mayur waited for Aisha, thinking about their growing friendship in the last two years. Aisha had been cooperative and worked well for him. She never hesitated to go with him outside Hyderabad to investigate the cases. Aisha had a curious mind and took interest in every case they worked on. *Having her around makes the day goes faster. Aisha has been supportive of my ideas which have been encouraging to me. I don't need to worry about a woman's companionship as long as Aisha works with me. But I need to turn our friendship into a permanent relationship. I should decide about our marriage soon.*

An approaching taxi caught Mayur's attention. He looked at the passenger in the rear seat. The vehicle stood beside the curb in front of Mayur. Aisha stepped out; in her dark blue embroidered sari, she looked beautiful. Mayur's heart lightened.

"Hi, Aisha." Mayur smiled.

"Good morning," Aisha smiled back. She paid the driver and came closer to Mayur. She hugged him, sending a cold shiver down his spine. Her well-cut medium hair, entwined into a braid, beckoned him. A small jasmine string adorned the braid. The awful smell of flowers hit Mayur's nostrils.

"Why didn't you pick me up on your way to the airport?" Aisha loosened her hug.

"Well." Mayur shrugged. "You never told me you wanted to come with me."

"Should I tell you about it?" Aisha grimaced. "I thought you would understand."

"Okay, okay." Mayur tried to clear the air. "Next time, I'll make sure we go to the airport together." He smiled. "Let's go now. We'll miss the flight, otherwise."

He walked her inside the airport lounge and towards the check-in counter. Mayur handed the tickets to an official and received the boarding passes.

He walked alongside her towards the seating area. They sat down on chairs.

"Prakash should've joined us," Aisha said. "His presence would've made a difference in our investigation."

"Yes," said Mayur. "I can understand that. But he will remain preoccupied with some other work here."

"What if we need police help at Bangalore? Don't you think Prakash would've helped us in those situations?"

"But he can still help us by staying at Hyderabad. He has some contacts with the Bangalore Police and can talk to them over the phone."

Aisha remained silent; she seemed to have convinced after hearing what Mayur had to say.

"Did you call Mr. Shekar Bedi?" she asked

"Oh, no," said Mayur. "Thanks for reminding me about this. It's wise to call him now." He took the phone from his shirt pocket and called Mr. Bedi.

22ND OCTOBER 1:30 PM - Bangalore

Mayur and Aisha arrived at Bangalore airport and decided to go to Mr. Bedi's house first. They hailed a taxi and told the driver the destination.

At Mr.Bedi's residence, Priya's body lay inside a glass casket, that sat in the main hall.

Julia, who had traveled a few hours before Mayur, sat beside Priya's body.

A girl in her mid-twenties with oblong face and sharp nose sat beside a sturdy boy. He was of average height and in his late twenties. A middle-aged woman with an oval-shaped face and almond eyes sat beside the girl. They were staring at Priya's body, their eyes red. The woman often wiped tears from her cheeks. *Are they Priya's sister Poonam, her fiancé Chirag, and Mrs. Bedi?*

Mr. Bedi approached and hugged Mayur, sobbing aloud.

Julia rose and approached Aisha and Mayur. They spoke about their flight journey from Hyderabad. She introduced Mayur and Aisha to Priya's sister, Poonam, Poonam's fiancé, Chirag and to Mrs. Bedi.

Mayur tried to calm their growing grief and emotions along with Aisha. They placed the marigold garland on the casket.

Mr. Bedi told Mayur the cremation would be later in the evening. Mayur needed to book a hotel room and freshen up. He preferred staying in a hotel instead of at Mr. Bedi's house. He also needed some privacy when talking with Aisha and stay in solitude.

22ND OCTOBER 2:30 PM

Mayur checked into the hotel room along with Aisha. The three stars hotel was luxurious. a large-sized bed with a thick cushioned mattress sat in the center of the room. A flat-screen LED TV perched on the wall in front of two sofas, which stood in an L-shape. A chandelier hung from the ceiling and the lamp lit the room with the yellowish-brown hue. An entrance to the balcony was on the right side and the purple curtains covered the windows.

Mayur told the room-boy to put their luggage down and ordered a pot of tea. He went to the bed and then collapsed on it. His back muscles and the entire body soothed because of the soft mattress.

"I am very much tired," Aisha said. She approached him towards the bed, smiling and relaxed beside Mayur.

Mayur turned to her and held her hand. "I don't feel fatigued if you're with me."

Aisha blushed.

Mayur's heart raced. It had been several weeks since he made love with Aisha. He always looked for such opportunities to sleep with her. He held both her arms and kissed her lips.

Aisha tried to protest his advancements, smiling. "I would like to freshen-up." Her heart too was beating faster and her breath had increased. Her chest wavered in rhythm.

"I can't wait, Aisha. Let's make love. You can go to the bathroom later." He climbed on top of her and continued kissing her lips and cheeks.

Aisha laid herself flat below him and showed her interest in making love by kissing him his lips.

Mayur removed his clothes and helped her to unbutton her dress. They made passionate love for the next fifteen minutes until the doorbell rang.

"It must be a room boy." Mayur waited for Aisha to put on her clothes. He too wore a night suit and then walked towards the door.

22ND OCTOBER 4:30 PM

Mayur ate snacks with Aisha in the hotel cafeteria. They hired a taxi to go to Priya's home to attend the funeral.

"What's your opinion after seeing Mr. Bedi?" Aisha asked as the taxi sped on the main street.

"He seemed to be a loving father. No doubt he is in shock about the loss. But he needs to be more cooperative with us in finding the culprit."

"Yes," said Aisha. "I too think so. He is fair and transparent enough. He didn't seem to be hiding any facts. You may need to spend more time with him and interrogate him."

"I know," said Mayur. "I will question most of them when we go to their home. It's better for us to get some vital information before it's too late."

Aisha nodded. "You are correct."

Mayur corrected his white kurta which was fluttering in the wind. His plain white dress suited the occasion. Aisha too wore a white sari for the event.

He got out of the taxi outside the Bedi's house. A large crowd dressed in white gathered inside the main gate. Wailing filled the air.

No doubt the Bedi family had a good number of social contacts. They were well respected as the attendees seemed to be affluent. The cars parked outside were expensive and everyone in the verandah wore sunglasses.

Mayur walked past the people and entered the porch. Priya's body placed in the main hall for the visitors to pay their homage. Mayur placed a marigold garland on her and walked out of the main hall along with Aisha.

They cremated Priya in the Bedi's farm. The atmosphere was tense and Mr. Bedi vowed he would not live in peace until they find the murderer.

22ND OCTOBER 5:30 PM

It was almost evening when Mayur came back to the hotel after attending the funeral. He made love with Aisha for the second time and relaxed on the bed, watching a sports channel on the TV.

"Did you get a chance to see Priya's sister, Poonam?" Mayur asked.

"Yes," said Aisha. "She resembles Priya."

"Did you observe something else about her?" asked Mayur.

"What is it?"

"She appeared not that sad when compared to Priya's parents which intrigues me."

Aisha sat beside Mayur. "Yes, I did observe. In fact, I wanted to talk about it. And her fiancé too seemed quite stony and appeared oblivious to what had happened to Priya."

Mayur nodded. "We'll know more about them only after a thorough investigation."

"And Priya's fiancé seemed unfazed by the loss. I never saw any sadness in him because of the loss."

"No worries," said Mayur. "We're interviewing all the possible suspects. Keep your fingers crossed until then."

Aisha nodded in agreement.

Mayur held her hand and kissed her palm. "You look beautiful."

Aisha tried to shove his hand away.

"What's the matter?" Mayur hadn't expected she would behave so.

"How long should we remain like this, Mayur?"

"You mean, are you talking about getting married?"

Aisha nodded. "Don't you think we can spend a good time together if we get married? I will feel secured if I've a loving husband like you. You know, my mother is also insisting I get married soon."

"Aisha," said Mayur. "I don't want to commit and take accountability by falling into marital life. Don't you think we'd be more comfortable staying like this instead of being husband and wife?"

"But we need to respect what our elders suggest, right?" Aisha said.

Mayur didn't want to argue and disappoint Aisha. He nodded. "All right. Give me some time so that I can talk about it to my mother."

"How many days you need, Mayur? It's already more than two years since we started dating. What should I tell to my mother? Should I agree to her suggestion to see any other boys?"

Mayur's pulse quickened. He might lose Aisha if he failed to convince and assure her that he intends to marry her. *I don't get a girl like Aisha in my life. It's imperative for me to keep her hopes alive.* "Aisha, I love you. You need to trust me. I'm waiting for my younger sister to get married. I will talk to my mother when Apsara gets settled well with her family."

Aisha's eyes glinted. She seemed to have convinced after what Mayur said. She nodded.

Mayur's phone rang. He got out of the bed and grabbed his device from the coffee table. Julia's name flashed on the screen.

Chapter 18 - Mayur Interviews Sumitra and Poonam

22ND OCTOBER 6 PM

"Hello, Julia," said Mayur. "I was about to call you. Are you all right there?" He put the phone on speaker mode.

"I'm feeling okay," Julia said. "I've planned to leave for Hyderabad tonight. When are you both traveling?"

"You please go ahead with your plan. We'll stay for another few days as I need to question the suspects who live here."

"All right" Julia paused. "Priya's mother, Mrs. Sumitra Bedi, and Poonam would like to meet you. Why don't you talk to Mrs. Bedi now?"

There was a rustling sound before Mayur heard a female voice. "Hello, Mr. Varma. It's Mrs. Bedi speaking. I would like to meet you to discuss Priya." She paused. "Is tomorrow morning okay for you?"

"Um..." Mayur mumbled. "Sure." He paused and then said, "but what if we speak the matter over the phone now?"

"No, Mr. Varma. I want the discussion to be discreet. My daughter, Poonam is also eager to share some information with you."

Mayur didn't want to lose this opportunity. His meeting with Mrs. Bedi and Poonam would throw some light on the investigation.

"All right," said Mayur. He looked at Aisha and then said, "Where are we meeting? At your home?"

"Um...,"

Mayur waited for Mrs. Bedi to answer.

"What if we visit your hotel? We'll have more privacy there."

Mayur too thought he could interview better at his hotel. "All right. What time can you come over?"

"At nine o'clock tomorrow morning," said Mrs. Bedi.

"Okay," Mayur said. "We're eager to see you tomorrow at ten."

"I have a request for you, Mr. Varma," Mrs. Bedi said.

"What?"

"Please keep our meeting secret. I don't want anyone to know about it."

"Don't worry, Mrs. Bedi," Mayur said. "I'll keep the matter undisclosed."

"Oh, thank you, Mr. Varma. I'm looking forward to seeing you tomorrow."

Mayur ended the call and turned to Aisha. "I hope our meeting with Mrs. Bedi and Poonam will be helpful and they reveal to us some important details. I am eager to find out more. Also, did you notice something strange about Poonam's fiancé at the funeral?"

"Um...no? What was it?"

"Chirag maintained a stony silence and didn't show any signs of sadness," said Mayur. "And he stood quite away from Priya's fiancé, Nayan."

"You made a good observation. I also noticed the only persons who cried at the funeral were Priya's parents. I got surprised Poonam wasn't as sad as her parents."

"Can you guess what might be the reason?" Mayur asked.

"Well," said Aisha. "Poonam is Priya's sister and she should be very much saddened. I am also surprised about what might be the reason."

"Julia told us that Mr. Bedi is a wealthy and well-known businessman and has earned good wealth. And because he has no male heir, his daughters will inherit the entire assets."

"You mean," said Aisha, "Poonam had the motivation to kill Priya for the inheritance?"

"That's correct. If Poonam is not involved in the plan, her fiancé has the motivation to kill Priya. He tried to make Poonam a sole proprietor."

"I admire you, Mayur," said Aisha. "And now I understand why Poonam didn't cry at the funeral. No doubt both she and Chirag should be on our suspect's list."

Mayur nodded. "I need to interrogate them and find out if they played a role in the murder."

"But why did Poonam volunteer to meet you if she is part of the conspiracy?" Aisha asked.

"Maybe she wanted to cover it up and trying to make us not treat her as a suspect."

"She must be very smart and think we're imbeciles." Aisha smiled.

22ND OCTOBER 7 PM

Mayur tossed the India Today magazine on the coffee table and looked at Aisha, who watched a horror movie. "Are we eating supper outside?"

Aisha took the remote and turned the TV off. "Yes, I'm interested in going out and eating at the restaurant."

Mayur rose. "Let's go then." He walked outside along with Aisha to the restaurant nestled within the hotel. They waited for a waiter to usher them to an empty table.

Aisha preferred eating North Indian food - tandoori rotis and masala curries. Mayur ordered a tomato soup to start with. He chose to eat tandoori rotis, palak paneer, and vegetable Palau.

The waiter took the order and left. Aisha propped her elbows on the table. "Coming back to our investigation," she said. "I wonder why Mr. Shekar Bedi is not coming along with Mrs. Bedi."

"They may be afraid that Mr. Bedi might prevent them from meeting us. And that makes me believe Mr. and Mrs. Bedi knows the perpetrator."

Aisha looked sideways, seemingly pondering over the matter. She removed her elbows from the table. "I tried to speak with Poonam at the funeral, but she avoided me by distancing herself from me. Your theory that the inheritance is the motive makes me understand why Poonam behaved so."

"It's good that you shared this information with me. It strengthens my guess that Poonam and Chirag did it. It makes me put them on the top of the suspect's list."

"It's good that Poonam is accompanying Mrs. Bedi. We need to interrogate her and understand her mind. By the way, is it not the correct time and opportunity for us to prepare the suspects list?"

Mayur nodded. "Yes, we should no doubt prepare the suspects list and continue the interviews."

"I guess we'll be busy here, interviewing the suspects for the next few days."

"You're correct," Mayur said. "No doubt our meeting tomorrow with Mrs. Bedi and Poonam will be a crucial one."

The waiter served them supper. Mayur ate sumptuous food, discussing their personal matters and about the case.

"Aisha, you have been like a Godsend for me. I wouldn't have come this far in my profession without your support. I admire you for helping me as a junior detective."

Aisha finished chewing her food. "Thank you. I too think I'm lucky to work with you. You've been considerate and encouraged me to do good work."

"I'm sure we solve many cases going forward and make the 'Dolphin Detective Agency' as a well-known name."

Aisha smiled. "Yes, we will."

22ND OCTOBER 8:30 PM

Mayur returned to the room from the restaurant along with Aisha and sat on the couch. He lit a cigarette while Aisha was lying on the bed with her back towards Mayur.

His cell phone rang. He took the device from the coffee table. It was Prakash. "Hi, Prakash. I'm sorry I couldn't call you after arriving here."

"That's okay," said Prakash. "Do you've any update for me?"

"We attended the funeral and currently relaxing at the hotel. Mrs. Bedi and her daughter, Poonam, would like to meet us tomorrow morning."

"What about Julia?"

"She is traveling back to Hyderabad tonight."

"Oh, that's okay," said Prakash. "Did you get a chance to question anyone at the funeral?"

"Um... unfortunately no. It's good that Mrs. Bedi and Poonam are meeting us tomorrow. We may get some leads after interviewing them."

"Okay," said Prakash. "I have an update for you. I've Priya's call details from her telephone service provider. She spent most of the time on her phone talking with her mother and her fiancé, Nayan."

Mayur inhaled a heavy breath. Did Priya argue with her mother over the phone? Maybe Mrs. Bedi wished to tell something about her phone conversation with Priya.

"Your findings of Priya's call details are timely. I'll mention it to Mrs. Bedi when we meet her tomorrow."

"Also," said Prakash. "Julia's project manager, Krishna Raj, called me this afternoon."

"What did he say?"

"He said he suspects Praful based on his observations in the last one month."

"Did he say anything more about Praful?"

"Well, he wants us to consider Praful as a prime suspect," said Prakash.

Mayur considered. It was evident that Praful was a strong suspect after interviewing him in Hyderabad. "Don't worry. We'll get a clear picture in the next few days when we interview all the suspects involved."

"Mayur," said Prakash, "I wish you and Aisha the best of luck. We need to close this case soon as people are starting to press me about this. We need to get something very soon. I hope we can make an arrest in the next few days."

Mayur hated rushing the process. He didn't want to arrest someone without proper evidence against him. But he remained silent, not to hurt Prakash. "Let's hope so."

Aisha approached, buttoning her nightdress. She kissed Mayur's cheeks and pressed her chest to his.

Mayur told her about the conversation he had with Prakash. He told her they were leaving for Hyderabad soon after meeting Mrs. Bedi.

Aisha instilled confidence in Mayur, saying he would solve the case very soon.

MAYUR TOSSED AND TURNED, contemplating the case. How did Krishna know Priya was close with Praful? Did he guess because Praful got sacked from his previous employer? He also thought about the possible involvement of Poonam and Chirag. He knew well that every fortune had a crime behind it. He would find about the matter only after interrogating each of them.

23RD OCTOBER 8 AM

Mayur took a hot shower which comforted him from exhaustion. He wrapped a Turkish towel around his waist and walked out of the bathroom.

Aisha, seated on the couch, smiled at him. Her deep-set eyes sparkled and her chubby cheeks reddened. She rose and sauntered into the bathroom.

Mayur sprayed deodorant under his armpits. He picked out a formal cream shirt and some dark blue pants and put them on. He needed to appear professional as he was meeting Mrs. Bedi and her daughter. He chose a pale blue tie and wore it. Standing in front of the dresser mirror, he combed his hair.

His fair, not so oblong and well-chiseled face shone in the fluorescent lights. His arched brows appeared prominent below his medium-sized forehead. He stood tall—above six feet. He made sure his attire was in order before he sat on the couch.

Aisha arrived from the bathroom with a green Turkish towel wrapped around her chest. Her black and not so thick hair formed into a bun. A blue and white napkin wrapped around it.

Mayur flipped through the magazine while she got ready. She approached him. In her dark blue embroidered sari, she looked beautiful. Her heart-shaped face and chubby cheeks shone in the fluorescent lights. Her full, but open lips got smeared with red lip gloss.

"Are we going out for breakfast?" Mayur asked, smiling at her. He placed the magazine back on the table.

"What if we eat here?" Aisha said.

"Okay," Mayur ordered two plates of idlis over the phone. He turned to Aisha. "Mrs. Bedi and Poonam will be here in the next thirty minutes."

When they finished eating their food, Mayur received a call from Mrs. Bedi saying they were on their way. Aisha preferred to have tea along with Poonam and Mrs. Sumitra Bedi.

The doorbell rang. "It must be them." Mayur opened the door. He smiled at Mrs. Bedi and Poonam. "Please come in."

Mrs. Bedi appeared younger than she actually was. Her black, dyed hair contrasted well with her fair, oval-shaped face. Her black, almond eyes and sharp nose stood out from the rest of her facial features.

Poonam resembled her father. Her fair, oblong face shone in the daylight that streamed through the windows. Her nose was like her mother's, sharp and long. Poonam seemed to be fond of jewels. A diamond necklace that glittered in the lights hung on her tender neck. A set of gold and diamond earrings adorned her earlobes. Her nose appeared prominent with a diamond ring in it.

Mayur gestured for them to take seats on the couches. When they had made themselves comfortable, Mayur ordered coffee over the phone.

"I hope Julia traveled back to Hyderabad yesterday night," Mayur said.

"Yes," said Poonam. "I went to the airport to send her off."

"That's good to know." Mayur checked her out from head to toe. Though her voice sounded shaky, she was confident. Her chest wavered as she breathed, but her facial features appeared courageous. Her face was ashen.

But Mayur didn't want to conclude anything before he interviewed her.

They all exchanged small talk before Mayur decided to come to the point. "Mrs. Bedi," said Mayur. "What made you consult me on the very next day after Priya's funeral?"

Mrs. Bedi looked sideways. She swallowed. "I would like to share some information about Priya so that it will help you in your inquest."

"Pray, go ahead," Mayur said.

"You know," she said. "Priya was not so well mentally after she went to Hyderabad. She often expressed her worries about her future and became emotional."

"Did she give any reason why she felt so?" Mayur asked. He waited for Mrs. Bedi to answer.

"No." Mrs. Bedi sounded confident.

"Did you ask her what bothered her?"

"Yes, I did," said Mrs. Bedi.

"What did she say?"

"Nothing and that's what worried me. She had been hesitating. She appeared scared to tell me the reason. She often cried whenever she called me or saw me when she visited Bangalore." A teardrop trickled down Mrs. Bedi's cheek.

Mayur waited for her to compose herself and gain control of her emotions. He looked at Poonam who seemed eager to say something. "How was her relationship with Nayan? Was she happy about her engagement to him?"

Poonam shot a glance at her mother before she looked back at Mayur. "They were getting along well." She paused. "Because Priya stayed in Hyderabad, I was not able to find out how their relationship was working out."

"How often did Priya visit Bangalore?" Aisha asked.

"Almost every month," Mrs. Bedi said.

"Did she meet Nayan whenever she visited Bangalore?" Mayur asked.

"Yes," Poonam added.

"If not with your mother, did Priya share any of her private information with you?" Mayur asked Poonam.

"Um...well... I don't think..."

"Yes, tell me," Mayur said, trying to sound encouraging.

"Poonam," said Aisha. "You need to tell us whatever information you have. We need your cooperation."

"Priya didn't share anything with me."

No doubt Poonam is concealing some private information. Is she scared of her mother? I should talk to Poonam in private so that she could tell me the truth.

"Poonam," said Mayur. "Do you agree with what your mother said?"

"What did she say?"

"That Priya was unhappy since she moved to Hyderabad."

"I don't know the reason." Poonam shrugged.

"Did you notice recently anything unusual in Priya's behavior?"

Poonam put her fingers on her lips, seemingly contemplating. "I did notice she was not happier after she went to Hyderabad."

"You mean she was sad after her engagement?" Mayur asked.

"She was all right when she got engaged."

"That means something went wrong after she moved to Hyderabad," said Mayur.

Poonam nodded.

Mayur shifted his glance to Mrs. Bedi. "Do you think Priya had any enemies?"

"Priya and enemies?" said Mrs. Bedi. "No. She was friendly with everyone at home and outside." She looked at Poonam with a 'do-you-agree' expression on her face.

Poonam narrowed her brows. "No, Priya didn't have any enemies in her life. She got along well with others."

Mayur considered. Neither Bedi nor Poonam gave any clues about why Priya felt unhappy after she moved to Hyderabad. He sensed Poonam knew something which was important to the case. But she tried to hide the fact which annoyed him.

"All right," said Mayur, darting his gaze between Mrs. Bedi and Poonam. "Did Priya love anyone before she got engaged?"

Mrs. Bedi and Poonam looked at each other with their eyes wide. Mayur waited to hear from them. When they remained silent, he said, "You need to answer, Mrs. Bedi."

"She didn't have any outside affair, but she was affectionate towards my brother, Rahul."

Mayur leaned forward. "Did she desire to marry him?"

"Well," said Mrs. Bedi. "I can only say they were very close and behaved like good friends. But, everyone at home and our close relatives knew Priya and Rahul were made for each other. I too took interest in their union, but my husband opposed it."

"Priya got forced to become engaged to Nayan, then," Mayur said.

Mrs. Bedi nodded. "Yes, you're correct."

Mayur turned to Poonam. "Do you agree that Priya and Rahul loved each other?"

"Well, I'm not sure if Priya loved Rahul, but she-" Poonam stumbled for words.

"Yes please tell me."

"Priya was in love with one of her classmates, Harsha," she blurted out.

Mayur sighed; no doubt Harsha would be another prime suspect.

"Are you sure she was in love with him?" Aisha asked.

Poonam nodded. "Yes. Priya considered Rahul a close relative and a good friend, but she loved Harsha."

Mayur turned to Mrs. Bedi. "Did Priya ever talk to you about her affair?"

"No," Mrs.Bedi said. "Had she told me, I would've helped her in uniting with him." She wiped a tear from her cheek.

"Poonam," said Aisha. "How do you know Priya was in love with Harsha? Did she ever talk with you about her affair?"

"I had seen her once at the Forum mall along with her lover. Later, when I asked her, she said she was in love with him and said she wasn't interested in Nayan. But she didn't want to hurt my parents. She loved Dad and that forced her to accept Nayan as her future life partner."

"All right." Mayur heaved a sigh of relief. "Thank you." He looked at Aisha and then back at Mrs. Bedi. "You gave us some vital information that will help us in the investigation."

Mrs. Bedi rose along with Poonam. "Mr. Varma, I want you to find that scoundrel who killed my daughter." She paused. "Please let us know if you need any further information from us."

"Sure. I will." Mayur ushered them towards the door.

Chapter 19 - Poonam's Revelations

23RD OCTOBER 9 AM

Mayur sat back on the couch, heaving a sigh of relief. His heart lightened after his meeting with Mrs. Bedi and Poonam. The meeting was a fruitful one and it helped in preparing the suspects list. He could now zero in on the people connected to the murder.

"Would you like to have another coffee?" He asked.

Aisha flipped through her notes and shifted her glance to Mayur. "Sure. I would love that." She smiled.

Mayur ordered the beverage over the intercom. He stretched out his legs. "We're now clear about the suspects who committed the crime"

Aisha nodded. "I've written down the list. We suspected Poonam and Chirag of murdering Priya to inherit the wealth. But the mystery deepened when Mrs. Bedi and Poonam met us."

"Now, we have Priya's ex-lover, Harsha, in our suspect's list. Also Mrs. Bedi's bachelor brother and Priya's uncle, Rahul. Also, I hope you have included Praful, Priya's colleague at Hyderabad."

Aisha flipped a page. "Yes, he's on the list." She closed the notepad. "We thought Poonam did it along with her fiancé, Chirag. What do you think about her, after questioning her for forty minutes?"

Mayur looked towards the window before shifting his gaze back to Aisha. "I would still like to keep her and Chirag on the list as Poonam appeared to conceal some information. She didn't appear concerned and disappointed by the loss of her sister, unlike Mrs. Bedi. I still believe she did it along with Chirag. But we may have to remove her name from the list if she has evidence that proves their innocence. But we need to interrogate Poonam and Chirag in private to get more details. Do you remember Poonam gave some personal information about Priya?"

"That Priya loved someone else before her engagement, right?"

"Correct," said Mayur. "And she tried to shield Chirag by concocting a story for us."

"But she told us the name of Priya's boyfriend was Harsha, right? She wouldn't have mentioned the name if she were lying to us."

"I agree. But we need to find out if Harsha exists. If so, then we should interview him."

"Yes, we should," Aisha said.

"But I still think Poonam has more information to tell us which she is trying to conceal."

"What's your feeling about the case?" Aisha asked.

"This case is not an ordinary one and is not a suicide or robbery as assumed by Prakash," Mayur said. "I have been saying from the beginning, the murder was well planned. It needs a thorough investigation. And I hope Prakash will wait with patience until we find the real murderer."

"I also thought Priya committed suicide. But the chain of events which followed after our visit to the crime scene proved my assumption was wrong."

A room boy arrived. He placed the tray containing two steaming cups of coffee on the wooden tea table.

Mayur took a cup and sipped the drink. The beverage invigorated his mood. He took a couple of more sips. "Mrs. Bedi told us Priya was unhappy after she moved to Hyderabad. But she wasn't sure who was responsible for Priya's unhappiness."

"Do you think she too tried to conceal something or was afraid, to tell the truth?" Aisha placed her cup on the coffee table.

"Well," said Mayur. "She didn't try to hide anything or feared someone. She seemed to be innocent and got shocked by the incident."

"That way," said Aisha, "Poonam seemed cooperative to me. She told about Priya's boyfriend, Harsha, and his involvement in the case."

"I agree with you, but—"

"I know," said Aisha. "Poonam protecting her fiancé by bringing Harsha onto the scene. But she told us everything. And I would like to put Harsha on the top of the list because he got betrayed and has a clear motive to commit the crime."

"Oh, yeah," said Mayur. "I forgot to talk about Rahul. Mrs. Bedi told us one more important suspect who has a clear motive."

"But Rahul is Mrs. Bedi's younger brother, right? How can he-"

"Rahul is a close relative, so he would be more heartbroken than Harsha. Mrs. Bedi said Priya and Rahul grew up playing together. Everyone talked about their wedding since childhood. "

"And they couldn't marry because Priya's father opposed their union," Aisha added.

"You are right," said Mayur. "And no doubt Rahul got hurt. Mrs. Bedi also told us Priya loved her father. Priya might've angered Rahul by refusing his proposal to get married to him. And that might have made him commit the crime."

Mayur's phone rang. Poonam's name lit the screen. He showed the screen to Aisha. She narrowed her brows with a 'why-had-she-called' expression. Mayur answered the call and put the phone on speakerphone.

"Hello, Poonam." *Why has she called so soon?*

"Hello, Mr. Varma." She said with her voice a bit shaky. "Do you have some time to speak with me?"

"Sure." Mayur straightened in his seat. "Pray, please proceed."

"Thanks for meeting us this morning," Poonam said.

"It's my pleasure. You and your mother gave us some vital clues about the case. I know you're eager to know who committed the crime. And thanks for cooperating with us."

"You know already Priya was unhappy since she became engaged and went to Hyderabad."

"That's what your mother told me."

"There was a reason why she was unhappy."

Mayur, his pulse quickened, remained silent and waited to hear from Poonam. *Does she have any important message to tell me?*

"There are two things. First, Priya had been dating Harsha before her engagement to Nayan."

"I'm sorry for interrupting you," Mayur said. "How long had Priya been dating her boyfriend?"

"I came to know about their affair only after seeing them in the Forum Mall. Later, I asked Priya about Harsha. She said she had been dating him for one year."

"Did you see her at the Forum Mall before the engagement?"

"Yes, a couple of months before she got engaged to Nayan."

"Did Priya ever ask your help in uniting with Harsha after the engagement with Nayan?"

"No, she didn't. She loved my parents, especially my father and she was ready to sacrifice Harsha to please my Dad."

"So, she broke with Harsha to keep your father happy, then."

"Yes."

"Why didn't she tell you about her interest in Harsha before becoming engaged to Nayan? Priya knew your parents loved her and they would agree with her marrying Harsha, right?"

"She did tell me about her interest in Harsha. But she feared my father who wanted her to marry Nayan, his friend's son."

"But still, Priya could've spoken to your mother, right?" Aisha asked, her voice curious.

"There is a reason. Harsha belonged to a different caste. And my mother came from an orthodox family background. My father too wouldn't have accepted the alliance. The inter-caste marriage would tarnish his image in society."

"Okay," Mayur said. "What's the other issue you would like to reveal to us?"

"Well, I was coming to that point. Priya told me once that Nayan wanted to cancel the engagement."

Mayur leaned forward. The plot was thickening. "What?"

"Yes, Priya told me Nayan had hesitated in telling her. When Priya insisted, he told her about his affair with some other girl."

Aisha gasped. "Oh, my God!" Her mouth fell open.

"Did Priya tell him she too wanted to break the alliance?" asked Mayur.

"Yes, Priya did tell Nayan he speak with the elders. But at the same time, she loved my father. She never wanted to tarnish his image by breaking the alliance."

"Okay," said Aisha. "Did you offer your help in solving her problem?"

"I did, but she never wanted to break the alliance from her side."

"Did you speak to Nayan about the matter?"

"No. But I came to know that Nayan too was afraid to talk to his parents. He seemed to have told Priya that he wanted to commit to their relationship. He suggested they forget their ex-lovers for the sake of their elders."

Mayur needed to verify Poonam's claim by interviewing Nayan and Mr. Bedi.

"Okay," said he. "Have you ever met Nayan's girlfriend? How long had he been dating her?"

"Well, I don't-" Poonam stumbled for words.

Mayur waited in silence. Poonam seemed to wonder if she should talk about the matter or not.

"Go ahead, Poonam," said Aisha. "You need to speak your mind and help us with the inquest."

"No," said Poonam. "I haven't seen Nayan's girlfriend. Whatever information I know about him is only from Priya." She sounded shaky. Was she concocting a story that Nayan had a girlfriend?

"All right," said Mayur. "Do you've anything else to tell us about Priya?"

"No, Mr. Varma," said Poonam. "I wanted to tell you that Nayan's girlfriend might have been a bone of contention between Priya and Nayan. And I thought this information may help you in the investigation."

"You made a wise decision to call us and give us more details." Mayur shifted his glance to Aisha. "Your information will help us in our investigation."

"Thank you, Mr. Varma."

Mayur bade her goodbye and heaved a sigh of relief.

"Interesting, isn't it?" Aisha smiled.

Mayur nodded.

"Should we trust her?"

"Well," said Mayur. "I'm finding it hard to trust Poonam ever since we met her this morning. We should cross-check her claims as soon as possible."

"Questioning Nayan is going to be important for us to make progress in the investigation."

Mayur nodded. He needed to speak with Prakash and update the facts. He took his phone from the table and called him.

He updated him about the progress made in the investigation after he came to Bangalore. He read out the list of suspects and listened to what Prakash said before ending the call.

Aisha, who was busy reading her notes, turned to Mayur. "What did Prakash say? Is he happy with the developments so far?"

"He is, but he still wants to hasten the process."

"Is that so?"

"Yeah," said Mayur. "He believed the case belonged to robbery, but now he is suspecting Praful as a perpetrator. I don't like his way of handling the case. He theorizes and believes in anything without proper evidence."

Aisha's face lit up with a grin. "Don't get upset over what Prakash says. He finally needs your help in solving the case. He will realize he is wrong once you find the real perpetrator."

"Who knows," said Mayur. "Prakash may be correct and Praful did it. Let's come to a conclusion only after questioning all the suspects."

Aisha smiled. "Sure."

Chapter 20 - Poonam Argues

23RD OCTOBER 11:30 AM

Mr. Bedi collapsed on a couch in the living room, beside his wife. *No, this shouldn't have happened to my daughter.* He wiped the tears rolling down his cheeks. *Who did this to my innocent child?* "I won't rest until the police find the culprit." He coughed for a few moments.

His wife offered him a glass of water. "You remember what Mayur told us at the funeral?" she paused while Mr. Bedi took a sip of water. "They need our cooperation in finding the murderer. Julia said Mayur has taken a good interest in the case and is working with the Hyderabad police. I'm sure he'll catch the murderer soon. Try to be patient."

"I am trying." Priya's father wiped his eyes with a handkerchief. "God shouldn't have been so harsh towards Priya."

Footsteps echoed in the hall. Poonam entered along with her fiancé. Chirag had been staying with Poonam at their house ever since Priya had died. Though it irritated Mr. Bedi, he remained silent not wanting to upset Poonam. He had already lost his first daughter. He didn't want to annoy Poonam by complaining about Chirag's overnight stay.

Her face lit with a smile. "Hello, Dad."

"Hi, Uncle," said Chirag. "Good morning, Aunty."

"Dad, are you unwell?" She looked at her mother, before shifting her gaze back to her father. "Are you thinking about Priya?" She touched his arm. "Come on, Dad. We need to move on. Priya's soul will rest in peace if we try to forget what happened to her."

"But I'm shocked about your sister's death," said Mr. Bedi

Poonam swallowed and touched her throat. She paused and then said, "Don't worry, Dad. I'm sure Mayur and his colleagues will tell us some good news very soon."

"Yes, Uncle," said Chirag. "I too am hopeful that detective Mayur will find the culprit."

Mr. Bedi sighed. "Let's hope so." He looked at his wife. "We made a mistake by sending Priya to Hyderabad. Had she remained with us, she would still be alive."

"I told you not to send her," she said. "It's you who suggested she go there." She darted her gaze between Poonam and Chirag. "If not this job, she could've found some other work here in Bangalore and stayed with us." Teardrops rolled down her cheeks.

Poonam went and hugged her mother. "It's all right, Mum. Priya isn't coming back. We need to move on. And I'm with you, all right?"

Her mother wiped the tears and snot using a handkerchief. She held Poonam by her shoulders. "That's right, beta (daughter). You're with us." She paused and then said, "I would like to see you get married to Chirag as soon as possible."

"Yes, Aunty," Chirag said. "I don't want to delay anymore."

Mr. Bedi felt hot all over. How could Poonam think of her marriage when Priya's death was still fresh in their minds? Didn't she and Chirag have any feelings towards the loss of Priya? He controlled his urge to say anything which would upset them.

"Dad," said Poonam. "What do you say?"

"About what?" Mr. Bedi touched his temple. He pretended he had not heard them talking about their marriage.

"We would like to get married soon."

"I don't have any objections, beta. We'll speak with Chirag's parents about it." Mr. Bedi was not in a mood to talk about the matter when they were still bereaved about Priya's death. He didn't want to disappoint Poonam.

She looked at Chirag. Their faces lit up with smiles. She turned to her father. "Dad," Poonam said, "Priya is no longer with us and I'll become the sole inheritor of the whole property. Don't you think you need to think about the matter, now?"

Mr. Bedi didn't like Poonam talk about the inheritance when they still bereaved. When Priya was alive, she had argued over the asset allocation. Mr. Bedi had calmed her by giving her a large sum of money in cash. It seemed Poonam's greed for money hadn't diminished.

"Is it the right time for us to talk about it?" Mr. Bedi grimaced.

Poonam's face reddened while Chirag's brows narrowed.

"Why don't you think so, Dad?" she said. "I already told you not to live in the past. I want-"

"I know-" Mr. Bedi snarled. "I know what's your intention. How you can think of the wedding and inheritance when Priya's death is still afresh in our minds? Don't you have any feelings towards your sister?" He bit his lip. Even though he had tried not to feel harsh, Poonam had crossed her limits, which forced him to vent his anger.

Poonam ran her eyes over everyone with her brows raised. "Dad, I wanted-"

Mr. Bedi's phone rang. Priya's fiancé, Nayan's name flashed on the screen. *Why has he called* now? "Hello, Mr. Bedi speaking."

"Hi, Uncle."

"Tell me, Nayan. What do you want?"

"I wanted to meet you along with my parents this evening."

Why do they want to meet? "You can. I'll make myself available after five o'clock. Is that okay?"

"That's all right, Uncle. Thank you."

Mr. Bedi looked at his wife. "Nayan and his parents are coming here at five o'clock."

"Did Nayan say anything else?" his wife asked.

"No."

"Perhaps, they want to spend some time with us as they didn't get any chance to speak during the funeral."

Mr. Bedi nodded.

"Dad," Poonam said, "You didn't answer my question."

"I will donate Priya's share of the property to a charity."

"What are you saying?" Poonam said, her brows knotted.

"Yes, that's what I'm going to do." He looked at his wife.

"How can you think of doing that, Dad?"

"It's the right thing to do," he said. "What do you do with so much wealth? Don't you think it's good for us to donate some of the assets to charity and feel happier?"

"Dad," she said. "You're not doing any such thing. I've all the rights to own Priya'property."

"Yes, Uncle," Chirag said. "You need to think of us."

"You will let me decide what I should do with it. I don't want either of you to interfere in this matter."

"Mum," Poonam said. "Why don't you talk? I don't know what's happened to you both." She rose and stormed towards her bedroom.

Chirag followed her.

Mr. Bedi sighed. He looked at his wife. "I don't understand why Poonam is behaving so selfishly after the engagement. She fought over the ownership of the jewelry showroom when Priya decided to go to Hyderabad. And now she is demanding Priya's wealth."

"It's not Poonam who took interest in all this," she said.

"Who is it, then?"

"It's Chirag or her in-laws."

"Why would they? They have enough property of their own to care for, right?"

"Maybe they are greedy. I'll talk to Poonam in private and find out why she's behaving that way."

MR. BEDI WAITED FOR Nayan and his parents to arrive. His gaze often shifted towards the wall clock. It was quarter to twelve and Nayan and his parents should be here anytime soon.

He couldn't catnap because of Poonam's rude behavior that morning. He was further disappointed when Poonam insisted he makes her the heir to all the assets. He would consult his lawyer before he made any decisions.

The doorbell rang. "It must be Nayan." His wife went to the door and opened it.

Nayan entered along with his parents. In his navy blue suit with a gold chain hanging on his neck, he looked handsome. His father wore cream pants and a purple shirt and his mother was in a traditional pink silk sari.

Priya's father rose and welcomed them. They all sat.

"We're sorry for what happened to Priya," said Nayan's father. "Our prayers are with you."

"Yes," said Nayan's mother. "We're always with you. Don't feel that you're alone."

Mr. Bedi tried to control surging emotions.

"Yes, uncle," Nayan added. "It's a great loss for me also. I hope Priya's soul rests in peace."

Mr. Bedi wiped teardrops from his cheeks. "It's all right. Everything is in the hands of the Almighty. We don't have any control over our lives."

"Is Poonam here, uncle?" Nayan asked.

"No," said he. "She has gone out with Chirag."

Mr. Bedi stared at Nayan. He was as cheerful as he used to be when Priya was alive. Why wasn't he affected by the loss? He remembered one of his colleagues saying Nayan loved his classmate. He intended to call off his engagement to Priya. But Mr. Bedi had become aware of it only after the engagement. Though he thought of breaking the engagement, he didn't want to tarnish Priya's image. He remained silent as Nayan had been trying to grow his relationship well with Priya. Yet, was he happy about Priya's death? Was Nayan happy to return to his girlfriend?

Chapter 21 - Mrs. Sumitra Bedi Meets Her Mother and Rahul

23RD OCTOBER 2:00 PM

Priya's mother, Mrs. Sumitra Bedi, stood in front of a dresser mirror. She curled her sari around her and tucked its frills in her waist. She put the loose end of the sari on her shoulder. She rubbed jasmine talcum powder over her face and applied red lip gloss.

"Hi, Mum." Poonam entered, diverting Mrs. Bedi's attention away from her reflection in the mirror.

"Hi, dear," she said. "I know you're hungry. I've prepared cheese sandwiches for you. They're in the fridge." She corrected her sari frills near her waist.

"Where are you going?"

"To your grandmother's home," Mrs. Bedi said. "Would you like to join me?"

"How can you go there, Mum?" Poonam asked.

"It's all over now. I sometimes feel we lost Priya because of hating each other. Now, it's time for us to set right the broken relationships and move on."

"Did you forget the abuse your brother, Rahul, yelled at us when Priya got engaged to Nayan?"

"Yes, I still remember, but he behaved so furiously because he got hurt. He'd loved Priya and wanted to ask for her hand in marriage. He didn't do anything wrong. You would've behaved in the same way if you were in his place."

"Don't you remember when he was drunk and abused Dad?"

"Let's not talk about the past," Sumitra grimaced. "Are you coming with me or not?"

"Um... no, Mum," said Poonam. "You can go. I don't want to see Rahul's face."

"But can you come for your grandmother's sake?"

"Yes, but not now," said Poonam.

Not wanting to force her anymore, Mrs. Bedi bade her goodbye and walked out of the room.

The chauffeur was waiting for her. He opened the rear door for Mrs. Bedi.

She sat, heaving a sigh of relief. Poonam had been behaving strangely these days. She had hated her parents ever since she got engaged to Chirag. Mrs. Bedi hadn't expected she would refuse meeting her grandmother.

It had been many days since Mrs. Bedi had visited her mother's place. She had often talked to her over the phone and enquired about her health. She used to meet Rahul, and her unmarried younger sister, Snehal, before Priya got engaged.

They all had decided to unite Rahul with Priya. Mrs. Bedi had tried her best to convince her husband to agree to the alliance. She gave up when he told her he wouldn't see Priya married to Rahul as long as he was alive. Priya's decision to abide by her father's intention also made Mrs. Bedi not want to pursue the matter.

She looked through the window when the driver stopped in front of the traffic lights. The evening traffic was heavy. The red and yellow city buses stood beside her car with the fumes coming out of their exhaust pipes. The cars and motorbikes lined up behind the buses and waited for the signal to turn green. A flock of parakeets flew above the electric wire and they sat on a large banyan tree that stood beside the street.

The driver parked the car outside Rahul's house and opened the rear side door. Mrs. Bedi stepped out and opened the main gate. The house had a large open area in which roses and bougainvillea were in full bloom. The smell of wet grass and soil surrounded the air. An Alsatian dog, which got secured to the porch railing, started barking.

Rahul opened the door and shouted at the dog to be quiet. He approached his sister. "Welcome." He smiled. He wore pale blue shorts and a red checkered shirt. He appeared rather young in his casual dress.

"Did you come early from work?" Mrs. Bedi asked.

He walked her towards the porch. "I'm not feeling well."

"What's wrong? Fever?"

"Yes," said Rahul. "Met with the doctor. Should be all right by tonight."

Mrs. Bedi entered the living room. Her mother, Usha Bhatt, sat on the couch. She reduced the TV volume. "Sumitra. What a surprise!"

Mrs. Bedi hugged her mother. She sat on a couch. Her glance shifted towards a framed photograph of Priya. A sandalwood garland adorned it. Nausea coursed through Sumitra's stomach. She couldn't control her sob. She broke out, hiding her face in her mother's chest.

Her mother ran her hands over her head. "You need to steel yourself. Whatever happened has happened. Let's not live in the past."

Rahul stood in front of Sumitra. "Mum is correct."

Sumitra wiped her tears and straightened in her seat. She looked at Rahul. Though he stood upright, his face was ashen and he seemed to have scared. His eyes were wide as he saw a wild animal.

He broke eye contact with Sumitra and looked at the floor. He went back and sat on the wooden chair.

"Let me prepare coffee," Sumitra's mother said.

Sumitra continued to stare at Rahul. His face was stony. She had observed him even during the funeral; Rahul had remained impassive.

Is there any reason for Rahul's behavior? He should've been more affected as he loved Priya more than anyone else.

Sumitra shook her head. She shouldn't interpret anything without proper evidence. The police had begun the investigation and it was their responsibility to find who did it.

Mrs. Usha Bhatt offered some coffee. She sat back in her seat.

Sumitra took a couple of sips in silence.

Sumitra's mother placed the cup on the table. She cleared her throat. "How is Shekar?"

"Doing well," said Sumitra. "He is busy with his business these days because of the wedding season."

"I'm very sorry for whatever happened to Priya," Rahul said. "Had Uncle Shekar not permitted Priya to go to Hyderabad, she would still be alive."

Sumitra's chest constricted. She wanted to forget the incident and that was the reason why she had visited her mother's place. She remained silent, not to encourage Rahul to say anything further.

"Rahul," said Sumitra's mother. "Let's not discuss the matter."

"All right," said Rahul. "I'm sorry if I've hurt you." He paused. "But we need to bring the perpetrator to justice so that Priya's soul would rest in peace."

"That's the job of the police," said Usha. "Why do you worry about it?"

Sumitra's heart raced. She too was keen to find out who committed the crime. She agreed with Rahul saying Priya's soul would rest in peace only when they find who did it.

"Sumitra," said Rahul. "I'm sorry to ask about the investigation. Did the police approach you and Uncle Shekar to question about the case?"

"Yes, Detective Mayur Varma is handling the case." She controlled her urge to ask Rahul why he was showing some interest.

"Is he from Bangalore?"

"No, from Hyderabad."

"Did he interview you?" asked Rahul.

"Yes," Mrs. Bedi said. "I hope detective Varma is able enough to bring the perpetrator to justice."

"If possible," said Rahul. "Tell me how the case is progressing. I would like to know if Mr. Varma can make good progress in his investigation. If not, we can hire a different private investigator and find out who the criminal is."

Sumitra nodded.

"Uncle Shekar would've acted sensibly," said Rahul. "He made mistakes by refusing to arrange my marriage with Priya and sending her to Hyderabad." He paused and then said, "Was Priya's job that important when compared to her personal life?"

"Rahul," Usha grimaced. "I told you not to talk about the past, right? Don't you think it would hurt your sister?"

Sumitra needed to calm her mother. "It's all right. In a way, Rahul is correct. Shekar made a mistake."

They sipped the coffee in silence and placed the empty cups on the tray.

"How is Poonam?" Usha asked.

"She is doing well. Her fiancé, Chirag is getting along well with her."

"When is their marriage?" Rahul asked.

"Well," Sumitra said. "We've not decided yet. But soon."

"It's wise not to delay the wedding after the engagement," Usha said. "Who knows if Chirag and his parents will change their minds?"

Sumitra's heart raced. It was possible that Chirag's parents might not go ahead with the marriage. Even though Chirag and his parents hadn't shown any signs of parting, Mrs. Bedi should be cautious. She needed to speak about the matter with her husband.

"I agree with you, Mum," she said, looking at her mother. "I'll talk to Shekar soon after going home."

"Sumitra," Rahul said. "Please keep me updated whenever the detectives interview you and Uncle Shekar."

Mrs. Bedi controlled her urge to ask the reason behind Rahul's interest. Was he eager to find the killer by hiring a different Private Investigator other than Mayur?

Chapter 22 - Evidence of Mr. Bedi, Poonam and Chirag

23RD OCTOBER 10:30 AM

Mayur grew contented after meeting Priya's mother and Poonam. He stood in front of the dresser of the hotel room and made sure his attire was perfect and then walked to the balcony. A morning cold breeze that swept down the balcony of the hotel room area rejuvenated him.

A few white and grey pigeons took flight above the building. Occasional honks of motorbikes and buses disturbed the otherwise calm ambiance.

He leaned on the railing thinking about the previous night spent with Aisha. She never refused his lovemaking. She believed in Mayur, who assured her he was serious about their marriage.

The bathroom latch clicked. He turned around. Aisha came out with her fair face glistened in the fluorescent light.

He stepped back into the room and closed the balcony door behind him. After switching on the TV, he sat on the couch, watching a cricket match while Aisha got dressed.

Aisha sat beside him. In her dark purple salwar kameez, she looked beautiful. Her heart-shaped face with not so chubby cheeks was rubbed with talcum powder. Her dark eyelashes, applied with mascara, appeared prominent on her face. Red lip gloss glistened on her full, open lips.

Mayur took her in from head to feet. "You look so pretty, Aisha."

"You look handsome in your new suit."

Mayur smiled. "Thank you."

"As per our plans, we're meeting Mr. Bedi at his house," said Aisha.

"Yes, but before that, let's go to the Swagat Restaurant to have some snacks."

They went inside the eatery and sat at a table.

Mayur leaned forward. "It's important for us to question Mr. Bedi about the suspects and seek his help in the interrogation."

"I agree. We should meet Mr. and Mrs. Bedi first."

"We may also meet Poonam and Chirag. We could interview them too."

"Sure," said Mayur. "That's a perfect plan."

The waiter arrived and took their orders. Mayur preferred to eat vegetable cutlets while Aisha ordered masala dosa.

"Should we call Poonam and tell her we are visiting her house?" Aisha asked.

"Yes," Mayur said. "It's better if she remains at her home. Poonam has been quite cooperative so far and we should continue to seek her help."

"But she and her fiancé Chirag are on our suspect's list, right?" Aisha asked. "How can we expect them to help us?"

"I know," Mayur said. "We'll treat her as a suspect while we question her. And I want her to help us in finding out more about the remaining suspects."

He took his phone from his shirt pocket and called Poonam.

"Hello, Mr. Varma," said Poonam.

"Hi, Poonam," Mayur paused. "May I know where you are?"

"Well...err...I am at my home."

"Okay. Aisha and I are visiting your house in an hour or so."

Poonam remained silent.

Why is she silent? "Are you there, Poonam?"

"Oh, I am sorry," she said, sounding startled. "I'm listening. Yes, you're most welcome."

"I want you to be at your home as I need to talk to you to find out a few more information." Mayur paused and then said, "Is your fiancé in Bangalore?"

Poonam cleared her throat. "Yes. Chirag is here with me."

"Oh, that makes my job easier," Mayur said. "Thank you and I'll see you soon."

"You're welcome."

The waiter arrived. He placed the food on the table and left.

Mayur cut the idlis. "We have yet to investigate two clues which we have collected at the crime scene."

Aisha took a bite of dosa and chewed. "The Pizza Hut cap and the footprints, right?"

"Yes," said Mayur. "We need to ask Prakash about the progress he has made with those two clues. But I wonder why he hasn't heard anything from the Pizza Hut outlets yet."

"Prakash has told us Priya hadn't ordered pizza on that eventful evening, right?"

"Yes, I remember that," said Mayur. "But where did those clues come from?"

Aisha chewed her food. "What if the murderer placed it there to misguide us."

"No," said Mayur, his tone reassuring. "Do you think someone would place more than one clue to misguide us? And about the footprints, why they are not from somebody from Pizza Hut?"

Aisha placed the fork on the plate. "It is better to remind Prakash to pursue the matter with the Pizza Hut outlets. It is possible it's a delivery boy who did it."

"Let's call Prakash." Mayur took his phone and swiped on its screen to call him.

"Hello, Mayur," Prakash answered. "How is everything there?"

"We've planned to meet Mr. and Mrs. Bedi in the next half an hour." Mayur paused. "Have you enquired with the Pizza Hut outlets about the clues we've recovered at the crime scene? I am sanguine we may get some useful tips to proceed in our investigation."

Prakash remained silent for a moment. "Well," he said, "we know from all the Pizza Hut branches that Priya hadn't ordered the food on that eventful night."

"And did you contact them again?"

"No, I haven't."

"We should. Let's not ignore those important clues - Pizza Hut cap, its uniform shirt button, and the footprints."

"Sure. I'll contact them today."

Mayur bade Prakash goodbye. He ate the last bite of his snacks. "We will hear something positive from the Pizza Hut because the DNA of the hair is not a match with Praful or Hemant. I suspect the culprit is from Pizza Hut."

Aisha raised her brows. "Why would someone from Pizza Hut-."

"Sexual favor," Mayur said. "I'm sure Priya had ordered pizza many times and the delivery boy had seen her before. Priya's petite figure would attract anyone who is so lecherous. No doubt the perpetrator got tempted to seek a sexual favor and killed her when Priya resisted."

"Aha," said Aisha. "That means the delivery boy went to Priya's flat even though she had not ordered the pizza."

"Yes," said Mayur.

"In that case, the perpetrator might've delivered the pizzas to other residents as well. We need to find out who delivered the pizza to any of the residents on that eventful evening."

"The perpetrator has not delivered any pizza to any of the residents before he struck Priya."

Aisha widened her eyes. "He didn't? Why?"

"He would know he would get caught if he visited the apartment officially. He came to the Majestic Apartments without a pizza and tried to rape Priya."

MR. BEDI OPENED THE door for Mayur and Aisha and ushered them into the living room.

In his loose-fitting white pajama and cream kurta, he looked younger than his actual age. His fair, oval and long face glistened in the daylight light streaming through the window.

"Did I keep you waiting?" Mayur said as he sat beside Aisha on a couch.

"No, Mr. Varma," said Mr. Bedi. "You didn't."

Mrs. Bedi smiled. In her pale red and green sari, she looked charming. Her black-almond eyes glowed as she looked into Mayur's.

Poonam, wearing pale blue jeans and a V-neck blue top, arrived along with Chirag. Chirag wore a white kurta and pajamas. They all exchanged pleasantries.

Mayur came to the point. "Poonam, we need privacy to interview your parents. Would you mind leaving us alone for a few moments?"

Poonam nodded. She rose along with Chirag.

"We need to interview you too after we're done with your parents," Mayur said.

Poonam's face filled with a light smile. She walked towards her room along with her fiancé.

Mayur turned to Mr. Bedi. "You know-"

Mr. Bedi raised his hand. "Before you start, I would like to know the progress you've made in your investigation."

Mayur swallowed. Though Mr. Bedi's words annoyed him, he needed his cooperation. He needed to answer him. He cleared his throat. "We're doing our best to nab the perpetrator, Mr. Bedi. So far, we've interviewed two strong suspects, based at Hyderabad. But I don't want to reveal to you the outcome at this stage. I hope we will make further progress out of our visit to Bangalore."

Aisha straightened in her seat. "Let's hope for the best, Mr. Bedi."

Mrs. Bedi's face fell. A teardrop rolled down her face.

Mayur waited for her to compose herself. "I'm sure we'll be successful in our investigation. We'll bring the perpetrator to justice if you cooperate with us. Now, can I ask a few questions?"

Mrs. Bedi wiped her cheeks and said, "Please, pray proceed."

"We found that Priya's age was twenty-five?" Mayur said."Is that correct?"

"Yes," said Mr. Bedi. "She turned twenty-five three months ago. I still remember the birthday party we hosted here."

"Can I know something about her childhood?"

Mr. Shekar Bedi looked at his wife before fixing his gaze back on Mayur. "Can you be specific about what you would like to know?"

"Well," said Mayur. "Did Priya jell well with her friends and loved ones?"

"Yes," said Mrs. Bedi. "She was quite friendly to everyone. She had spent most of her evening's time playing with her friends and did her classwork in the night. She was such a lovely girl, you know." Mrs. Bedi broke down.

Mayur paused. "Mr. Bedi," said he. "Please be patient. I need to know if any of you or your family members beat her when she was a child."

"Never," said Mr. Bedi, his voice raised. "Priya was our lovely daughter and we cared her more than anyone else."

"How about her teachers?" asked Aisha. "Did they treat her well?"

"Yes," said Mrs. Bedi. "Priya was in the top ten and was punctual in doing her class assignments. Her teachers never complained about her performance and treated Priya well."

"She was fond of playing basketball and participated in state-level tournaments."

Mayur heaved a sigh of relief. Priya was no doubt brought up well and she wouldn't have had anyone who held a grudge against her. "So, you assure me that Priya was much loved by her loved ones and didn't have any enemies."

They both nodded.

"You said you loved Priya more than Poonam," said Mayur. "Was there any conflict of interest between the sisters over this matter?"

"No," Mrs. Bedi said. "They didn't have any conflict over the matter. In fact, Poonam understood Priya deserved the extra love and affection as she was the elder."

"Mr. Bedi," said Mayur. "You mentioned Priya's friendship with someone before she got engaged to Nayan."

Mr. Bedi nodded.

"I would like to know whether Priya was happy with her engagement."

Mr. Bedi looked at his wife for a moment before fixing his gaze back on Mayur. "As I said, Priya loved everyone at home. She loved us more than anyone else. She didn't want to defame the family status and so, she accepted Nayan as her would-be husband."

"That's correct," said Mrs. Bedi. "I've seen Priya going out with Nayan and they had developed a close relationship very soon. In fact, she visited Bangalore almost every fortnight to see him and she was eager to get married to him." She grew emotional and burst into a light sob. "Oh...no...Mr. Varma...had she not transferred to Hyderabad, she would've married Nayan by now."

"It's all right, Mrs. Bedi," said Aisha. "Please console yourself. We're here to know the facts so that we can find the culprit."

Mayur sighed. He hoped he had collected enough information. But Poonam and Mrs. Bedi had told him Rahul loved Priya since their childhood and he desired to marry Priya. And he was one of the main suspects on his list with betrayal as his motive.

"Mrs. Bedi," said Mayur. "You and Poonam had told us when we met last that your brother Rahul liked Priya and wanted to marry her."

Mrs. Bedi nodded. "Yes, I did tell you that."

"Do you think he got upset over Priya's engagement and would have harmed her?"

"No," said Mrs. Bedi. "My brother wouldn't have thought something so heinous." She looked at her husband for a moment before she turned to Mayur. "Rahul indeed loved her and I still believe he loved her in spite of her engagement with Nayan."

So, Rahul might not have tried to kill Priya. He looked at Mr. Bedi. "What about Harsha?" said he. "You'd said that he had vowed to avenge her for the betrayal. Do you think he held a grudge and harmed Priya?"

"Quite possible," said Mr. Bedi. "Quite possible, Mr. Varma. He indeed was angry over Priya's betrayal when he met me at my showroom."

Mayur smiled. "That's what I wanted to know." He paused for a moment. "One last question, Mr. Bedi. Did you ever visit Hyderabad while Priya stayed there?"

Mr. Bedi looked at him and seemed to have startled. "No, but-"

"I'm curious to know," said Mayur.

"We wanted to," said Mrs. Bedi, "but Priya came to Bangalore almost every fortnight. So, we didn't feel it was necessary."

"All right," said Mayur. "Can you please send Poonam and Chirag to us?"

"Of course. I will."

Mrs. Bedi accompanied him out of the room.

Mayur continued to watch Mr. and Mrs. Bedi leave and looked forward to seeing Poonam and Chirag. He was eager to question them to find out if they conspired the murder.

Approaching male and female voices and the sound of footsteps echoed in the hall. Poonam and Chirag arrived.

She had applied facial cream to her fair and oblong face and it shone in the daylight. A dimple formed on her cheeks when she smiled. "Good morning, again." She sat on the couch.

Chirag, his semi-dark face ashen a bit, made himself comfortable beside her.

Poonam seemed confident, her chin upwards. There was no sign of sadness or melancholy on her face, unlike her parents. Chirag seemed eager to face the questions and leaned forward. He often twisted his watch which was on his right wrist showing a sign of anxiety.

"I'm sorry for what had happened to your sister," said Mayur. "And we need your cooperation so that we can bring the perpetrator to justice."

Poonam's face fell and grew pallid. "Please let us know how we can help you."

"How close were you with your sister?" Mayur asked.

"I don't understand what you mean by that."

"Well," said Aisha, "did you both share your secrets and private information with each other? Or were you like distant friends?"

Poonam looked sideways. She seemed to be contemplating. She paused for a few moments. "I'm not sure if she shared her private matters with me, but I was quite open-minded with her. I also sought her help in whatever way possible, whether it was academic or about my future. I didn't hide anything from her."

"And what about her affair with Harsha?" asked Mayur. "Did Priya tell you about it?"

"I've told you about it already. I saw both of them at the Forum mall. And I insisted she tell me about her friend. She said she had been dating Harsha."

"So, Priya didn't volunteer the information about Harsha," Aisha said.

"That's correct."

Mayur straightened. He needed to enquire about the inheritance that was a prime motive for Poonam and Chirag. "We know that you both were the sole heirs of the property that your father owned. Am I correct?"

"Yes," Poonam said.

"Was there a dispute over the matter?"

She narrowed her eyes. She looked at Chirag for a second before fixing her gaze back on Mayur. "With whom? With my parents?" Poonam sounded shaky.

"Yes and also with Priya if ever there was a dispute," Mayur said.

"We did have a couple of disagreements over the asset allocation. But I did rectify them before Priya moved to Hyderabad."

"That means those disagreements surfaced after your engagement, right?"

"Yes."

"That's what I wanted to know, Miss Bedi," Mayur said. "After your engagement, did you ever go to any place outside Bangalore?" He smiled. "I would like to know how well you got along."

Chirag leaned forward. "We wanted to visit Mysore and the surrounding areas, but Priya moved to Hyderabad. That put an end to our plans."

"Yes," said Poonam. "That's right."

Mayur paused. "Do Nayan and Chirag know how much you would inherit after your father?"

Poonam looked at Chirag, her face lit with a light smile. She nodded, looking back at Mayur.

Why did her face grow cheerful again?

"All right," said Mayur. "One last question, Miss Bedi. Two guys loved Priya other than her fiancé: Rahul and Harsha. Do you think they ever held any grudge against her?"

Poonam swallowed. "Yes, as they both got hurt and betrayed. And you remember my mother said Priya wasn't that happy when she spoke to her when she visited Bangalore. She worried about the matter though she had accepted Nayan as her husband to be."

Mayur's pulse quickened. He needed to probe more into this matter which he had ignored. He paused and composed himself. "Thank you, Miss Bedi. That's all we wanted to know from you." He needed to find out if Poonam was a left-hander and she wore size nine shoes.

"Poonam, can you write your full residential address for me?" He handed her a pen and a notepad to her. Poonam took the pen with her right hand and wrote the details.

Mayur asked her the size of her shoes which she wears. Poonam said it was size nine.

He looked at Chirag and then back at her. "Thank you, Miss Poonam. Would you mind leaving Chirag alone with us for a while?"

Poonam rose. "Sure. I hope I helped you." She walked out of the room.

Mayur looked in the direction in which Poonam went. When she disappeared, he shifted his gaze back to Chirag.

Chirag seemed rather less courageous. His pale face contrasted with the brightness of his purple kurta.

"May I know your full name?"

He swallowed. "Chirag Bakshi."

"Where do you work?"

"At Wipro, as a software engineer."

"May I know where you were on the 19th of October between 7 pm and 10 pm?"

"Um... You know er...it was Sunday and I had lunch with Poonam here along with my would-be in-laws. In the evening, I went to Lalbagh along with Poonam and was at the MTR Restaurant until nine. We had dinner there together. It was around half-past ten when I arrived at my home."

"All right," said Mayur. "Do you know the worth of property that Priya and Poonam would inherit after her father died?"

Chirag nodded. "Poonam did tell me about it."

"And you're well aware that now Poonam is the sole proprietor."

Chirag drew in a heavy breath. He nodded.

"Do you think Priya and Nayan got along well with each other?"

"Yes, but-" Chirag stumbled for words.

"Yes, tell me. You need to be honest with me."

"Poonam told me that Priya loved her classmate, Harsha. And Priya struggled to forget him even though she tried to develop a close friendship with Nayan."

Mayur paused. He remembered Mr. Bedi and Poonam saying Priya had indeed found it hard to forget her ex. Now, Mayur needed to check if Chirag was a left-hander. He took a piece of paper from his pocket and held it in front of Chirag.

"Chirag," said he. "Can you write your phone number on this? I may need to contact you if needed." He took a pen from his shirt pocket and gave it to him. Chirag took the paper from him, held the pen in his right hand, and wrote his phone number. He gave the paper back to him.

When Mayur asked him his shoe size, Chirag told him it was size eight. Mayur, not convinced, told Chirag to remove his slippers which he was wearing. The number 'eight' was printed on it.

"Thank you very much." Mayur put the paper back in his pocket. It was unlikely that Chirag committed the crime as he was a right-hander and wore size eight shoes. But Mayur needed to verify his alibi. "That's all, Mr. Bakshi. Thank you for cooperating with us. Can you go and send Mr. and Mrs. Bedi to us?"

Chirag nodded and rose. He disappeared.

Aisha flipped through the pages of her notepad. "Are we saying goodbye? We can because we've collected enough information."

"I have got a couple of more questions to ask Mr. Bedi before we leave," Mayur said. His glance shifted towards the place from where Mr. and Mrs. Bedi entered. They approached and sat in their usual places.

"All right, Mr. Bedi," Mayur said. "Before we leave, we need to know a couple of things from you."

"Please ask," Mr. Bedi said.

"Post engagements, was there any discord between Priya and Poonam over the property?"

Mr. Bedi bit his lip. He paused. "Yes, sort of," he said. "Poonam was not happy because she didn't inherit my primary jewelry showroom. I compensated her with extra money. But she wanted an equal share in the showroom and I had opposed her on this matter."

"Did you settle it, finally?" Aisha asked.

"Yes. I offered her more money."

"Was Poonam happy with the settlement?" Mayur asked.

"Yes, sort of," Mrs. Bedi said. "But the matter got closed now as Priya is no more."

"On the 19th of October, were Chirag and Poonam at Bangalore?"

Mr. Bedi remained silent for a while, seemingly contemplating and then said, "Yes. They both were here."

Chapter 23 - Miss Bedi's Greed

23RD OCTOBER 12:30 PM

Mr. Bedi gestured Poonam and Chirag to take a seat on a couch. He looked at his wife, who sat on a recliner in the living room.

Poonam's fair and oblong face glistened in the fluorescent light. Her black, large eyes shone as she looked into her father's eyes. A dimple formed on her right chubby cheek when she smiled.

Chirag's semi-dark, oblong face contrasted with that of his fiancée's. His average height almost equaled to Poonam's. Being of a heavy build, he occupied more space on the couch than anyone else seated in the hall.

Mr. Bedi straightened in his seat. "I'm planning to arrange a special pooja—prayers to God—at home." He turned to Poonam. "I would like you both to attend the ceremony."

Poonam shrugged. "When are you planning it for?"

"This Sunday and it's the most auspicious day this month to perform it."

Poonam leaned forward. "But Dad, I'm attending my close friend's wedding on Sunday."

"Where is the wedding?" Mrs. Bedi asked. "Here at Bangalore?"

"No, Mum," Poonam said. "It's at Mysore." She turned to her father. "Can we have the pooja some other day, Dad?"

Mr. Bedi raised his eyebrows. "No. We need to have it on this coming Sunday. Panditji has told us not to postpone it and we should listen to his advice."

"But Dad, I can't miss my close friend's wedding." She paused and then said, "What if you and Mum perform the pooja? I'll be coming back from Mysore by evening."

"Poonam," said Mr. Bedi's wife. "Listen to what your dad says. And it's good for you to attend the pooja. All the family members should be present when it's performed."

Chirag leaned forward with his eyes glowing. "What Poonam is saying is correct, Aunty. She has to attend the wedding as the bride is a close friend. All her classmates are going to Mysore together."

"Yes, Mum," Poonam added.

"Poonam," Mr. Bedi's wife said, her voice raised. "Don't you think you need to listen to what your Dad is saying? It's not good going against his wishes."

Poonam rose, her nostrils flared. She breathed heavy. "You never care for what I need in my life. You can't be so pushy, Mum." She stormed out towards her bedroom.

Chirag sat on the edge of the seat for a moment and then followed Poonam.

Mr. Shekar Bedi's chest constricted. He looked at his wife with his pulse quickened.

His wife widened her eyes. "I don't understand what has happened to Poonam these days." She stared down for a moment before fixing her gaze back on Mr. Bedi. "She is behaving rather adamant and impatient."

Mr. Bedi sighed. "There is a reason why Poonam is acting so."

His wife looked at him with a questioning expression on her face.

"Better I don't tell you about it," he said. He waited for a moment. "She wants me to change my will."

"Change the will?"

"Yes. She would like to become the whole proprietor of the family assets because Priya is no more now."

His wife remained silent seemingly contemplating.

"No doubt she will inherit most of my property as Priya is no more." He paused and then said, "But her pushy attitude has annoyed me. The sad incident of Priya is still afresh in our minds. Why is Poonam hurrying? I don't understand her manners."

His wife looked at him, her brows narrowed. "She is hurrying to arrange her marriage. She told me if this marriage season passes, she has to wait for another eight months to one year, that she doesn't want to do."

"How can you say that? Isn't she affected by the loss of Priya?" said he. "And that Chirag. He is also behaving quite erratic. He is no friendlier with me than he used to be before Priya's death. Both Poonam and he are behaving unfriendly after I refused their advice to change the will."

"Maybe they're afraid of not inheriting the family business," said his wife. "You may need to tell Poonam she would get her share of property and not to worry."

"I did, but she is quite greedy and impatient." Mr. Bedi looked at his wife. "Have you noticed Chirag is staying in this house for the last two days? What's the need for him to remain here?"

"And they're dining out and avoiding eating at home," his wife said.

Mr. Bedi's heart raced. "I'm not sure what has happened to them."

Chapter 24 - Evidence of Nayan

23RD OCTOBER 1:00 PM

Mayur bade Mr. and Mrs. Bedi adieu and walked out of their home along with Aisha, contented. "Let's catch a taxi on the main street and go to the hotel."

Aisha walked alongside Mayur. The afternoon sun was less intense. The leaves of the peepal tree fluttered. The branches of the Gulmohar trees with their red-edged flowers shook in the wind,. The breeze was cold and comforting. A few pedestrians took a stroll in a residential area. A couple of them walked their pets alongside the street.

They hailed a taxi and it took about half an hour for them to arrive at their hotel room. Mayur collapsed on the couch and stretched out his legs to unwind. Aisha sat opposite him on a smaller couch.

He poured a glass of water and drank. "Would you like to have coffee?"

Aisha nodded.

He spoke to the room boy over the intercom and ordered.

"What do you infer after interrogating the Bedi couple, Poonam and Chirag?" Aisha asked.

"Well," said Mayur. "Priya was well taken care of by her parents when she was a child and her parents loved her more than Poonam. Priya wouldn't have committed suicide because she had received affection from her parents."

"Do you think Poonam and Chirag have a role in this crime?"

"What's your opinion?" Mayur asked.

"Poonam did mention the discord they had over the property allocation."

"Yes," said Mayur. "I too am thinking along those lines. No doubt they'd a considerable amount of differences over the matter. Mr. Bedi also confirmed to us that Poonam was unhappy about it."

"But he also mentioned both Poonam and Chirag were at Bangalore on that eventful evening. There was no evidence of guilt or embarrassment on their faces barring a sign of nervousness. Maybe they were nervous because they faced a police investigation for the first time."

"But the greed for money will motivate anyone to make untoward decisions," said Mayur. "Who knows. Poonam got determined to own her father's primary jewelry showroom and murdered Priya?"

"You mean," said Aisha. "Poonam killed her own sister?"

Mayur nodded. "If not she or Chirag, they must've hired some supari killer to murder Priya."

"Oh my God," said Aisha. "Are you sure they did it?"

"It's quite possible. You remember that we have been seeing Poonam and Chirag since Priya's funeral. They appeared less affected by the incident. They haven't shown any signs of sadness or melancholic, unlike her parents. If Poonam had loved Priya, she would've cried at least once."

Aisha widened her eyes. "You may be correct. We should compare their DNA against the clues we've collected."

Mayur nodded. "Yes, we should. We'll call Prakash soon and tell him to make arrangements for the tests."

"You said Poonam and Chirag might have hired a professional killer to kill Priya," said Aisha. "Then, why would he don a Pizza Hut uniform and forget to take the cap with him? The entire scenario puzzles me."

"I've been thinking about it from the beginning. That is why I told Prakash not to neglect the Pizza Hut related clues and pursue the matter with the branch."

Coffee arrived. They sipped their hot and aromatic beverage in silence. Mayur placed his half-empty cup on the table. "We should interview the remaining suspects before Prakash arranges for the DNA tests."

"Whom will you interview next? Rahul or Harsha?"

Mayur took the cup and sipped. "I would go with Nayan. He seems a strong suspect with greater motive as he loved someone else before he got engaged to Priya." He paused. "I hope you've their contact numbers."

Aisha nodded. She read the numbers.

Mayur saved them into his phone contacts list. "We now have all three contact numbers. We'll start with Nayan and before we call him, I would like to speak with Prakash."

He called Prakash.

"Hello, Mayur," Prakash said. "How is everything going?"

"Going well," Mayur said. "We met the Bedi couple, Poonam, and Chirag. We're happy with the way things went."

"Congratulations," Prakash said. "Tell me, how can I help you?"

"Did you contact any of the Pizza Hut branches? I would like to know if you have made any progress."

"Yes," said Prakash. "I've found that Priya's phone number got registered with the Hi-Tech City's Pizza Hut branch. We already know that she didn't order pizza that night. But I've told the owner to report to us if he has noticed anything suspicious in any of the Hyderabad branches."

"That's good to hear. I'm sure we'll be successful if we follow up the Pizza Hut uniform clues and will be able to arrest the perpetrator."

"Sure," said Prakash. "I'll spend more time investigating along those lines."

"What if you ask them if anyone has lost their cap? I'm sure the owner of the outlet should be able to help you."

"It's a good point," said Prakash. "I'll call immediately and find out."

"Also about the footprints. The forensic team has concluded that the delivery boy wore size nine shoes. You can get the names of those who wear a size nine shoes so that we can interview them when I return."

"Sounds good." Prakash paused. "Have you guys got any other lead?"

"Poonam and Chirag were unhappy over her father's asset allocation. It's possible that they might have committed the crime to get Priya from their way. But they have a strong alibi. Her parents have confirmed to us that they were at Bangalore on that evening."

"What if they'd hired a professional killer?" asked Prakash.

"It's quite possible," said Mayur.

"What about the remaining suspects?" asked Prakash.

"We are finishing the interviews in two days. You need to arrange for the DNA tests of all the suspects based at Bangalore. When do you think we can get the results?"

"Very soon. And you finish the interviews. I'll arrange for the tests soon after you arrive here."

"Sure," said Mayur. "By the way, I have all the suspects' phone numbers. I want you to get the cell site data so that we can find out if any of them visited Hyderabad."

"That's a good idea," said Prakash. "Please send me the details."

Mayur told Aisha to text the phone numbers to Prakash.

She did so and went on: "Why are you so particular about the DNA tests? Is there any possibility of a DNA match?"

"It's quite likely," said Mayur.

"You mean someone from Bangalore-" Aisha's eyes widened.

"Yes," said Mayur, "Correct. One of these suspects wore the uniform and entered the apartment. Do you remember what the security guard said? The delivery boys entered the apartment without writing their details? It's quite possible the suspect knew the loopholes and Priya's stay on that weekend. And it should be one of these suspects who committed the crime."

"We shouldn't delay questioning the remaining ones, then," Aisha said.

"Yes," said Mayur. He took the phone from the table and called Nayan.

"Hello."

"Hello, Mr. Nayan. I'm Detective Mayur Varma. I'm calling about Priya's murder."

"Oh, yes," Nayan sounded shaky. "Please tell me how I can help you."

"I would like to meet you and ask questions related to the case," said Mayur. "I hope you can spare some time for us."

"Um...sure...I will."

"I want you to come to my hotel room so that we can talk privately," said Mayur. "I hope you don't mind meeting us here."

"Oh, why not? May I know where are you lodged?"

Mayur told him the address and looked forward to meeting him at his place.

AN HOUR LATER, THE hotel room bell rang. "It must be Nayan." Mayur rose, walked to the door and opened it.

A young man in his mid-twenties smiled at Mayur. "Mr. Mayur?"

Mayur smiled back. "Detective Mayur." They shook hands. Mayur stepped away, making room for Nayan to enter. "Thanks for coming."

He asked Nayan to remove his shoes near the entrance, for he wanted to check Nayan's shoe size. When Nayan took off his footwear, Mayur bent down a little and read the shoe size; it was size nine.

He ushered Nayan towards the couch and introduced him to Aisha.

In his white cotton shirt and blue jeans, Nayan appeared handsome. His fair, oval face shone with face powder on it. His button nose contrasted to his long neck that suited his more than average height".

"Mr. Nayan," said Mayur. "You know we're here to investigate Priya's murder. We're trying to interview all the possible suspects based at Bangalore. We may get some leads that would help us find the perpetrator."

Nayan swallowed. He touched his nose and narrowed his thick-black eyebrows.

"And I hope you'll cooperate in our investigation," Aisha added.

"Sure," said Nayan, "why not? Please let me know the questions you have."

Mayur paused. "May I know your full name?"

"Nayan Chabra."

"What do you do for a living?"

"I own clothing business."

"Did you inherit the business?" asked Mayur.

"Yes. I opened a couple of more shops after I took over my family business."

"Are you living with your parents?"

Nayan nodded. "Yes."

"What's your opinion of Priya?"

"Oh, I better not talk about her after what happened to her. She was such a lovely girl, you know. I'm unfortunate to lose her and I will never get a girl like Priya in my life."

"That means you were happy over your engagement with her," said Mayur.

"Yes."

A bead of sweat formed on Nayan's forehead. He often swallowed. A feeling of embarrassment and lack of confidence was evident in his voice. But he tried to answer without hesitation.

"Did you ever visit Hyderabad to see Priya?"

"Um...no."

"Why? Didn't feel eager to see her?"

"I was eager, but..."

"But what?" Aisha asked.

"Priya visited Bangalore almost every fortnight. I was also busy with the business that prevented me from going there to meet her."

"Okay," said Mayur. "Were you getting along well after the engagement? Or did you have a dispute about anything else?"

"Well," said Nayan. "I'm not sure why you're asking this, but I can say we were getting closer day by day and developed a good relationship."

"I know you had been engaged for six months," said Mayur. "Didn't you ever go to a tourist spot with her?"

"Um... as... I said I was busy with my business, but I did have in my mind to go for a honeymoon. I remember talking to Priya about it, but God disturbed our plans, you know." Nayan paused. "I didn't expect this would happen in my life."

"It's okay," said Mayur. He waited for Nayan to compose himself. He said, "Mr. Nayan, we want to know if you ever loved someone else before you got engaged to Priya."

Nayan swallowed with his Adam's apple bobbing. "Well...I..."

"Yes, Mr. Chabra," said Mayur. "You need to tell us the truth." He looked into Nayan's eyes. "Did you love someone else before your engagement?"

"No," said Nayan, his voice shaky. "Priya was the first girl whom I ever loved in my life."

"Are you sure, Mr. Chabra?" Aisha asked.

"Yes."

"After your engagement, did you come across any disagreement between Priya and Poonam?"

"Oh, yes," said Nayan with his face lit up with a slight grin. "Priya told me once about it. In fact, it was Poonam and Chirag who started the argument. I often suggested to Priya not to fight over the matter and jeopardize her relationships."

"What did she say?"

"She was such a well-mannered girl, you know, she remained neutral and allowed her father to decide about it. Now, with her death, Poonam owns Priya's share of the property."

"Do you think Poonam and Chirag did it for the sake of an inheritance?" Aisha asked.

"Um... I'm sorry. I can't answer," said Nayan.

"A couple more questions before we conclude the interview," said Mayur. "Did you know Priya had a boyfriend before she got engaged to you?"

"What?" Nayan narrowed his brows; he opened his mouth wide. "She had a boyfriend? I can't believe it."

"Yes," said Mayur "But are you sure you didn't know?"

"Yes. I'm telling you the truth."

"Can you tell me where you were on the 19th of October between 7 pm and 10 pm when Priya got murdered?"

"I was at work until 11 pm."

"Do you have any close friends who live in Hyderabad?"

"Um... no. I don't."

Mayur continued to look at Nayan and there was no sign of guilt or fear on his face. Mayur needed to check if Nayan was a left-hander.

"Would you like to have some water?" Mayur poured him a glass of water.

Nayan nodded. He took the glass from his left hand and drank.

He is a left-hander. Mayur took a glance at Aisha, who looked at him with her chin up and eyes wide.

Nayan took out his handkerchief from his pants pocket and wiped his mouth, using his left hand. It further confirmed Mayur that Nayan was a left-hander.

"Thank you for meeting with us, Mr. Nayan," said Mayur. "I'll get back to you if necessary."

"Thank you," Nayan said with his voice shaky. He rose and said bye to Aisha.

Mayur went up to the door and sent him off. He came back and sat beside Aisha.

Chapter 25 - Mayur is Attacked

23RD OCTOBER 3:00 PM

Mayur poured a glass of water and sipped. "What do you think about Nayan?" He placed the glass back on the table. "Is he innocent?"

"He is a left-hander and it's possible that he did it. Also, his footwear size matches the one found at the crime scene. But why he would go to Hyderabad and kill Priya, disguising himself as a Pizza Hut delivery boy?"

"The same logic applies here which we thought earlier. He needed to get into the apartment building without being questioned."

"Oh, I see," said Aisha. "Should we verify his alibi in that case?"

"Yes, we should," said Mayur. "But it will be difficult to get his correct alibi as Nayan is a businessman."

"We can visit his place of business and talk with the workers," Aisha said.

"His workers might lie to us to protect their boss." Mayur paused and then said, "Do you remember what Nayan said when I asked if he loved someone else?"

"Yes, I do," Aisha said. "He lied to us."

"That's correct. We must tell Prakash to use his men to trail Nayan and find out if he meets his girlfriend. If he is seeing her, we should question him further until he confesses."

Aisha nodded. "What's your gut feeling? Do you think it's him?"

"Well, I can't rule out his involvement, but I can't be convinced until we further probe the matter."

"My head is spinning," Aisha said. "The murder took place in Hyderabad, but the suspects live in Bangalore. The chance that anyone of these suspects went to Hyderabad and killed Priya is very unlikely."

"I don't think so," said Mayur, smiling.

Aisha looked at him, seemed to have puzzled. "You asked Nayan if he has any relatives and friends at Hyderabad. Is there any significance associated with that?"

"Yes," said Mayur. "I can talk about it more after we interview the remaining suspects." He didn't like to reveal all the details until he further probed the matter. He grabbed the phone from the table. "Let's call Prakash."

He swiped on the screen and called.

"Hello, Mayur," said Prakash.

"Prakash, I hope I didn't disturb you."

"It's all right. We can talk for a few moments."

"We interviewed Nayan a while ago. We found that he is a left-hander and he wears size nine shoes which makes him more suspicious. He also lied when he said he didn't have a girlfriend."

"Oh, that's good progress you've made." Prakash sounded elated. "Now, tell me how can I help you? Do you need any help?"

"Yes. I want someone from the Bangalore police to trail Nayan and find out if he meets his girlfriend. Also, I want his call records so that we can know more about him."

"Sure," said Prakash. "I'll arrange for someone to shadow him."

Mayur exchanged a few more words before he ended the call.

23RD OCTOBER 5:00 PM

Mayur spent time romancing Aisha and took a catnap until the evening. After having coffee with her, he liked to spend some time outside. He told her he would return soon and walked to the reception.

He sat on a couch in the lobby, picked up *India Today* magazine from the table and flipped over the pages. A cricket players' auction for the Indian cricket tournament caught his attention. While he was reading, his cell phone rang. The screen was lit with an unknown number. Who might it be? Mayur always answered anonymous calls thinking the caller might be known to him.

"Hello, Mayur speaking."

"Hello, Mr. Varma," said a male voice. "You had fun with your secretary?"

Goosebumps popped up on Mayur's skin. The caller indeed touched Mayur's raw nerves. *Is he the same person who threatened me a few days ago?*

"Hey, who you are? It's none of your business to poke into my private life. If you have guts, tell me who you are?"

"I hate seeing your face, Mr. Mayur. All I ask you is that you stop investigating Priya's murder, all right? This is your second warning. Heed my words or there will be consequences."

"Do you think you can scare me? I've seen-" before Mayur completed his sentence, the line went dead.

Mayur shrugged. Though nervousness overwhelmed his thoughts, he composed himself. *I don't want to give in to all these threats. No doubt it's the perpetrator and he is afraid of getting caught and convicted.*

He rose. A few minutes of walking should rejuvenate him. He placed his phone in his shirt pocket and walked out of the hotel.

The evening traffic was heavy. The street was crowded with cars, motorbikes, city buses, and rickshaws. The exhaust smoke filled the surroundings.

Mayur tasted fumes and craved fresh air. He ought to enter into the residential area to breathe fresh, clean air. But he needed to cross the road. He looked towards the right, standing beside the road and waited for the traffic to lessen. While he waited, a heavily built dark-complexioned man caught his attention. This person wore soiled white pajamas and a black banyan. A thick silver chain surrounded his neck.

Mayur sprinted across the road when the traffic lessened. He walked towards a path that led to the colony of houses. Large peepal and neem trees were growing alongside the pathway. A fresh breeze that swept down the area comforted Mayur. Cars stood in front of houses and beside the street. An occasional sound of a dog barking and the whistle of tropical birds filled the atmosphere.

An image of the man in pajamas reappeared in Mayur's mind. *Why did he stare at me with his eyes widened? Is he trailing me?* A sixth sense arose in his mind. He slowed down and looked back. His heart missed a beat. The man was walking behind with his eyes fixed on him. Mayur needed to either go back or take the next left turn and see if the man would continue trailing him. He looked ahead and walked a few more steps. A faint sound of approaching footsteps announced the person had come nearer to him. Mayur got alerted. He looked back; the man holding a pen knife stood a few inches away from him. His hand was raised high and was ready to strike Mayur at any moment.

Mayur's heart pounded. He waited for the man to approach him. When the man tried to stab his shoulder, Mayur held his hand and prevented him from stabbing.

Mayur applied his full strength and twisted the man's hand. Unable to bear the pain, the man loosened his clutches on the knife and it fell. Mayur seized the opportunity and pinned the man's hands behind his back.

He needed to know who he was and who had sent him. He kicked the knife on the ground and it fell into roadside drainage.

The sound of an approaching vehicle filled the surroundings. The man, heaving a heavy breath, crushed Mayur's left foot and ran away.

Mayur groaned in pain. He limped towards the pathway to enable a vehicle to pass. He waited there until he recovered from the shock. He then walked back towards the hotel, limping.

There is no point in searching for the man as I'm not familiar with the surroundings. I'm sure one of the suspects know about the investigation and the progress we have been making. Maybe he got scared of conviction and sent a rowdy to do away with me.

Mayur managed to return to the hotel room. Aisha opened the door for him. He forced a smile. He didn't want Aisha to know what had happened.

"Where have you been, Mayur?" Aisha asked, her eyes wide.

"I took a stroll."

"I hadn't expected you'd be out for so long." She paused, staring at Mayur's arm. "What is that bruise on your arm? And you're limping also. Did you fall down somewhere?"

"Um...no... I happened to rush through a crowd of people while coming back and someone crushed my toe. I'm all right." He hobbled towards the closet to change his clothes.

Though he wished to reveal the truth, Mayur didn't want to scare Aisha. He knew threats like these ones were common in his profession. He should not heed to these cowardly acts by his opponents.

Chapter 26 - Mayur Calls Rahul

24TH OCTOBER 9:00 AM

A hot shower relieved Mayur from his overnight stress. He made love to Aisha a couple of times in the night, and his body ache got after a comforting shower.

He came out of the bathroom with a pale purple Turkish towel wrapped around him. Aisha was still lying on the bed; no doubt she too got tired after their extended romance. Mayur went to her and told her to get ready.

When Aisha went into the bathroom, he put on his underwear and chose his pale blue business suit from the closet. He donned it and stood in front of a dresser mirror. His not so oblong, but well-chiseled face appeared fair. His dark almond-shaped eyes sparkled in the fluorescent lights.

He combed his black silky hair and applied a facial cream. After making sure his make up was in order, he walked towards the balcony to breathe in some fresh morning air.

A cold breeze that swept down the balcony rejuvenated him. He leaned on the balcony railing, looking at the busy street below.

The traffic was stalled and an inspector in a khaki uniform hooted to clear the congestion. A couple of crows took flight above the building; a few sat on an electric wire, oblivious to the chaos on the road.

Mayur needed to return to Hyderabad after he finished interviewing the remaining suspects. He ought to discuss his findings with Prakash and find out if Prakash had made any progress in the case. Mayur hoped that Prakash had some useful leads after he had met the owners of the Pizza Hut branches.

Aisha approached him. In her teal and white silk sari, she looked beautiful. An intricate necklace glistened in the sunlight and it matched her heart-shaped face. Her full open lips got smeared with pink lip gloss.

"Are we calling Harsha and Rahul now?" she asked.

"Yes." Mayur took his phone out of his shirt pocket and called Rahul. The phone rang and rang. Rahul didn't answer.

Aisha continued to look at Mayur with an expression on her face that said, 'what's the matter?'

"Rahul is not picking up the phone."

"Why don't you try again?" Aisha said. "Maybe he saw your number as unknown."

"You may be correct," said Mayur. "He doesn't have my phone details." He called Rahul for the second time.

After a prolonged ring, he answered. "Hello, Rahul here."

"Hello, Mr. Rahul. I'm detective Mayur Varma speaking from Bangalore." He waited for Rahul to say something.

"Detective Mayur?" Rahul said, inquisitively. "Are you sure you called the right number?"

"Yes, Mr. Rahul," said Mayur. "It's about your niece, Priya who was murdered in Hyderabad."

"Oh, I see." Rahul sounded shaky. "I'm pleased to speak with you, Mr. Varma. How can I help you?"

"We would like to meet you and ask a few questions related to the case. Are you free today?"

"Well...you...know..." Rahul stumbled for words.

Mayur remained silent, allowing Rahul to compose himself.

After a few moments of silence, Rahul said. "Sure, where would you like to meet me? At my office?"

"Can you come to my hotel?"

"Um...What if we meet at my home? You can also meet my mother there."

"All right," said Mayur. "May I know your home address?"

"Sure. I'll message you the details soon." He paused. "Is there anything else you would like to know?"

"No," Mayur said. "I'm looking forward to seeing you soon." He ended the call.

Aisha straightened. "Are we meeting at his house?"

Mayur nodded. "Yes."

"You should've insisted he come here." Aisha frowned.

Mayur smiled. "I have good reasons."

"What are they?"

"Rahul said we can meet his mother - Priya's grandmother. Don't you think we can get more information from her?"

Aisha's eyes glinted. She smiled. "You made the right decision. No doubt Priya's grandmother will help us."

Mayur's pulse quickened. "But it was Rahul who suggested the place, you know."

"Um...do you think there-?" Aisha sounded curious.

"Yes. I can understand his psychology. Rahul was nervous when I introduced myself. But he sounded confident after I agreed to come to his home."

"Well, I don't understand what-?"

"Rahul feels comfortable and safe in the presence of his mother. He doesn't want to show any sign of guilt and maybe he would succeed in hiding his emotions."

Aisha remained silent. She seemed to have understood the motive behind Rahul's interest in inviting them to his home.

"Do you think he did it?" she asked.

"I can't say anything until we have a shred of proper evidence to prove his involvement." He put his hand on Aisha's back. "Let's go and have breakfast. We'll finish our interviews tonight."

They walked into the restaurant and ordered Uthappa—a thick pancake with onion toppings.

The place was half full, and the muffled conversation of customers filled the air. The hot and spicy smell of sambar masala wafted in the air.

The waiter in a white uniform served the food.

Mayur took a bite of Uthappa. He chewed and then said, "The injury to my leg yesterday was not an accident."

Aisha widened her eyes. She finished chewing the food and said, "What is it then? Did..." she stumbled for words.

"Someone who is involved in the murder is closely watching us and monitoring our progress."

"Do you remember I got a hoax call in Hyderabad a few days ago?" Aisha widened her eyes. "I think the perpetrator doesn't want to let us know whether he lives in Bangalore or Hyderabad."

"I agree with you," said Mayur. "The perpetrator is quite clever in trying to mislead us. Do you remember the clue which got planted to misguide us?"

"You mean the cigarette butt?" asked Aisha.

"Yes," said Mayur. "No doubt the perpetrator had picked up the butt from the apartment and left it at the crime scene."

"That makes Hemant innocent, then," Aisha said.

"Possibly so," said Mayur. "If he is the culprit, why would he leave the cigarette butt near Priya's body?"

"And he also has a strong alibi as told by Dhananjay," said Aisha.

"That's correct," Mayur said.

They finished eating their breakfast, exchanging a few more words. While having coffee, Mayur's phone jingled. "Rahul must have sent his home address."

Chapter 27 - Evidence of Rahul

24TH OCTOBER 10:00 AM

Mayur and Aisha hired a taxi to Rahul's house; he was eager to see and question him. The car stopped outside the gate. Mayur paid the driver; the intricate iron gate squeaked as he opened it and stepped in. An Alsatian dog, secured to a pole by a steel chain, barked.

"Let's wait for someone to escort us," Mayur said.

The latch sounded. An elderly woman with a fair complexion and wrinkles around her eyes opened the door. She regarded Mayur and Aisha intently for a few moments. Her face lit up with a slight grin as she stepped from the porch. "Rahul is freshening up. Please come in."

Mayur smiled back. His glance shifted towards the blooming red roses growing in the flower pots. The smell of wet soil and the fragrance of flowers wafted in the air.

The old lady walked into the living room. Mayur noticed a pair of brown shoes, placed near the closet. He bent down to unlace his footwear and glanced at the shoes, which Mayur thought belonged to Rahul. He read the number nine printed on them.

"Please sit down." The old lady gestured them to wooden cushioned chairs. "Rahul should be here at any moment." She walked out of the room.

Mayur sat in silence, looking at the modern art hanging on the wall. A small chandelier hung from the ceiling. The flower-patterned blue curtains draped the windows. The showcase in front of him contained wooden artifacts and plastic flowers.

A man, wearing blue pants and a white shirt approached. He stared at Mayur with a questioning look.

Mayur rose and bowed. "Hello, I'm Detective Mayur Varma." He looked at Aisha. "And this is my assistant Aisha Mishra."

"I'm Rahul." He smiled. "Nice to meet you."

They all shook hands.

Rahul sat on a cushioned chair. "I remember seeing you both at Priya's funeral. Didn't you attend it?"

"Oh, yes," said Mayur. "We did, but I don't remember seeing you. What about you, Aisha?"

She shook her head. "No, I didn't."

Rahul bit his lips and averted his gaze.

"Rahul, I need to ask you some important questions about your niece's murder."

Rahul nodded. "Sure...um...why...not?" He swallowed.

"What is your full name?"

"Rahul Bhatt."

"How old are you?"

"I celebrated my twenty-seventh birthday last week."

"Late greetings." Mayur forced a smile. "What do you do for a living?"

"I own a business - a computer training center."

"Your qualifications?"

"I'm an engineer in Computer Science."

"Why did you choose to teach instead of working as a software engineer?" asked Aisha.

"Well," said Rahul. "I'm passionate about teaching. A few personal matters prevent me from working as a software engineer."

"We understand that Priya's mother is your sister," said Mayur. "Is that correct?"

Rahul nodded. "That's correct."

"Is she older than you?"

"Yes."

"Do you have any other siblings?"

"Yes, I've got a younger sister who is yet to marry."

"What does she do?"

"She is a software engineer."

Mayur paused. "Why have you not thought of getting married yet?"

Rahul raised his brows. "That's my personal matter, Mr. Varma." He shot an intense gaze at Aisha and then looked back at Mayur. "I don't want to discuss this with you now."

But Mayur persisted. "You don't want to talk about it because you were betrayed by Priya, right?" He tried not to mock.

Rahul shrugged. "Who told you I was betrayed?"

"Your elder sister, Mrs. Bedi," Mayur said. "Do you agree you were hurt knowing that Priya got engaged to some other guy and you held a grudge against her?"

"I agree that I loved Priya." Rahul stared down. "But-"

"And you thought of vengeance because Priya broke your heart," said Mayur.

"No, that's not correct." Rahul bit his lip. "How could I harm my niece?"

"Yes, you indeed thought so, Mr. Bhatt," said Mayur with his voice raised.

"No, Mr. Varma," Rahul said. "No...I didn't kill my niece." He paused. "God shouldn't have been so harsh on her, you know."

Mayur composed. "Mr. Bhatt, if you loved Priya, why didn't you talk to your elders in the family? Why didn't you act when you heard Priya was getting engaged to someone else?"

"I did raise my concerns and told her parents about my interest in Priya. But her father was a hard nut to crack. You know, Mr. Varma, I didn't want to put myself down by begging Priya's hand in marriage."

"What did Priya say?" asked Aisha. "Did she talk to you before she got engaged?"

"Priya didn't want to disappoint her father. I insisted she reconsider her decision, but she refused to go against her parents."

"How did you feel, Mr. Bhatt?" asked Mayur. "I'm sure you got hurt when you heard that from Priya."

Rahul rubbed the back of his neck. "I told you already. I indeed got hurt, but I'm not involved in the murder. I loved Priya and I'll continue to love her," Rahul said, his voice raised.

Mayur sensed a tone of fury in Rahul's voice. *Is Rahul trying to hide something from me?* "All right," he said. "Did you go to Hyderabad after Priya moved there?"

"No, I didn't."

"Did you know Priya was working in Hyderabad for five months before she got murdered?"

"Um...yes." Rahul's lips trembled. "My mother did mention me about it."

"Okay," said Mayur. "One last question, Mr. Bhatt. Who do you think murdered Priya?"

Rahul swallowed. He paused for a few moments, "It must be her classmate and boyfriend, Harsha."

Mayur looked at Aisha who was jotting the details of the interview on a notepad. He shifted his gaze back to Rahul. "All right. I'll call you if I need any further information. Now, do you mind sending your mother?"

Rahul rose, nodding. He walked out of the room.

Rahul's mother arrived. She sat opposite Mayur, smiling.

"Before we proceed, I would like to know your full name."

"Usha," said she. "Usha Bhatt."

"Okay, Usha," said Mayur. "Now I would like to ask a few questions about your granddaughter's murder."

"Pray, please proceed."

"Do you agree that Rahul loved Priya since their childhood and wanted to marry her?"

Rahul's mother nodded. "Yes. We thought of arranging their marriage when Priya and Rahul began earning money."

"What prevented you from doing so?" asked Aisha.

"It was because of Priya's father." She swallowed. "He was dead-set against her marrying Rahul and wanted her to get married to Nayan."

"Did you protest?"

"I did, but I fought a losing battle as Priya also took her father's side. I didn't want to put myself down by begging them. Instead, I told Rahul to forget Priya and seek another girl."

Mayur stared down, contemplating. *Did Priya love Rahul? What about her friendship with Harsha?*

"Did you know Priya had a boyfriend?"

"No," said Usha. "I wasn't aware of it."

Mayur waited for a few moments for her to compose herself. "When your husband died?"

"We lost Mr. Bhatt when Rahul was six. Priya's mother and I raised Rahul. Yes, he missed his father and fatherly affection in his life."

Rahul was affected first by losing his father and then by Priya for her decision to marry Nayan. What if his father's death has influenced him to commit the crime? "Did Rahul share with you any plans to get married?"

"Um...no. I've been persuading him to see girls other than Priya and get married soon."

"What's he saying?"

"Well, he has been procrastinating, citing several reasons," said Usha. "I'm hoping he will respond to my request positively without much delay."

Mayur leaned back. "Thank you, Usha. That's all for now."

"You are welcome." She smiled.

He and Aisha bade Usha and Rahul goodbye and walked out of the home. The sun was hot in the middle of the sky, but the winter cold breeze minimized the effect of intense sun rays. A couple of kids took a ride on their bicycles. A young girl with a scarf wrapped around her head and face, sped on her scooter, ignoring the speed limits. Mayur walked past the residential area and arrived at the main street. A coffee shop caught his attention. He stopped and turned to Aisha.

"What if we discuss everything over a cup of coffee?"

Chapter 28 - Evidence of Harsha

24TH OCTOBER 11:00 AM

They entered the glass-walled coffee shop. It had a wooden desk from where they served beverages and snacks to patrons.

Mayur looked at a board that had the list of food items and their prices. He turned to an attendant at the other end of the desk and asked for two coffees. When the server handed over the steaming cups, Mayur went and sat opposite Aisha. He placed the cups on the table.

They took a couple of sips in silence.

Aisha placed the beverage back on the table and referred to her notes. "We're calling Harsha next."

"Yes," said Mayur. "We are. He is the last suspect based in Bangalore and I don't want to delay any further." He took his phone from his shirt pocket and called Harsha.

He didn't answer.

Mayur sighed. He called again.

After many rings, there was an answer. "Harsha here."

"Hello, Mr. Harsha. It's Detective Mayur Varma."

"Detective Varma?" Harsha sounded surprised. "Tell me how can I help you?"

"This is in connection with Priya's murder. I would like to interview you as part of our investigation."

"Priya?" asked Harsha, sounding astonished. "Who ...is ...she...? I really..."

"Mr. Harsha," said Mayur. "We have heard that you had been in love with Priya and interested in getting married to her."

There was a pause. Harsha cleared his throat and went on: "Oh, are you talking about Priya Bedi, my classmate?"

"Yes, I need to find out a few details about her."

"All right. Can we continue to discuss the matter over the phone?"

"No, Mr. Harsha," said Mayur. "I prefer seeing you to discuss the matter. Can you come to my hotel for an hour or so? We can meet in the restaurant."

"Sure, I'll be glad to meet you. Can you give me the hotel details?"

Mayur told him the room number. "I'm looking forward to it."

He ended the call and placed the phone back in his shirt pocket.

"Thank God, he's agreed to come here," Aisha said. "Was he reluctant?"

"Yes. Though I didn't notice any nervousness in his voice, why he pretended he didn't know Priya?"

"Maybe he didn't pretend. But we can conclude only after interviewing him and finding out more about the case," Aisha said.

IT WAS HALF PAST ELEVEN o'clock sharp when the doorbell of the hotel room rang. "It must be Harsha." Mayur and Aisha rose and walked toward the entrance. He opened the door.

A young man in his mid-twenties looked at Mayur with his eyes wide. "Detective Mayur Varma?"

Mayur stretched out his hand. "Yes. And you are..."

"Harsha Ahuja."

"Oh, it's nice to meet you." Mayur shook his hand. "Meet my assistant, Aisha Mishra." Aisha smiled and also shook his hand.

"Let's go to the restaurant," said Mayur.

Inside the café, Mayur located a less crowded area near a window and got a table. Harsha sat opposite Mayur and Aisha.

When the waiter arrived, Mayur ordered coffee for all.

"Mr. Ahuja," said Mayur. "As part of Priya's murder case, we would like to learn certain facts from you."

Harsha leaned forward.

"You said your last name is Ahuja?"

"That's so."

"Okay, Mr. Ahuja," Mayur said. "What do you do for a living?"

"I am a software engineer at Cisco."

"For how long had you known Priya?"

"I met her first at the engineering college. We studied our course together."

"Did you both like each other?"

"Um...I can say we were good friends. We studied together and shared class notes."

"What was your opinion of Priya?"

"She was a lovely girl," said Harsha. "It's a great loss for us and I miss her a lot."

"Were you interested in marrying her?"

"Well, yes."

"Was Priya interested in marrying you?" asked Mayur.

"Yes, but she was under pressure from her parents to get married to Nayan."

"So, she didn't commit to you."

"That's right."

The waiter returned with coffee and placed the steaming beverages on the table. Mayur's pulse quickened as he was eager to find out if Harsha was a left-hander.

Harsha took the cup from his left hand, sending a shiver down Mayur's spine. *If he wears a size nine shoes, he will be a strong suspect and I need to get his call records from Prakash as soon as possible.*

Mayur sipped the coffee then placed the cup on the table. "Did you threaten Priya's father when she got engaged?"

"I...do...not...remember..."

"You need to tell the truth, Mr. Ahuja. Did you threaten Mr. Bedi?"
Harsha grew pale. He stared down, nodding.

"Did you vow revenge on him?"

"No, Mr. Varma," said Harsha, his eyes wide and brows pulled together. "I'm not that kind of person. I agree that I got disappointed to lose Priya, but didn't hold any grudge against her."

Mayur's pulse quickened as Harsha didn't show any sign of fear or low confidence. He answered him with determination. *Is he innocent?*

"Who do you think murdered Priya?" asked Aisha.

"Well.... how...can...I..."

"Did you meet Priya after she got engaged to Nayan?" asked Mayur.

"I wished to," said Harsha, "When I asked her intention, she said 'I don't want to go against my parents, Harsha. If you love me, I beg you to look for some other girl. Please stop calling me and don't try to meet me as I'm committed to Nayan.'"

"Do you know anyone in Hyderabad?"

"Well..." Harsha placed his cup on the table.

Mayur sensed evidence of guilt in him. "Do you have any friends there?"

"No...I don't...have anyone there."

"Are you sure?"

"Yes, I am."

Mayur paused and then said, "Where were you on the 19th of October when Priya got murdered?"

"I was at my workplace until seven in the evening," said Harsha. "Then, I went home and spent time with my parents."

"Mr. Ahuja," said Aisha, "it was Sunday. Did you work on that day?"

"Yes," said Harsha. "I had some more work to finish that weekend."

"Are you *sure*, Mr. Ahuja?" asked Mayur.

"Yes, I am. You need to believe me."

"All right," said Mayur. He paused for a moment contemplating if Harsha had planned to get married after he got betrayed by Priya. "Have you planned your marriage?"

"Well...I...haven't"

"You need to answer," said Mayur. "Have you planned anything?"

"Mr. Varma, I haven't planned anything yet."

"Is Priya's betrayal haunting you?"

"Well...I... agree with ...that..."

No doubt Priya's betrayal had hurt him. Mayur didn't want to go deep into the matter and upset Harsha as he needed to find out some more details from him.

" Mr. Ahuja," said he. "Did you ever speak with Priya after her engagement?"

"Yes, I did."

"What did you talk about?"

"I insisted she refuse her parents' advice to get married to Nayan. I begged her to return to me so that we could lead a happy married life."

"What did she say?" Aisha asked.

"She denied everything and cut the call."

"One last question, Mr. Ahuja," said Mayur. "Can you tell me the size of your shoes?"

"Um...it is size nine."

"Thank you. That's all I've for you now," said Mayur. "We'll call again if needed."

They bade him goodbye. Mayur looked in the direction in which Harsha left until he disappeared.

Aisha cleared her throat. "What's your opinion about him? All three suspects, Nayan, Rahul, and Harsha, are left-handers. They all wear size nine shoes and they have clear motives."

"That's what is interesting, you know."

"I don't believe Rahul is involved even if he is left-handed."

"Why?" Mayur asked.

"He was a close relative of Priya," said Aisha. "And he'd known her since their childhood."

"But he has been more betrayed than Harsha as he knew Priya since childhood." Mayur paused and then said, "Our next step should be to verify their alibis."

Aisha nodded. "That's a correct decision." She paused. "I observed Harsha lied more than Rahul."

"You are correct," said Mayur. "At first, Harsha said he didn't threaten Mr. Shekar Bedi. I was sure he was hiding something from us."

Chapter 29 - Check The Alibis

24TH OCTOBER 12:00 NOON

Mayur returned to his hotel room along with Aisha. He craved coffee and ordered some over the intercom. They changed into their night suits and watched a TV serial. The room-boy arrived and placed the coffee pot, cups, and saucers on the table.

Mayur poured the steaming beverage into the cups. "We should verify the suspects' alibis instead of assigning the task to Prakash." He handed the coffee to Aisha, looking into her eyes.

"I agree with you," Aisha said, holding the cup at chest level. "We're already in Bangalore and it saves a lot of time."

Mayur took a sip. "We'll do it by the end of the day today" He took another sip and placed the cup on the table. "We've all the three major suspects' telephone numbers, their residential and business addresses. Don't we?"

Aisha flipped through her notepad. "Yes, we have their information."

"We'll visit their work or residential places when they are not present there," said Mayur.

"You mean we'll meet someone else to verify their alibis?" asked Aisha.

"Yes. We can talk to their co-workers and parents. The suspects might corrupt the facts if they are present."

"Oh, that's a good idea," said Aisha.

"So," said Mayur. "Let's visit Nayan's business center in the afternoon when he is out for lunch."

IT WAS AFTER ONE O'clock in the afternoon.

Mayur and Aisha stepped out of the taxi a few meters away from Nayan's business place. "We'll see from the distance whether Nayan is at the counter or not." He looked around and spotted a neem tree. "We can watch his shop without being seen by standing under that tree."

Aisha nodded.

When they crossed the road and stood under the tree, Nayan was at the counter. He was busy collecting money from the customers and giving them the receipts.

"I hope he will leave for lunch in the next half an hour," said Aisha.

"Let's hope so," said Mayur, continuing to look at Nayan.

A green city bus, loaded with the passengers, passed by. A man in white soiled clothes pulled a cart, which was loaded with the large-sized jaggery cubes.

Mayur heaved a sigh of relief when Nayan spoke to one of his workers and then walked out of the shop. No doubt he is going out for a lunch break.

"It's good that Nayan didn't keep us waiting for long," said Aisha.

Mayur nodded. "Let's go."

They stepped into Nayan's garments shop.

A man in white pajamas and Nehru shirt, that extended up to the knees, approached. "Please come in." He paused. "How can I help you?"

Mayur knew it was imperative to talk. "I'm Mayur Varma, a private detective from Hyderabad. This is my assistant, Aisha Mishra."

The man's lips trembled and his brows narrowed. "Why are you here?"

"We've got a few questions to ask you," said Mayur.

"But I'm not the right person, sir," said the man. "I suggest you contact-"

"We already met with Nayan yesterday," said Mayur. "What we want to know is whether Nayan was at work on the 19th of October?"

"I don't remember, sir." The man looked at the calendar. "The 19th of October was Sunday." He paused and looked at the counter and his face lit with a smile. It appeared something flashed through his mind to prove his statement. "I haven't been absent for the past few Sundays."

"Are you sure?" asked Mayur.

"Yes, sir, I remember it. We were quite busy that day and sold a lot of clothes because it was a wedding season. I remember we all worked until eleven o'clock that night."

Mayur noticed no hint of fear or evidence of guilt. But he needed to make sure the man was telling the truth.

"Are you telling us the truth?" asked Mayur. "If you're lying, we'll prosecute you in the court of law and punish you."

The man shivered. He swallowed. "You need to believe me, sir. Why should I lie? I know the consequences if you find that I lied to you."

Mayur stared at him. The man might be telling the truth as he stood straight with his chin high. He didn't fidget and his voice was full of confidence.

"All right," he said. "Is there any other proof you have showing Nayan worked late on the night of 19th October?"

The man put his fingers to his lips and rolled his eyes. "Yes." He walked towards the cash counter and brought a long and thick book—a register. He flipped over its pages and showed it to Mayur.

"See here, sir." The man pointed at the entries in the register. "Nayan had signed against each of these entries. And the date is registered here."

Mayur sighed. There was no time recorded, but the volume of sales confirmed that Nayan had worked there for long hours. "Thank you. That's what we wanted to know." He glanced inside the shop, whose racks were loaded with colorful clothes. He walked out along with Aisha. "Let's go to Harsha's home and meet his parents," he said.

"But Harsha may be at his workplace now," Aisha said.

"That's what I want."

They hired a taxi. After a bit of inquiry with a passerby, the driver located the house. Mayur paid him and entered the house. It was built of stone and part of it was painted in pale green. A variety of gardening plants—Asoka and coconut trees—were growing alongside the compound wall. Mayur stepped onto a small porch and rang the doorbell.

An elderly man in his white pajamas and blue kurta opened the door. He looked at Mayur and then at Aisha with his brows pulled together.

"I'm Detective Mayur Varma and she is my assistant, Aisha Mishra."

The old man's face lit with a smile. "Harsha told me about you. But I never expected you would come now." He backed away, making room for them to enter.

Mayur removed his shoes and followed the old man into the living room. He sat on the couch according to the gesture of the old man's thin arm.

An aged lady in her traditional cotton sari entered. She sat beside the old man. They all exchanged pleasantries.

"Mr. Ahuja, do you know of Priya Bedi, who was killed in her apartment in Hyderabad?" Mayur considered. "Your son was in love with her."

Mr. Ahuja's face grew red. "Do you mean my son killed her?"

"I didn't say so, Mr. Ahuja."

"What are you saying, then?"

"I would like to know if Harsha was with you on Sunday, the 19th of October when Priya got murdered in Hyderabad."

Harsha's father looked at the old lady, his mouth opened and eyes widened. "Yeah, he was with us. And I tell you my son is quite innocent.

You make sure not to suspect him and make his life miserable. Don't ask me again if my son loved her or murdered her, all right?"

"Mr. Ahuja," said Mayur. "I am not saying Harsha has committed the crime. I wanted-"

"Why did you ask whether my son loved her?" Mr. Ahuja said.

Mayur remained silent for a few moments. He needed to diffuse the tension which was building up between them. "It's good to know that Harsha was with you on that eventful evening. And mind you, Mr. Ahuja. If the information you provided proved to be untrue, we'll prosecute you in the court of law and punished."

Mr. and Mrs. Ahuja's face grew ashen. They looked at each other.

"Do you have anything which proves Harsha was with you?" asked Mayur.

The old man leaned forward. "I remember Harsha went to a movie along with his cousin later that evening." He rose and walked towards the door that led to the bedroom.

What proof does he have? Mayur continued to look at the door with his pulse quickened.

Mr. Ahuja came back. He gave two pieces of paper to Mayur. Mayur glanced at them. They were movie tickets. The dates and times printed on them were 19th October, 8 PM.

The old man cleared his throat. "I can give Harsha's contact details. You can inquire with him."

Mayur noticed a sign of nervousness in him, but there was no sign of guilt. "I hope you're telling us the truth."

"Yes, Mr. Varma," said Mrs. Ahuja. "You need to believe me."

"All right," said Mayur. "That's all we have for now. Thank you, Mr. Ahuja, for your cooperation. We'll contact you if needed." Mayur bade them adieu.

While stepping out of the main gate, Mayur said, "Let's go to the hotel and relax."

"When are we verifying Rahul's alibi?" asked Aisha.

"We'll visit his institution after six o'clock when he won't be there."

IT WAS JUST AFTER HALF-past four when Mayur came back to his room along with Aisha. He ordered snacks and coffee as they missed eating lunch.

They both lay on the bed.

"What do you think about Nayan's alibi?" Aisha asked.

"We can trust Nayan's and Harsha's alibi. But we need to check if any of their DNA samples match with the clues we have collected at the crime scene."

"Yes, we should." Aisha turned towards him. "But it's quite strange that all the three suspects—Rahul, Harsha, and Nayan—are left-handers. I'm sure any one of these three must-have committed the crime."

"But at least two of them so far have strong alibis," said Mayur. "Though I don't want to depend entirely on their alibis, I want Prakash to check the DNA samples against clues. Let's not assume anything until we've checked Rahul's alibi and seen the DNA test results."

At six o'clock sharp, Mayur got ready to go to Rahul's institution. He waited on the balcony for Aisha to get ready. They hired a taxi and arrived at Rahul's institution, 'Excellent Computer Training Centre.'

Mayur paid the driver and they went to the help desk. A lady receptionist in her early twenties smiled at them.

"Hi, I'm Detective Mayur Varma from Hyderabad and she is my assistant, Aisha Mishra."

The lady introduced herself as Shilpa. "Are you interested in meeting Rahul?" she asked.

"Um....no," said Mayur. "We would like to ask a few questions to you."

"Me?" Shilpa widened her eyes. "Why?"

"This is about the murder of Rahul's niece, Priya Bedi," Aisha said. "We would like to know if Rahul was here on that day, the 19th of October when the murder took place."

"Well, you must ask Rahul about it." Shilpa narrowed her eyes. "Why are you asking me?"

"Rahul told us he taught here between seven o'clock and ten o'clock on the 19th of October," Mayur paused. "Was he here on that day?"

Shilpa swallowed. She remained silent.

"Shilpa," said Mayur. "I would like to make it clear to you that if we found you are hiding the truth, we'll arrest and charge you."

Shilpa swallowed. "Yes...he was...here."

"May I ask how long you've been working with Rahul?"

"For four years."

"Do you record your attendance in a register?" Mayur asked.

Shilpa opened the drawer and took out a long notebook. She showed it to Mayur. "This is where we log our attendance."

He read the details. The dates and times of the entry and the departures were logged against the employees' names. Each entry was signed in the last column.

Mayur looked at Shilpa's entry on the 19th of October. She had left the institution at ten o'clock. But there was no entry of Rahul in the book. Mayur looked at Shilpa with his pulse quickened. "Where is Rahul's name?"

"He is the founder, sir," said Shilpa. "He doesn't have to log in."

Mayur looked at Aisha before fixing his gaze back at Shilpa. "So, on the 19th of October, Rahul worked till ten in the evening?"

"Um...I ...do not..."

"Shilpa, you need to answer my question."

"Yes," said Shilpa. "He did work late that night."

"Are you sure?"

"Oh, yes," Shilpa said, her voice shaky. "I'm sure."

"All right," said Mayur. He shifted his gaze towards the glass-walled classroom. A teacher, in her green sari, was teaching a few students. What if I ask a couple of those students to verify Rahul's alibi?

"Shilpa," said Mayur. "Has Mayur been teaching those students this semester?"

She nodded. "Yes." But her face quickly fell.

"Can you bring two students out of that classroom to me?" Mayur said. "I would like to meet them."

Shilpa seemed hesitant. She waited for a few moments and then rose. "Sure. I will." She went to the classroom and spoke to the teacher; she returned with two female students.

Mayur gestured them to take their seats.

The students sat with their eyes slightly wide and brows knotted.

Mayur exchanged greetings. He paused for a moment and then said, "Do you remember Rahul took the class on the 19th of October, a Sunday?"

The students looked at each other. They referred to their notebooks and then, one of them said, "No, sir. Rahul didn't conduct the class on that day."

"That's right," the other student said. "On Saturday, he told us he wouldn't be teaching on Saturday."

"Did Rahul usually teach you on Sundays?"

"Yes, sir. He taught us on Saturdays and Sundays, but not on Wednesdays."

Mayur looked at Shilpa, whose face became pale. "You said Rahul worked late in the night on Sunday, right?"

"Yes, sir. He was in the institution, but he didn't teach on that day because he needed to work on the project reports. I remember helping him get the reports ready until ten at night."

Mayur looked at Aisha, his brows narrowed.

Aisha stared at him with an expression 'something is suspicious about Rahul's alibi'.

Chapter 30 - Returen to Hyderabad

25TH OCTOBER 8 AM

Mayur was contented after interviewing the suspects and verifying their alibis. Now, it's imperative for him to travel back to Hyderabad. He should continue his work with the information gathered so far.

It was evident from the revelations made by the suspects that the plot was deeper than Mayur had thought. He shouldn't delay compiling the case details and discuss them with Prakash.

A hot bath in the hotel bathroom comforted him. It soothed his fatigue-filled, aching muscles. He donned formal dress—a dark maroon T-shirt and navy blue pants—while Aisha walked into the bathroom. After a quick makeup, he made sure his clothes were in order and then strode towards the balcony.

He wanted to give Aisha some privacy so she could get dressed. He opened the balcony door and stepped onto it. A mild winter breeze ruffled his hair; he inhaled some fresh outside air. The pleasant weather and invigorating freshness elevated his mood.

Mayur stared down at the street, leaning on the railings. He was standing nine floors above. The vehicles on the road, city buses, and cars along with a few motorbikes, appeared like toy vehicles. A blue police Jeep with a red siren lamp flashing reminded him of a past incident. He was a superintendent of police two years ago.

It had been an interesting case. The murder of a journalist. Mayur's boss, Mr. Suresh Reddy, wanted to close the case as early as possible. He was ready to make all the resources available to Mayur. After working for a fortnight on the case, Mayur was close to succeeding and was ready to arrest the culprit. He thought his successful investigation would boost his career. Mr. Reddy would be pleased to know about the progress.

But, on one fine morning, when Mayur had arrived at his office, his boss had summoned him. Mayur had been a bit disappointed as Mr. Reddy sounded rather upset over the phone. He had disconnected the call without saying anything much. Guessing something was wrong, Mayur went to his office.

Mr. Reddy had appeared more serious than he usually did and he didn't even tell Mayur to take a seat. Instead, he had shocked Mayur by insisting he stop the investigation and hand over the case file. Mayur guessed his boss was under pressure from the Home Ministry. He had asked the reason why Mr. Reddy wanted to close the case. Mayur had told his boss he was one step away from solving the mystery, but Mr. Reddy didn't listen to his appeal.

He had told Mayur there would be a threat to Mayur's job and even to his life if they continued working on the case. With goosebumps on his skin, Mayur had cursed the red tape bureaucracy and had stormed out of the office.

That bitter incident was one of the reasons why Mayur resigned from his post. He started his own brainchild—Dolphin Detective Agency. Though he was angry at his boss and a few co-workers, Mayur had made sure he remained cordial when he bade adieu to his job.

The police department realized they'd lost an intelligent young officer. That was the reason his close colleague Prakash consulted Mayur to handle the cases. Prakash knew Mayur's way of functioning and his accommodating nature.

Being his own boss, Mayur liked to work as a private detective and as a consultant. Though he had teething problems with his agency, he had steered it towards success in the last year. In its third year, Dolphin

Detective Agency had made considerable progress. Mayur was getting cases not only from Prakash but also from local families to solve their feuds. The corporate organizations approached him to investigate the background information of their employees.

Mayur jerked when Aisha put her arms around his neck from behind. He inhaled a quick breath and turned around, holding her right hand. A jasmine scent from her hit his nostrils.

Aisha smiled wide with her neatly arranged white teeth glistening in the daylight. A dimple formed on her left chubby cheek. She kissed his lips, preventing him from speaking. The smell of red lip gloss, smeared on her full, open lips cheered him a bit.

"I love you," said Aisha. "You look so handsome."

Mayur put his hands around her neck and said, "You too look so beautiful in this green sari."

"Thank you," she said, loosening her grip on his neck. "I'm fortunate to work with you and have you as my close friend."

Mayur nodded. "I've never regretted having you as my junior. And thank you for the support you've been offering in the last two years." He walked her inside the room, closing the door behind him.

"I'm glad that you're happy with my work," Aisha said. "Please try to be open-minded if you've anything to suggest for me to improve myself."

He sat on a sofa and gestured her to take a seat beside him. "No doubt you're doing a good job and taking interest in the cases." He paused for a moment, looking sideways. "But I want you to be more proactive when I question the suspects. You're asking a couple of questions, but I want you to be more enquiring."

"I've been thinking my interference during the interview might annoy you. That's the reason why I concentrate more on making notes," Aisha said. "I will try to ask more questions now on as you rightly suggested."

He nodded. "Your well thought out and intelligent questions would definitely help us."

"Okay," said she. "I'm apprehensive of our stay which got extended by a day and I'm not sure how to convince my mother."

"I too am thinking of how to calm my sister and mother. My sister wanted me to return soon because of her college work."

"When are we leaving for the airport?"

"Soon," Mayur said. "Would you like to eat some snacks? I'm feeling hungry."

"Sure, I too am hungry."

Mayur picked up the intercom receiver and said, "What would you like to have?"

"Whatever you like." Aisha smiled.

Mayur punched in the numbers on the telephone and waited for someone to answer. He said, "Two masala dosas and two cups of coffee, please." He paused and then said, "Please get it soon. We need to leave for the airport." He placed the receiver back on the phone.

Aisha looked at him with her eyebrows raised. Mayur told her the boy would be here in fifteen-twenty minutes.

Aisha scooted closer to Mayur and rested her head on his shoulder. Mayur's heart raced. Aisha might get dejected over some matter. Was she remembering her mother and felt depressed? "Are you all right, Aisha?" Mayur rubbed her shoulder.

"I wanted to ask you a question," she said, her voice lowered.

"What is it?"

"Mayur," she paused, stumbling for words.

"Yes, please go ahead. I'm listening."

"How long should we continue like this?"

Mayur realized Aisha was speaking about their union. "Like what?" He didn't sound like he was pretending.

"It's been more than two years and we've understood each other well."

"That's correct."

"Don't you think we need to change our friendship into a permanent relationship?"

Mayur sighed. "I've already told you I can't commit to our relationship so early in my career." He inhaled. "Why are you so bothered about it? Are you not comfortable staying like we are now?"

Aisha shrugged.

Mayur needed to calm her down. "Please, don't get upset. I suggest you build your career for the next two-three years. We should establish our name so that we get more cases to investigate. You know our agency is still in an incubation period and we need to grow it further."

Aisha looked into his eyes. She seemed to have convinced about Mayur's concerns about their profession.

"I agree with you," said Aisha. "But are you open to our alliance soon?" She sounded eager.

Mayur didn't want to promise as he liked his current solitary life. But he didn't want to disappoint and lose Aisha, either. He pulled her closer and kissed her forehead. "Let's not think too much about it. I can assure you that you'll be well taken care of as long as you're with me."

Aisha loosened her hug and her eyes sparkled. Without fatherly or brotherly care and support, Aisha felt insecure. *My love and affection surely would've comforted her.*

"I agree with you, but I'm worried about my mother," said Aisha. "She has been insisting I get married this year."

Mayur forced a smile. "Aisha, you still have ages to get married as you're just twenty-six years old, right? I suggest you convince your mother and make her wait. Getting married is an important decision in your life and I don't want you to rush."

Aisha smiled.

Mayur hoped she wouldn't bring the matter up for discussion again as she was now convinced. Maybe Aisha was pressured by her mother and opened up the matter for a discussion. Mayur was content to see Aisha happier while he conveyed his decision.

The doorbell rang.

Mayur walked over and opened the door. A room boy entered and placed the snacks on the table. Mayur gave him a tip and then retreated to his seat.

Aisha opened the food wrapped in the aluminum foil. The smell of hot masala wafted in the air. When Aisha thanked Mayur for ordering the mouth-watering food, his cell phone rang. He took the phone from his shirt pocket. Aisha stared at him with a 'who-is-it' expression. He whispered it was an unknown number.

"Hello, Detective Mayur here."

"Hello, Mr. Mayur Varma. I know you're having a good time with your beautiful and loving junior."

Goosebumps popped up on Mayur's skin. "Who is this?"

"I want this phone call to be brief, Mr. Varma. You escaped last time, but don't expect that you'll be unhurt the next time around. Better you stay away from Priya's murder case."

"Are you threatening me?" He winced.

"Mr. Varma, you'll face dire consequences if you continue investigating the crime."

"Do you think I'd be afraid of your threats?"

"You're risking your life, Mr. Varma. Goodbye."

"Hey, scoundrel." Before Mayur completed his words, the line went dead.

"Who was it, Mayur?" Aisha said.

He remained silent and composed. "A rascal tried to intimidate me."

"Oh, no," said Aisha. "What did he say?"

"Don't get scared. You know such calls are common in our profession. I don't think he will do any harm. His voice trembled like he was afraid. I'm not sure if he's used to making threats."

"We've to tell Prakash about this"

"Yes, good thinking. We'll tell him when we return."

"Do you suspect anybody who lives in Bangalore?"

"I don't want to speculate about it, you know. It's a waste of our time."

"But, Ma-"

"Aisha," said Mayur. "Let's not take the matter so seriously." He smiled. "Aren't we eating dosas?"

Aisha poured two glasses of water and cut the food with a fork. "I can understand that such threats are common in our profession. I hope Prakash will protect us with some security."

"He will if it's necessary," Mayur said.

25TH OCTOBER 11:45 AM - Hyderabad

It was just before noon when Mayur arrived at Hyderabad airport along with Aisha. The temperature was a bit higher than that of Bangalore.

"I'll meet you again at the office, then," Mayur said as he waved to a taxi.

"Oh, come on, Mayur." Aisha came closer to him. "I want you to come with me to my house."

Mayur plastered a smile. "Not now. I'm too tired."

"Wouldn't you like to meet my mother?" Aisha said. "She'll believe me when I tell her about our extended stay if you give her the facts."

"Doesn't your mother trust you?" Mayur needed to go home and see his mother. "What if I meet her tomorrow?"

"Come on, Mayur," Aisha said, her voice pleading. "You must come with me."

Mayur didn't want to upset Aisha. He paused for a while and then said, "All right. But you should make it very brief as I need to see my Mum soon."

Aisha smiled and nodded. "Yes, you can talk to my mother over a cup of tea."

The taxi approached. Mayur sat in the rear seat, beside Aisha. She told the driver the destination.

She paid the driver and walked Mayur inside her home. Aisha lived in a villa. The house was built of stone. The front porch had several gardening plants growing in clay pots. The smell of wet soil and the jasmine fragrance wafted in the air. The colorful roses, daisies, daffodils, and bougainvilleas soothed his eyes.

She rang the doorbell and waited for her mother to open the door.

Aisha's mother glanced through the window and then opened the door. She smiled at Mayur. "Good evening, Mayur. How are you both?"

He entered the living room. "We're tired, Aunty. You know about our hectic work schedule."

"Was the trip successful?"

"Yes Mum, it went well," Aisha said.

"Why did you extend your stay there?" Aisha's mother winced.

"We met a couple of more suspects and questioned them, Aunty," Mayur said. "I hope Aisha's absence didn't trouble you."

"I became anxious when you didn't return as per your previous schedule. She told me about your extended stay rather late, you know."

"I'm sorry, Mum," said Aisha. "I was busy discussing the case with clients and with Mayur during the day."

"Whatever. You tell me about any change in plans so that I don't get worried." She paused and said, "I am glad that you had a successful trip."

"Yes," said Mayur. "We've crossed an important milestone, Aunty."

"Oh, did you?" said Aisha's mother.

"Yes, Mum," said Aisha. "It was indeed a successful trip."

"I'm glad you both returned safely," Aisha's mother smiled. "I was worried about your safety, you know."

"Don't worry, Aunty," said Mayur. "Aisha will be safe with me."

Chapter 31 - Mayur With his Family

25TH OCTOBER 1 PM

Mayur exchanged a few more words with Aisha and her mother before he bade them goodbye. He needed to rush home. His mother was disappointed over his extended stay in Bangalore. His younger sister, Apsara, also wanted him to get home sooner.

He hired a taxi and reached his house. When he stepped onto the porch, the smell of jasmine flowers and wet soil hit his nostrils. He rang the doorbell and waited. Apsara should be out of the house attending her school.

Apsara opened the door, leaving Mayur surprised. She wore a white mixed sky blue nightdress. Her round and fair face shone in the fluorescent light. Her small, black eyes narrowed; her thin brows were knotted. Her black and short hair was tied into a medium-sized bun. She smiled and stepped back for Mayur to enter.

"Didn't you go to your school?" Mayur asked.

Apsara winced. "First, tell me why you are so late?"

"Okay, Okay." Mayur ran his hand on her head. "Don't get angry at me, dear." He removed his shoes. "We can sit and talk the matter over, all right?"

"You promised me you would return two days before. Why are you late?"

Mayur forced a smile. "May I know how that affected my dear sister?"

"I didn't submit my assignments because you were not here to help me," said Apsara. "My ma'am wanted to meet you today."

"Okay." Mayur flopped on a couch. "I'm sorry, dear. I promise that I'll help you finish your assignments today." He paused. "Now, tell me why your ma'am wanted to meet me?"

"There was a parent meeting. I didn't go because you weren't here."

"Oh, I see." Mayur sighed. "Why didn't you take Mum with you?"

"She is unwell."

There was a sound of approaching footsteps. Mayur's mother entered the room. Her gray hair was messy and her round face was ashen. "When did you arrive, Mayur?" she asked.

"A while ago, Mum," he said. "Are you not well?"

She sat on the couch, beside him. "A mild fever; should be all right soon." She gestured for Apsara to take a seat.

"Tell me why are you late?" Mayur's mother asked.

Mayur narrowed his eyes. "Okay, everyone is unhappy because of my late arrival." He looked at Apsara. "I'm very sorry, dear. My job requires me to stay away from home. Even so, I'll help you finish your homework. We're going to meet your ma'am tomorrow. Is that alright?"

Apsara nodded, smiling.

"You informed us about your change of plan so late." His mother grimaced.

"I was busy, Mum. I'm sorry."

"I still caution you not to continue with this profession, Mayur," said his mother, eyes welled up with tears. "We know what tragedy befell your father. I don't want the same to happen to you."

Mayur's chest constricted. "Why are you remembering the past, Mum? I'm no longer with the police department."

"I know," said she. "Your life will be still at risk because you're helping the police."

"I wouldn't have studied criminal justice if I wanted to work in some other profession. I want to bring justice to Dad's departed soul by nabbing the lawbreakers. I'm committed to my current profession, Mum. I'm passionate about it."

"I know you will not listen to what I say. You'll be getting us in jeopardy, you know."

"Yes, brother," said Apsara. "We're dependent on you." A teardrop rolled down her cheek. "I agree with Mum. Dad will also be happier in heaven if we stay in comfort."

Mayur sighed. He found it hard how to convince them. He was passionate about facing challenges in life. He enjoyed working as a detective. Though he was apprehensive about what befell his father, he had faith in God.

He remembered the incident which had claimed his father's life:

Mr. Varma had been working as a superintendent of police. He was an efficient officer who chased and nabbed the lawbreakers. He was working on a case of a politician who was brutally murdered. He started getting threatening calls while he interrogated the suspects involved.

After he made the first arrest in the case, Mr. Varma was brutally attacked while he was going to his office. Mayur was in his second year of law school when the incident happened. It forced Mayur to study criminal justice. His father's demise etched in his mind permanently. He decided to work as a detective in the police department.

But he never imagined he would open up his own agency. After three years of successful work with Aisha, Mayur was contented. He never regretted his decision to quit his previous job. Aisha had been a Godsend to him.

Mayur convinced his mother, promising them that he wouldn't stay away from home for more than two days. He walked to his bedroom.

Chapter 32 - Mayur Discusses the Case

25TH OCTOBER 3 PM

Mayur entered his glass partitioned office and offered prayers to Goddess Saraswati. He lit a couple of incense sticks; the sweet smell of burning sandalwood filled the room.

Aisha would arrive soon. But Mayur was waiting for Prakash. He had told Mayur the DNA tests results of Bangalore suspects would be available by that evening. Mayur was tired of the case which lasted for longer than he had expected. He was eager to close it soon.

His glance shifted towards the main door. Aisha, in her white and cream embroidered sari, entered, smiling.

"Good evening." She pulled a chair in front of Mayur and sat.

"A very good evening."

A facial cream covered her face. Her fair skin glistened in the fluorescent lights. A red lip gloss shone on her open lips. A golden necklace adorned her neck.

"At last," said Aisha. "We finished interviewing all the suspects. I can say our Bangalore trip was a success."

Mayur nodded. "Yes, it was helpful for us to know a lot of information from the interviews."

They exchanged small talk before Aisha said, "What do you think of Shilpa, Rahul's secretary?" She cleared her throat. "Do you think she was hiding something?"

"Yes, I think so. I did notice she was mumbling at times. But do you remember I told her she would get punished if she lied to us? How could she lie to us despite my warning? How would she enjoy shielding Rahul? She must have something to gain to save her employer."

"What if she is dating Rahul?" asked Aisha.

"That's a good point. Rahul is already disappointed about losing Priya. No doubt he fell for Shilpa, who is more attractive and charming than his niece."

Aisha narrowed her brows. "Do you think Rahul is the one who-"

"Before making any conclusions, we need to wait for the DNA results. Combined with them and the suspect's alibis, we should be able to zero in on who did it."

"And what about Nayan and Harsha? Do you think their alibis are strong compared to Rahul's?"

"Nayan's alibi seemed strong after what we noticed in the sales register. He would've worked on that day until eleven o'clock. And about Harsha's alibi, we need to believe his parents unless we get any fresh evidence against him."

Mayur's phone rang. It was Prakash.

"Mayur, where are you both?"

"We're are at my office and waiting for you to join us."

"Do you have any updates for me?" Prakash asked.

"Yes. I've many items to discuss. Please come here as soon as possible."

PRAKASH ARRIVED. HE sat beside Aisha at the table. In his police khaki uniform, he appeared handsome and charming. His black, prominent mustache stood out on his square face. A bead of sweat appeared on his wide forehead. Prakash sat in silence, evidently trying to compose himself. His face grew ashen as he sat opposite Mayur.

"Welcome back to Hyderabad. I need to know about the progress made in the case." He sounded impatient.

Is Prakash once again under pressure from his boss? Better I remain patient and not annoy him further. "We've collected some useful information. But everything depends on the DNA tests."

Prakash's face lit with a smile. "Let's wait for a couple of more hours to hear from our Bangalore crime branch, then."

Mayur considered. "What about your inquiry with the Pizza Hut branches? Did you get any clues from them?"

Prakash continued to look into Mayur's eyes. "I went to each of the Pizza Hut branches and spoke to their owners." He paused. "They'll get back to me if they come across anything suspicious."

"The Pizza Hut clues we have got are quite important, you know," said Mayur. "We should tell the outlet owners to be watchful. They should report to us immediately if they found anything suspicious. I'm sure we'll achieve success if the owners of the outlets cooperate with us in the inquest."

Prakash turned to Aisha for a second before he fixed his gaze back on Mayur. "That's what I've told the branch owners. Can you tell me what else you've for me from your Bangalore trip?"

"We've verified the alibis of all the suspects and found their motives. Let's discuss the details after the DNA test results."

Prakash pouted.

Mayur inhaled a deep breath. "I would like to prepare a document containing the vital details of the suspects and show it to you both. It should help us where we've erred and what needs to be done next."

Prakash remained silent, seemingly satisfied with the reply.

A notepad and pen on the table caught Mayur's attention. He needed to prepare a report of the inquest and discuss the details with Aisha and Prakash. But he decided to defer writing it until the DNA test results were announced. It would be more appropriate to include them in the report.

Prakash's phone rang. He looked at the screen and his eyes widened. "It's from Bangalore Crime Branch."

Mayur leaned forward. He was eager to hear about the DNA test results.

"Hello, Inspector Prakash speaking. Oh...I am sorry?... That's right....negative...? Are you sure....All of them...? Okay, thanks..." Prakash ended the call. He tossed the phone on the table. There was a touch of dejection in his face.

Did something go wrong? "Is everything all right?" asked Mayur.

Prakash paused. "No. We have bad news."

"What?"

"The Bangalore crime branch has tested for a DNA match with the cigarette butt and the strand of hair. The outcome is negative."

"Negative?" Mayur's pulse quickened. "I can't believe this."

"But it's true."

"Damn it." Aisha thumped her fist on the table. "What are we going to do now?"

Mayur gestured her to remain patient by placing his forefinger on his lips. "All my guesses so far have been turned upside down. I had never expected we would hit a dead end."

"Have we?" Aisha asked.

"Yes. I had expected one of the four—Chirag, Nayan, Rahul, and Harsha—had come to Hyderabad on the 19th of October and did it. Now, the hair that the technician had found inside the cap doesn't belong to any of these men. Who then entered Priya's flat and committed the murder?"

"Was he a real pizza delivery boy who robbed and killed her?" Aisha asked.

"Maybe but if at all he wanted to rob her of her valuables, why would he murder Priya?"

Aisha nodded. "Yes, it's unrealistic."

"Ah," Mayur said. "Is it not a second misdirected clue, like a cigarette butt, which was placed at the crime scene to misguide us?"

"Maybe," said Aisha. "The perpetrator, so clever, might not have left the cap by mistake."

Mayur nodded. "Yes. It's quite likely." "It's a great setback for us to hear about the DNA results."

"Yes," said Prakash, "and I'm not sure what to do next."

"There are other ways in which we need to drive our investigation. First, let me know whether your police personnel at Bangalore trailing Nayan or not?"

Prakash nodded. "Yes. I'm told that Nayan is meeting his girlfriend almost every evening."

"Ah. It proves that he lied saying he doesn't have a girlfriend. Had the DNA been a match for him, we would've made an arrest."

"What must we do now?" Prakash asked, his chin lowered towards his chest.

"Wait, my friend. You always become nervous so soon. We need to exercise patience, and it's common to face the situation like this."

"But my boss-"

"I know," Mayur added. "I know that you're under pressure from your boss. But to please your superiors, we can't punish the innocent."

Mayur took a notepad and a pen from the table. "Allow me to write the findings of our investigation in a concise way. It won't take much time."

Mayur started writing as follows.

a) **Praful** - A software Engineer, colleague of Priya based at Bangalore.

Motives: 1) Womanizer. Wanted a sexual favor from Priya 2) Held grudge against her for noncooperation.

Alibi: He was at his home with his parents.

Suspicious circumstances: 1) He was sacked from his previous employers for sexual harassment.

2) He booked an air ticket for Priya to go to Bangalore the following Sunday.

Evidence against him: He is a left-hander,

Evidence that proves his innocence: He wears a size eight shoes. But the size nine footprints were found at the crime scene.

b) Hemanth: A security guard who worked on the apartment in the night shift.

Motive: Stole the jewels from Priya, sexual favor.

Alibi: He attended a meeting at his manager's place on that night between 7 pm to 10 pm.

Lie: He said he never returned to the apartment after the meeting.

Evidence against him: The cigarette butt found at the crime scene belongs to him. He wears size nine shoes.

c) Chirag: Poonam's fiancé

Motive: To make Poonam a sole heir to her paternal assets.

Alibi: He was at Bangalore with Poonam.

Evidence against him: 1) He started staying with Poonam at her house after Priya died.

Evidence that proves his innocence: He wears a size eight shoe.

Suspicious circumstances: He hadn't shown any sadness or felt a loss at the funeral.

d) Poonam: Priya's younger sister

Motive: to become a sole proprietor to her father's assets.

Alibi: She was at Bangalore with Chirag.

Evidence against her: 1) None, except she wears size nine shoes. But the one found at the crime scene is male footwear.

Suspicious circumstances: She blames Harsha and says he is the one who murdered Priya.

e) Nayan: Priya's fiancé, owner of a garment business.

Motive: He has a girlfriend and wanted to marry her. He knew Priya loved someone else and planned to return to his girlfriend by killing Priya.

Alibi: He worked at his showroom until 11 PM.

Lie: He says he didn't have any girlfriend before he was engaged to Priya.

Evidence against him: He is a left-hander, and wears size nine shoes.

f) Harsha: Priya's ex-lover, works at Cisco.

Motive: He is unhappy over Priya's engagement with Nayan.

Lie: He says he didn't threaten Priya's father, Mr. Shekar Bedi.

Alibi: His parents say he was at home and went to a theatre to watch a movie with his cousin.

Suspicious circumstances: He threatened Priya's father and vowed vengeance.

Evidence against him: He is a left-hander and wears size nine shoes.

g) Rahul: Priya's mother's brother, owns a computer training center.

Motive: Heartbroken as he loved Priya since childhood.

Alibi: He worked at his institution until 10 pm.

Suspicious circumstances: A couple of students say Rahul didn't conduct the class that evening. Also, the receptionist makes contradictory statements, seemingly to save her boss.

Evidence against him: 1) He is a left-hander and wears size nine shoes.

Mayur read the contents and made sure all the information was correct. He gave the report to Prakash. "Here are the details you wanted to know." He paused, allowing Prakash and Aisha to look at it.

"I wonder how the DNA tests are failing on these suspects when all have a clear motive. And most of them have clear shreds of evidence against them." Prakash looked at Mayur.

"Don't you think Praful has a greater motivation? Should we put him on the top of the list, considering the information you have?" Aisha asked.

"But he had booked an air ticket for Priya to go to her place on Sunday," Mayur said. "If he had planned to kill Priya, he would've waited till she came back. And he was not hurt by Priya, unlike other suspects. I strongly believe someone from Bangalore committed the crime."

Prakash glanced from Aisha to Mayur. "Where the hell did the Pizza Hut cap come from?" He sounded impatient. "I'm totally confused and my head is spinning, Mayur."

"Be patient, my friend. And that's the reason I told you to rely on the information the Pizza Hut outlets are going to give us. We won't make any progress in the case unless we get a clue from them."

Prakash's phone rang. He took it from his short pocket and glanced at the screen. His face lit with a smile. "It's from the Madhapur Pizza Hut outlet." He whispered to Mayur and Aisha.

"Hello, Inspector Prakash here."

"....."

"Okay. We'll be there in the next ten minutes." He ended the call and looked at Mayur. "The Pizza Hut owner of the Madhapur branch wants us to meet him soon," Prakash said. "Let's go and meet him." He rose. "He has something important to discuss with us."

Mayur's chest lightened. He hoped they'd get a breakthrough.

Chapter 33 - News About Parthiv

25TH OCTOBER 4 PM

Prakash slid behind the wheel of his Jeep. Mayur sat in the passenger's seat while Aisha sat in the back. He eased his Jeep out of the parking lot and headed down the main street.

The afternoon sun was bright, but the winter breeze, cold and soothing, was comforting. The street was crowded with cars and motorbikes. An occasional honking of red and green city buses filled the surroundings. A traffic inspector in white-khaki uniform struggled to clear the congestion.

"What do you think the Pizza Hut owner has to tell us?" Mayur asked.

"I too am curious. No doubt, he has some important information."

"Maybe," said Aisha, "they've found a record saying Priya had ordered pizza on that night."

"But why didn't they find it earlier?" Mayur asked. He waited for Prakash or Aisha to respond. When they remained silent, he said, "I am thinking of a new theory at this stage."

Prakash looked at him for a moment. "What?"

"I'm thinking about the Pizza Hut cap. I suspect that a delivery boy had helped one of the suspects with his Pizza Hut uniform."

"It is a possibility." Prakash passed a heavy vehicle. "The owner has called us after noticing one of his employees behaving suspiciously."

"There can be many possibilities," Aisha said. "It will be clear only after we meet the owner."

"But why should a delivery boy help a suspect with his uniform?" asked Prakash. "I believe he is the one who committed the crime and our suspects are innocents."

"If that's the case," said Aisha, "what's his motive?"

"Robbery," said Prakash. "What do you say, Mayur?"

"Well, I can talk about it only after meeting the owner."

Prakash parked his vehicle in the parking lot. They walked towards the main entrance of the outlet. A young boy wearing a uniform opened the glass door. They all entered.

A dozen tables sat in a large-sized hall and space was occupied by the patrons. The area was lit with fluorescent lights. The waiters in red uniforms were busy taking orders from the customers. The smell of spicy pizza wafted in the air.

The owner of the outlet smiled and ushered them to empty seats. They all sat with their forehead creased.

The owner introduced himself as Ankit Tiwari. "Mr. Prakash, you wanted me to tell you if I noticed something suspicious." He darted his gaze between Mayur and Prakash. "One of our delivery boys hasn't been to work since the 20th of October."

"What is his name?" Mayur asked.

"Parthiv Saha," Ankit said.

"Why didn't you tell us before?" Prakash asked.

"Well, I was hoping he would return soon. He is not even answering my phone calls."

"Is his phone turned off?" Mayur asked.

"Yes." Ankit nodded.

"How long had he been with you?"

"For two years."

"Did he behave suspiciously during his tenure?"

"No," Ankit said. "He behaved as normal as anybody else."

"What's your opinion of him?"

"He was quite friendly with everyone and was loyal to me. He was a hard worker, too."

"Is he from Hyderabad?"

"No. He comes from one of the districts in north Karnataka. He came to Hyderabad to work and earn money."

"Ah," said Mayur. "Can we have his telephone number and address?"

"Sure," Ankit said. He took his phone out of his shirt pocket and looked at its screen. He read out the details while Aisha jotted the information on her notepad.

"How old is he?" Prakash asked.

"Around thirty years old."

"Did Parthiv deliver pizza to any of the residents of Majestic Apartments on the 19th of October?" Mayur asked.

"I have already told you about it. He didn't."

"And did he work on that night?" Mayur asked.

"Yes, he worked and delivered pizzas to other locations."

"What's your gut feeling?" asked Mayur. "Do you think he is involved in the crime?"

Ankit widened his eyes, seemingly not wanting to comment.

"You need to answer me."

"I don't think he did it," said Ankit. "But I'm not sure."

Mayur's chest lightened. "Thank you, Mr. Tiwari, for cooperating with us in the investigation." He paused. "Prakash, I want your men to check if Parthiv is still staying at this address. I also want his telephone records and credit card history for the past two months."

Prakash nodded. "Sure."

They all bade Ankit goodbye and walked out.

"What do you think of Parthiv?" Prakash asked while he steered his jeep towards the main street.

"He left his job without informing Mr. Tiwari. That is suspicious."

"I'll inform my constable to visit his house soon," Prakash said. "Do you expect anything untoward happening?"

"If he is involved in the crime, directly or indirectly, he had put himself in danger," Mayur said. "We need to act sooner to catch him alive."

"I think there is a reason why he left his job without informing his employer," Aisha said. "He was scared that his missing Pizza Hut cap and uniform shirt button might get him in trouble."

"Yes, I agree with you," said Mayur.

"If the cap and button belonged to him, the hair found in the cap should also belong to Parthiv," Prakash said. "The DNA of the hair should match with Parthiv's."

"There can be two possibilities," said Mayur. "First, he himself committed the crime. Second, he had helped someone who held a grudge against Priya."

"The first possibility makes more sense," Prakash said.

Mayur inhaled a deep breath. "I still believe Parthiv may not be directly involved."

Prakash nosed his Jeep to the police station gate and parked the vehicle. Inside his office, he told a constable to go and inquire about Parthiv at the address given by Ankit Tiwari. He made a couple of calls to the crime branch asking for Parthiv's phone and credit card history.

Mayur told Prakash he would wait for the details to arrive before he took further action. He bade him goodbye and traveled back to his office along with Aisha.

With his mood upbeat, Mayur played an old Mohd Rafi song inside his car. The case would end when Prakash and his men found Parthiv and got his personal details. *I hope the police will find Parthiv alive.*

Chapter 34 - Parthiv Dies

25TH OCTOBER 5 PM

Mayur heaved a sigh, seated in his office. "I don't know why it's taking so much time for the police to find Parthiv."

Aisha, seated opposite, leaned forward. "Maybe Prakash hasn't heard anything from the constables. Otherwise, he wouldn't have kept us waiting over this important matter."

"I already told you, finding Parthiv alive or dead is important for us. I can say it's going to be a major milestone in our investigation."

"Why do you think so?" Aisha asked.

"I think so because the Pizza Hut cap and the shirt button might belong to Parthiv."

"Do you think he's guilty?"

"Yes, it's possible." Mayur paused. "It's him or someone who disguised himself as Parthiv."

"Why would somebody wear Parthiv's uniform-?"

"The guards at the Majestic Apartments didn't register the delivery boy's details. The perpetrator used this to his advantage."

"It's clear that the culprit wore the uniform, disguising himself as a Pizza Hut delivery boy. He then committed the crime."

"That's right," said Mayur.

"What about the strands of hair we've got inside the cap? Do you think they belong to Parthiv?"

"Maybe so, but let's wait for the DNA test results."

"If the DNA is a match for Parthiv, do you think it's him?"

"Yes, but we need to further probe by looking at his call history and credit card transaction details."

"You mean it's some other person-"

"Yes," said Mayur. "But we can't arrest Parthiv just because his DNA is a match. It's quite likely that he had helped one of the suspects."

"What would Parthiv gain by doing so?"

"There are a few reasons to substantiate it. First, Parthiv is a close friend of the perpetrator. He couldn't refuse his friend's request to lend his uniform. The second reason is money. The perpetrator has lured Parthiv by offering considerable cash. Or, Parthiv didn't realize his friend intended to commit the crime. He overlooked the impending danger and handed the uniform to the murderer blindly."

"I admire your reasoning." Aisha smiled. "Now, do you think the perpetrator is from Hyderabad? Or-"

"I think Parthiv's call details and his credit card histories should clarify it for us."

Mayur's phone rang; an image of Prakash lit the screen. He grabbed the phone. "Hi, Prakash."

"Hi, Mayur." Prakash sounded hurried. "I've something important to tell you."

"What?"

"The constables visited Parthiv's house."

"Okay, but is he all right?" asked Mayur.

"No, Parthiv has committed suicide."

"Oh, my God. I did expect this." He covered the phone with his hand and whispered the news to Aisha. "Can we come over there?"

"Yes," Prakash told Mayur to come soon and ended the call.

"Let's go to Prakash's office." Mayur rose. "We're going to the crime scene from there." He walked out of his office along with Aisha.

The traffic was moderate. A few motorbikes raced past Mayur's car. Yellow-black taxis carried their passengers alongside the red-green city buses. A flock of cranes took flight above the multi-storied building.

Mayur steered his vehicle to the police station premises. He stepped out of the vehicle and marched towards the main entrance along with Aisha.

Prakash was seated on his chair and was busy talking over the phone. He gestured Mayur and Aisha to a set of chairs opposite him.

Mayur sat. A newspaper article about Priya's murder caught his attention. He took the paper and read the contents until Prakash ended his call.

"The press is not happy with our investigation," Prakash said. "They think the case is getting delayed. The IT company where Priya worked is concerned about not finding the murderer yet."

Mayur folded the paper and placed it back on the table. "You know we've been working hard to nab the perpetrator. Some cases will take more time to solve like the current one. Let's not bother about what others say. We are continuing to work until we find the real culprit." He paused, looking at Aisha. "We've almost identified the perpetrator after finding Parthiv."

"Okay," said Prakash. "Let's go now."

Mayur nodded and rose.

"Do you think we made progress by finding Parthiv?" Prakash asked as they walked towards his Jeep.

"Yes," Mayur said.

"But it's unfortunate that he committed suicide."

"Never mind, my friend," said Mayur. "I'm sure the DNA of the strand of hair, found in the Pizza Hut cap, will be a match for him. It will surely help us in the investigation."

"I think Parthiv committed suicide to save face," Prakash said. "He somehow found out that the police were about to arrest him for the crime he had committed."

"But I have a different theory." Mayur smiled.

"You have a different theory?" asked Prakash. "What is it? Don't you think it is Parthiv?"

"I think he is innocent. And he didn't kill himself."

"Come on, Mayur. Are you not satisfied yet even after hearing about Parthiv? I'm sure we'll end the case once the DNA tests come in."

"You always think simple, my friend. The mystery is deeper."

Prakash sighed. He nosed his vehicle into a narrow street and parked the Jeep in front of a decrepit building.

A large crowd was gathered outside. A muffled conversation and a barking of a stray dog filled the surroundings. One of the constables approached and ushered them inside.

In one of the dimly lit rooms, a body of a youngster was hanging from the ceiling. A reek of alcohol and burnt cigarettes filled the room. A couple of beer bottles were strewn on the floor.

"Did anyone identify the body?" Prakash asked.

"Yes, sir," said a constable. "A neighbor has identified him. He is Parthiv Saha."

The forensic team was busy collecting clues. They held the magnifying glasses and wore white rubber gloves. Mayur noticed there was no chair or a table below the legs. How could Parthiv have committed suicide?

Chapter 35 - The Murderer

26TH OCTOBER 2 PM

Mayur, seated opposite Prakash and Aisha in his office, fiddled with a paperweight. He eagerly waited for the DNA test results of Parthiv. "Shouldn't we have the DNA test result by now?"

"Let me contact the forensic department." Prakash took the phone from his shirt pocket. He called and asked how soon the results would be available. He ended the call and said, "They should be ready within the hour."

Mayur heaved a sigh of relief. Everything depended on the DNA match. If the results were positive, Parthiv indeed was involved in the crime. He opened the table drawer and took out a sheet of paper on which he had written the details of the suspects. "You remember we started our investigation by questioning Praful, who worked with Priya. He is a strong suspect as he has a weak alibi and is a left-hander. There is no evidence to rule out his involvement in the crime.

"Next, we interviewed Hemanth, the security guard. Though the cigarette butt belonged to him, it's unlikely that he smoked in the living room. It's been placed there to mislead us. Two strong points to rule out Hemanth's involvement are—he has a strong alibi and is a right-hander.

"Next, Aisha and I went to Bangalore to interview the suspects who are living there. Chirag, Poonam's fiancé, is a right-hander and has a strong alibi. I don't think Poonam's parents would lie to protect him. But he has a strong motive—to make Poonam the sole heir to her father's assets.

"Then, I interviewed Poonam, who had not shown any sign of grief. She has an alibi saying she was with Chirag at Bangalore. But she too is suspected of trying to become the sole owner of the family property. She had an argument with her parents over inheriting the main jewelry showroom. It is on Brigade road, one of the busiest streets in Bangalore. Also, she blamed Harsha, Priya's ex-lover. She was confident that Harsha had killed Priya. I think she was trying to mislead us.

"The last three persons—Nayan, Harsha, and Rahul—topped our list of suspects. After a meticulous verification of their alibis, I found that Nayan has a strong alibi. He worked at his business until eleven o'clock in the night on the day of the murder. Harsha's parents are unlikely to lie to us. He was in Bangalore and he watched a movie with his cousin.

"But we found that Rahul's alibi is a weak one and is suspicious. The students said he didn't conduct the classes on that eventful evening. I found Shilpa stumbling and nervous while she told us Rahul worked until ten o'clock on that night. Maybe she had a reason to protect Rahul.

"Considering this and applying the principle of deduction, Praful, Harsha and Rahul should be on the top of the list. I'm sure one among these three has committed the crime."

"I admire you for your meticulous investigation," said Prakash. "But what do you think about Parthiv? Don't you think all the above suspects are innocent because it is Parthiv who did it?"

"Well, that's the reason why I'm awaiting Parthiv's DNA test results for a match against the strands of hair. Also his call details, and his credit card transaction history."

Prakash's phone rang. He glanced at the screen. "It's from the forensic department."

He spoke and his face lit with a smile. He ended the call and said, "Yes, it's a match for Parthiv. He is the killer." He darted his glance between Aisha and Mayur. "We now have strong evidence against Parthiv. We should close the case saying Parthiv is the murderer."

"Wait, my friend," said Mayur. "Don't rush. Parthiv wears size eight footwear. But the footprints collected at the crime scene are of size nine." He paused. "We should wait until we get Parthiv's call details and credit card transactions."

"You've got a lot of patience, Mayur." Prakash sighed.

"Patience pays, my friend. We need to wait."

26TH OCTOBER 4 PM

Mayur, seated in his office, was speaking with Aisha about the case when his phone rang. The screen was lit with an image of Prakash.

"Hello Prakash," said Mayur. He put his phone on speaker mode.

Aisha looked at him with her forehead creased.

"Parthiv's telephone call details and credit card transaction history are available," said Prakash. "He had not called any of the suspects using his phone. But using his credit card, he booked flight tickets from Bangalore to Hyderabad in the name of Rahul. The crime branch personnel at Bangalore have arrested Rahul based on the evidence. Rahul has confessed to the crime."

Mayur heaved a sigh of relief. "Yes, my friend. My hunch was indeed a correct one."

Aisha smiled. "Congratulations."

"Congratulations to you too." Mayur winked at her.

Chapter 36 - The Confession Letter

27TH OCTOBER 9 AM

Mayur was flirting with Aisha when his phone rang. He took it from his table and answered. "Good morning, Prakash."

"I wanted to update you about Priya's murder case. Rahul has been remanded to judicial custody. He will be trialed in the criminal court at Bangalore. And he has sent a letter to you."

"Letter? What is it about?"

"I don't know. I'm sending the sealed envelope to you through my constable."

"All right." Mayur ended the call.

"What did Prakash say?" Aisha asked.

Mayur told her the details. "Maybe Rahul wants to confess why he committed the crime."

"Maybe." Aisha nodded.

Mayur straightened in his seat. "It's been a challenging case to work on."

"Yes, I also enjoyed it."

The constable arrived and gave the sealed envelope to Mayur. Mayur opened it and read the contents:

Dear Mr. Varma,

I never expected you'd trace me and find out I committed the crime. You didn't seem clever at first, but I was surprised when the Bangalore police arrested me.

I confess that I killed Priya and hired a professional rowdy to murder Parthiv. You don't know, Mr. Varma, how much I loved Priya. We grew up together and known each other since childhood. Everyone talked about our union until Priya's father parted us. I begged Priya to elope and get married when the news of her engagement with Nayan spread in our families. But Priya was afraid of her father. She was so obsessed with her family name that she refused to bring disrespect to her parents. I told her no one could harm us and no one could separate us once we get married secretly, but Priya was unyielding.

After her engagement with Nayan, I came to know from a reliable source that Nayan had loved someone else. He was not happy with his engagement with Priya. I tried to make use of this opportunity to my advantage and tried to contact Priya. But she still took her father's side. At times, she avoided answering my calls, which made me violent. A sense of jealousy and hatred also filled my mind. I couldn't imagine Priya getting married to someone else and I needed to do something. I decided to make one last request to Priya in person and if she still refused, I decided to do away with her.

I knew one of my schoolmates, Parthiv, worked at Pizza Hut. I also checked security rules at the Majestic Apartments where Priya stayed. Parthiv told me that the guards were lenient in allowing the food delivery boys. They didn't write their details in a register book, unlike for the normal visitors or the guests. I spoke to Parthiv and asked if he would lend me one of his uniforms so that I could bypass the security and meet Priya. Parthiv hesitated, but I offered him fifty thousand rupees if he helped me with his uniforms. I also told him to book my flight tickets on the 19th of October in my name which proved to be fatal to me.

On the evening of the 19th of October, I traveled to Hyderabad and went to Parthiv's house. He helped me with his uniform and lent me his bike. It was around twenty minutes to eight when I entered the Majestic Apartments. I carried a corn knife fastened to my waist belt. I noticed a cigarette butt lying on the ground where I parked the vehicle. I collected *it, ascended in the lift, and rang the doorbell of Priya's flat. I knew from Priya that her flat-mate was out of the station and Priya was alone on that weekend.*

Though Priya expressed her surprise when seeing me, I managed to get inside her flat. After exchanging small talk, I pleaded with Priya to come along with me so that we could get married in a temple. And lead a happy married life. But so adamant, she stuck to her stance which annoyed me. And that eventually forced me to think violent. I pretended to make love and hugged her. I knew she wouldn't oppose my advances as she too was feeling emotional. I walked her towards the bedroom, hugging, and took out the corn knife fastened to my waist belt. I tactfully turned her around, hugged her from behind and slit her throat.

I regretted my dastardly act. But I thought it would be good to see Priya dead rather than seeing her leading a marital life with someone else.

To misguide the investigators, I took all the jewels Priya possessed. And dropped the cigarette butt at the crime scene. In the heat of the moment and chaos, I left the Pizza Hut cap. Though I remembered my mistake when I approached the bike, I couldn't risk going back to collect it. I was confident that I wouldn't be caught because I'd breached the security. I thought I had left almost no clues for the police to catch me. But I was wrong. I never thought your meticulous investigation would land me in jail.

About Parthiv's murder, I came to know from him that the police were searching for him. He was the only person who knew about my deed and I wanted to clear my way by eliminating him. I hired a rowdy to kill Parthiv. But I never expected he booked my flight tickets using his credit card instead of cash.

I tried to threaten you twice to make you stay away from the case, but that didn't help.

I thought my confession will ease my conscience and justify myself.
Yours sincerely,
Rahul Bhatt.

——-The End——-

Don't miss out!

Visit the website below and you can sign up to receive emails whenever Vijay Kerji publishes a new book. There's no charge and no obligation.

https://books2read.com/r/B-A-LDAI-UKZY

BOOKS 2 READ

Connecting independent readers to independent writers.

Also by Vijay Kerji

Mayur Varma Mysteries
The Mystery of a Techie's Murder
The Secret of a Strangled Woman
Mystery At The Mansion

Standalone
Love is Blind
A Friend In Need
The Ticking Clock
Lover's Courage
I Still Love You
Rohita - A Love Story

Watch for more at https://vijaykumarkerji.wordpress.com/.

About the Author

Vijay Kerji has written ten full-length novels (in both Romance and Mystery genres) in the last seven years and his books have received good reviews from the online readers. He is writing the fifth novel in Mystery genre as part of the Mayur Varma Mystery series.

Earlier, Vijay worked as a Software Engineer in various IT organizations, including Siemens and Intel. His best contribution is to the Siemens Corporate Research in New Jersey as a Senior Software Consultant. Later, he worked as a mentor in engineering colleges imparting technical knowledge to young students with his practical expertise. He has a degree in Electronics and Communication Engineering and post graduate degree in Computer Science and Engineering. He lives in India with his parents, wife, and children.

Read more at https://vijaykumarkerji.wordpress.com/.